The Molecule Thief

The Molecule Thief Book 1

LP Styles

ASTRO

Astro Books

ASTRO BOOKS
5840-5844 Malden Road, Unit 108
Lasalle, ON, N9H 184

For Jamie, Sean & William

Spencer Faceplants into a Fish

Spencer

I AM SPENCER NEWTON, and I *am* somewhere else. I'm hundreds of thousands of dandelion seeds spread out on the breeze. I'm years away while still standing in front of your face.

SEATTLE: A Past

The floor of my house rumbled and slid, and I laughed. Scared as hell, I laughed. Not a true belly laugh, but a nervous idiotic laugh with fits of nasal twittering.

Mom and dad shouted, I don't know what; they looked right at me, but I couldn't make out the words as cracks spread through the wall and ceiling.

I stood in the hallway in my underwear, glancing back toward my bedroom, wondering where I put my pants from the night before.

The house shook harder, and I fell.

"Spencer!" Dad screamed, seizing my wrist.

Instinctively, I jerked away. I stopped laughing and righted myself. The quake rolled the house in thundering waves and I stood in a rowboat in the middle of a turbid ocean.

I leaned against the wall and closed my eyes, palms sweating. Don't look. Don't look.

My dad grabbed my arm again. It hurt so much as he pulled me across the oak floor. I stumbled, landing hard on my face.

"Help him!" My mom's voice broke.

My dad reached under me and lifted, half-dragging me down the hall as blood trailed from my nose. Seeing the blood, I cried and flailed. I think I shouted. The tremors intensified. The vibrations were inside me, alive and trying to get out.

My dad fought me, wild eyes darting everywhere, jaw clenched tight. My mom joined in, trying to haul me somewhere safe, but I wasn't sure where safe was. Maybe under the table. Or under the bed. Maybe it didn't matter.

Safe is an idea, not a place.

Safe is a time. Like...

VANCOUVER ISLAND: Now

The beach is rocky and full of driftwood. Enormous bones of oarfish and other smaller fish are scattered everywhere. I squat, stroking a piece of blanched wood—so smooth.

There's a sound. I check the trees. Leaves rustle nearby, turning up one side to the sky. I watch them and see a tree that's dying. I can tell by the way the leaves move. The mountains from the east watch me back in layers that stretch higher and higher until their snowy tops melt into the sky.

I like being on the beach. I feel less hemmed in here. It's the only open spot on the peninsula where I'm not surrounded by towering pines. There are no trees, no buildings, no rows of employee housing.

I can see the peaks of Mt. Baker and Mt. Rainer. Open sky stretches to the west until it's swallowed by the ocean. Out in the water, clumps of rock hunch down in dense huddles that bind them together against the constant wearing of the waves.

When I was younger, before the quake hit, I took Vyvanse. Also Clonidine to help me sleep. I remember sitting in a chair by the dark window, unable to move, feeling my skin crawling, ready to run away from me.

Yeah, the drugs work. Yeah, they help keep my thoughts in order and attention focused. Yeah, I still need them. My mom keeps at me, but I just don't take them. Like so many other things, I just don't.

There's this one oarfish preserved in the water, floating where the sea's frosting meets the shore.

The fish is wild. It's like a shiny stone. It has a soapy substance on it and around it. I see something in one of its mirror-like scales—a color like no other color, a color I can't name that my mind can hardly hold on to. It sort of reminds me of the inside of a fire opal.

You can't just look at something. You have to look at it close, then far away. See it from different angles, then close your eyes and still see it in your mind. Look at it until it isn't there. Until it's something else. Everything is always something else. Even time.

I crouch down by the fish. The water laps at the rubber tips of my shoes. Next to it, my reflection stares at me, my signature shock of honey-colored hair, that untamed bedhead I can't comb the curl out of.

The water ripples and becomes a funhouse mirror. My face, as long and stretched out as the rest of me, appears distorted. The angles are all wrong, obtuse where they should be acute. You can't trust reflections.

The fish rocks between the crests and troughs of the water. On a whim I touch the scummy film that surrounds it.

"It's called grave wax."

The voice startles me. I lose my balance, face planting in the middle of the fish. It's as hard as a bar of soap, except where it's liquefied. The scales and ooze cling to my face.

I gag while I push myself up out of the ocean. It leaves a disgusting salt and rancid seafood taste on my lips.

I wipe my face, but there's nothing to do about my drenched clothes. I turn around.

A girl I recognize stares back at me. Maude Faraday.

I've seen her around. Our moms work in the same lab, and my mom suggested we get to know one another, but I can't exactly go up to a girl and say, "Hey, my mom says we should be friends," without her thinking I'm a total loser.

Maude's cute. She's skinny and wears tight jeans with no holes in them. Her hair is dyed the color of an oil slick and her uneven bangs are too long so they hang in front of one charcoal-underlined eye. She's pale except where her fingers are a kind of reddish-purple like she has poor circulation or something, and her fingernails are short and ragged. She wears a white tank under an oversized aviator jacket along with some kind of knock-off Chuck Taylors with no laces.

"It's called adipocere, actually," I say, straightening my posture.

She twists up one side of her lip, so I think maybe I amuse her. "Show off."

All wet and covered in fish slime, I don't feel like much of a show off. "Grave wax sounds cooler, though."

"The oarfish are massive, aren't they?" She steps closer.

I take a step back like an idiot. The way she looks at me, I'm sure she's sizing me up. She'll be disappointed.

I suppose I'm sizing her up, too. She gives me a broad smile. Her teeth are square and white, with a little space between the front two. This perfect gap, partly covered by the bow of her lip, glossed red, gives her a sensual, deviant look. I return the smile and think maybe her eyes brighten.

An osprey catches my attention; it drops into the water after something but comes up empty. It dives again a second later. An engine starts inland. Someone is cutting down trees, I think.

She takes another step toward me. "There's a Japanese myth that claims oarfish are underwater dragons."

"Dragons?" I love dragons. I imagine the oarfish changing, its ugly face lengthening, and the eyes deepening with fire. The tail stretches, whipping back and forth.

"They say when oarfish wash up from the deep, earthquakes follow."

"Who are 'they'?"

She raises an eyebrow; obviously, she hadn't expected that one. Her tone becomes at once imperious and conspiratorial. "The same 'they' that say oarfish are dragons. The same 'they' that say the underwater dragons control the tides with magic jewels."

"Then I guess 'they' were right. About the fish predicting the quake, anyway."

"You're Spencer Newton." She reaches out, and I duck away, but not before she's plucked an oarfish scale out of my hair. "It's funny we don't have any compulsory classes together, but I hear you're some kind of genius."

I don't ask what year she's in. She looks like a freshman. Maybe a sophomore. I can't judge, but then people always assume I'm older than I am. I'm told my brooding is quite mature.

Most kids my age are just starting high school, but I've blown through most of my undergraduate studies. I'm doing some graduate level work in physics. That wasn't offered as part of the program, but the teacher-scientists do their best to accommodate me.

They give me the problems they're working on, in a piecemeal way so I can't see the complete picture, but still, it's pretty cool to work on problems with no right answer.

"I am Spencer Newton," I confirm. "And you're Maude Faraday."

"Aha! We keep passing one another on campus. Maybe not by accident?"

I wonder what she's heard about me. I don't want to know. I've stopped talking and I'm listening to the surf. Seabirds keep attracting my attention, especially that osprey as it glides up and down this stretch of beach. I'm no good at small talk.

"Faraday and Newton," she says. "Those are some big names to live up to."

"What are you studying?" I ask.

She hesitates, grinning as if self-conscious. "I'd rather be creative than scientific. I play classical piano. My mom wanted me to play a stringed instrument, and I told her that's what a piano really is."

"Percussion. Piano's a percussion instrument," I say, then wish I hadn't contradicted her. But she only shrugs her shoulders, so maybe she doesn't mind.

"Wait," I say. "You're studying music? Here?"

"I know. I should be in Montreal. Maybe New York. We're from Edmonton. You're from Seattle, right?"

I always think people came from the same place I did. I don't know why. I've met a few Seattle people who relocated here, to Vancouver Island, after the quakes.

My mother and I lived in a FEMA community in Alberta for a short time. We might have headed east, but GERI, the Global Energy Research Initiative, contacted her about The Project. Sometimes I wish we'd stayed in Alberta. It wasn't so bad. Better than here. I don't like being on an island with no way off.

The osprey hasn't given up. He dives again. This time a dragon leaps from the waves, its enormous mouth open, jaws ready to snap shut. The bird pulls up just in time, and the dragon morphs into its oarfish form to sulk.

"We were in Alberta for a couple months." The words sound stupid. What if she thinks I'm just saying that?

I've talked enough. When I talk too much, I say things I don't mean to say, and I get in trouble. I like this girl, she's friendly, funny, and I would like to get to know her, but I have to be careful or my stupid mouth will mess it up.

I wait for her to say something, but she doesn't. I hold back.

The quiet between us thickens. She looks out to sea. I follow her gaze, thinking about the water.

"I miss Alberta," she says. "I don't mind it here, so much. I mean, the neighborhood is a bit sterile, but that's the way it is."

The neighborhood, the residential community where most of us live, is an orderly place that could pass for a suburb somewhere on the mainland. They did a good job designing it.

Some of the small homes, cottages really, existed before GERI arrived. Some prefab units were set up afterward, along with cookie-cutter landscaping.

"The Project is sending out some ships later this week," I say. "They're going to drop mini-submarines for exploration. They have equipment they want to set in place. They had some stuff there before the quake, for a different project I think, but it was destroyed. I heard two teachers talking about it outside a classroom."

She cocks her head. I'm talking too fast. I always talk too fast, and I don't know if she can keep up with me or make sense of me.

I press on even faster, like more speed will give me enough time to say all I need to say and somehow this will make her understand my thoughts.

"I work alone a lot, but I study in the rec center sometimes. Gets me out of the house and makes me feel less like a prisoner. I'm doing a lot of reading on refraction at the quantum level, but I don't know, I'm losing interest, because it wasn't what I thought it was going to be when I first started it, and the math that applies to modeling is only taking me so far. But I'm doing a lot of other work, too, so it keeps me going."

I stop talking again, from full speed to zero. It's like someone threw a switch and the words ended.

The waves keep talking though, and the birds, and the leaves. I listen. I smell the salty sea and although there are only a few clouds above, I can taste the beginnings of a storm.

On the island, I'm more sensitive to weather changes. I'm better at picking up on fluctuations in air pressure than I am peoples' moods. Maybe that's deliberate.

"Well, I gotta go," Maude says.

I nod and scan the water.

I'm blowing it. It's always a struggle to apply the *coping strategies* I worked on with my therapist, like checking in with people while I'm talking.

When I start revving up, I should pause and look at the other person's eyes, give them a chance to interrupt, or maybe plan what I'm going to say in my head before I let it spill out, set limits for myself. God, why is it so hard for me to have a normal conversation?

She's still there. I make eye contact, and she surprises me by not looking away.

I start to say something but check myself. Then she does something shocking. She bumps my shoulder.

"You going to be around later?" she asks.

I stop myself from babbling and nod instead.

She smiles and nudges me again, then extends a hand as if she expects me to kiss it. I wish I had the courage to. I give it a light shake.

"Nice to meet you, dah-ling," she says in an accent you hear in old Hollywood movies.

"Sure." Really? Sure?

"Cool. Watch out for dragons."

She turns, leaving wet prints of crimped sneaker tread in the sand as she dashes across the beach. She gives me a last glance over a shoulder and winks before sprinting over to a rocky cliff twenty feet high that she actually starts to scale. Madness.

She attacks the rock with a precise and hypnotic meticulousness. She's like a gymnast. She grips a ledge and pulls herself up. Maybe classical piano translates to amazing grip strength.

At the top, she silhouettes against the bright blue sky, oversized coat flapping in the wind. I watch her until she finally steps out of sight.

Maude.

I think she likes me, right?

I look out at the water, resisting the urge to overanalyze every microsecond of our conversation. Something beneath the surface grabs my attention. It's not a fish. It seems to come together and pull apart with the movement of the waves.

I'm drawn forward with the need to find out what I'm looking at until the sudden shock of cold water lapping at my ankles brings me to my senses. I watch the water closer in, where my image reflects on the surface in splashes of color. Only the reflection isn't moving in sync with me.

That's not supposed to happen.

In the mirror, okay, I've come to accept that, but it's never happened in the water.

It's just the ADHD. I'm hypersensitive, distracted by my imagination.

Something explodes from the water a few feet away. I stagger back, my arms windmilling to keep me from falling.

A liquid hand thrusts up and then shatters, raining back into the ocean.

My mind races, bounces over a thousand things. I stumble back, squeezing my eyes shut, afraid to look.

I didn't see a hand. I know I didn't. It's a trick my mind played.

Only I don't believe my rationalization.

It's not him. It can't be.

I don't believe that, either.

Elliot Versus The Wheeler Twins

Elliot

E LLIOT BORN WENT THROUGH the motions as the Wheeler twins charged down the basketball court.

Lucas dribbled the ball once, passed without looking at his brother, then set a screen in front of Elliot, feet planted wide on the ground.

Convinced he'd blocked any chance Elliot had to steal, Lucas smirked. Screw that. Elliot feinted left, then spun around him.

He had plenty of time to grab the ball and make a fast break. Instead, he slapped the ball from Jarod's hands, sending it arcing out of bounds.

Lucas sucked on a cigarette, and almost looked badass as Jarod retrieved the ball from the grass. In a classic jerk move, Jarod stepped in before Elliot was ready. He chucked the ball at Lucas, who nearly dropped it as it hit him in the chest. With the coffin nail dangling from the corner of his mouth, he went unchallenged and sunk the ball.

Elliot could have stopped him, could have rushed down and fouled or blocked him, but why bother? If he really tried, they'd stop playing, and there was no one else half as coordinated in this valley of nerds to challenge him.

"Want one?" Lucas pulled the cigarette pack from his back pocket and offered it to Elliot.

"Tastes like shit."

Lucas shrugged. He took a long draw on his half-smoked cigarette. "It calms me down."

"Yeah, you're the charged-up type," Elliot said.

Jarod snickered, punching his brother in the side. The brothers regularly exchanged blows, but never threw a punch Elliot's way. They didn't have the balls.

Both were homegrown, cornfed tenth-graders with meaty arms. Jarod had a weasel nose. Lucas had one partly scarred eyebrow, from a "shaving accident", that would never grow back.

"You know what we should do?" Jarod said. "We should make a couple bucks."

Elliot didn't have to wait more than a second for Lucas to pick up the question. The brothers were two halves of the same brain.

"How?" Lucas asked.

"We challenge three of the soldiers. Offer a bet."

"They're not going to play us," Lucas said.

"They're on the court all the time. They'll play."

Elliot nodded. "But they won't bet."

"Sure they will," Jarod said. "We're three spoiled rich kids. They won't think twice about it. We start with a twenty, then take them up to hundred. It's not a lot, but it'll be a rush. When we have enough cash on the line, Elliot can turn on the skills that got him scouted early by UCLA."

"National Player of the Year," Lucas mocked.

How did he hear about that? Elliot didn't respond. He hadn't won National Player of the Year. That award went to Hasan Mohammed from Dallas who had equal skills but better grades. Still, the nomination got him scouting attention. He never mentioned it, mostly because when he thought about where he could be and what he should be doing he wanted to break shit.

He still refused to believe the quakes had destroyed UCLA until he saw the rubble with his own eyes. Every time a chopper brought a mail delivery, he couldn't help but look for his scholarship offer.

"That true?" Jarod asked. "You were the best basketball player in the nation? As a freshman?"

Elliot smiled.

"That true?" Jarod asked again.

"I came in second."

"No shit." Jarod gave his head a shake. "How good are you?"

Elliot watched pinhead Jarod come to the realization he'd been holding back on them, playing with one hand tied behind his back. Either that, or Jarod was marveling at how good he and his brother were, keeping a basketball star in check.

Elliot snatched the cigarette from Lucas' mouth and considered launching it. Instead he let it drop to the pavement. Lucas scooped it back up, giving it a quick check before sucking in more nicotine.

"So what you think?" Jarod asked. "We go three-on-three and humiliate the goon squad?"

"What makes you think some of them didn't play first string at Duke or MSU?" Elliot said.

"Right," Lucas said.

Elliot stooped and retrieved the ball. He turned on full speed, pivoted, broke into a lay-up. He grabbed the ball again, pounded it around the court, then stopped and launched a long three-pointer. Nothing but net.

The Wheelers applauded. But now that he'd finished showing off, they didn't move into their starting positions for another game.

"Well, it's been a riot." Elliot dropped the ball and started for his overstuffed backpack.

He didn't want to do schoolwork, but he was already pissed off, so why not keep the mood going? He had shitloads of work from Mr. Labon. That prick had it in for him.

God, those assignments. Maybe the guy didn't like his attitude, or maybe he thought he was doing something noble by burdening him in an attempt to instill self-discipline.

"Where you going?" Jarod asked.

"It's getting late. I gotta quit. I gotta get stuff done for Labon or he's going to nail my ass tomorrow."

"Oh, he wants to nail your ass bad," Lucas grinned.

Of course he would give it that innuendo. Jarod and Lucas, the loveable Wheeler assholes. Totally interchangeable. Hopefully they wouldn't breed.

"I'm definitely getting screwed here, and not in the nice way."

"Forget the homework," Jarod said. "Get Mutant Boy over there to do it for you."

Elliot turned and saw Spencer bobbing along the path to the rec center. He moved like a chicken in meth withdrawal. He was a wiry kid, with long arms and clumsy legs. He didn't appear comfortable around people, but his shyness wasn't off-putting.

Spencer stopped at a picnic table. He leaned against it, not noticing the dried bird crap he was rubbing up against as he frowned in deep thought. Elliot watched him with a smile.

Whether he was a mad genius, or just weird, Elliot liked him. He couldn't say why. Spencer could be annoying as hell, but sometimes when he started talking, Elliot got a feeling the guy knew something he needed to know.

"Don't call him Mutant Boy," Elliot said.

"He's such an asshole," Lucas said. "Look at him."

"Look at yourself and shut the hell up. I mean it."

He couldn't believe he was defending Spencer. Or maybe he was still pissed they'd brought up his basketball history. Probably both. God, talk about assholes.

"Grow the hell up," Elliot said. "Just once."

Total Internal Reflection

Spencer

THE FIRST TIME I saw Elliot at Orientation, I didn't like him, not for any real reason except he was good looking and walked with an air of confidence.

We were the last to arrive; me because I spaced out, and Elliot because late is his preferred way to be.

Everyone else already gathered in little knots, forming groups of friends. Not that there were many newcomers.

There were maybe a dozen of us, plus a few others who'd arrived with their parents days or weeks earlier, like Maude and the Wheeler twins. And there were some younger kids who'd had individual Orientation with their families.

All our parents were scientists on the research team. The people living on the compound were kept at a minimum: a hundred people more or less, if you counted the kids and spouses. Fifty or so if you didn't, split almost evenly between the research scientists, some doubling as teachers, and a fluctuating crew of military personnel, usually counting around twenty.

When Elliot and I were paired up as Orientation Buddies I waited for him to harass me, but he didn't. At least, not until he got to know me better.

Now, he can be a real prick. We're friends, but I don't kid myself. We aren't the kind of friends who will look fondly back on our time together. We won't remember each other. Or more accurately, he won't remember me.

Elliot, on the other hand, is unforgettable. Years later, Maude will probably still dream about those washboard abs and pouty lips. Honestly, I might, too.

I wonder if they've met.

Elliot waves from the corner of the rec building as he spins a basketball on one finger. He stops and tosses it my way.

The ball of course bounces off my fingertips, off the picnic table, and into a flowerbed. I see the Wheelers roughhousing on the court, but they're not paying any attention to me, so I stoop to retrieve it.

"Good job," Elliot cracks. I throw the ball back to him. "Where you coming from? The beach? Anything going on?"

I don't want to share information about my exchange with Maude. And I definitely don't want to mention the hand in the water, even though it's all I can think about.

I shake my head.

He nods, like we've shared a cool secret, and says, "Newt, how about lending me your brain?"

"Uhh." My idea of witty repartee.

I sit cross-legged at the picnic table as he retrieves a backpack from the edge of the court. He comes over and slides onto the bench across from me.

From his bag, he takes out a tablet and a textbook. After he flips to the right page, he hands me the book. I look at the page and see what he's highlighted.

Light travels through a vacuum at a speed of 2.998×10^8 m/s. What would be the speed of light through the following: 1) Water (n=1.333) 2) Air (n=1.00) 3) Cubic zirconia (n=2.16) 4) diamond (n=2.419)

"Oh, it's Snell's Law." I start to rattle off the answer.

"How about slowing down, Newt."

I'm talking too fast again. I'm mumbling. "It means light follows the path of least time."

"That makes no kinda sense."

I open a graphing app on the tablet, then draw an angled line passing through a straight, dotted line. He frowns as he watches.

My mouth operates independently. "Do you know the Japanese believe oarfish are dragons?"

"What?"

"When I was a kid, I had a thing for dragons. I remember this film where a group of coal miners found a dragon egg and accidentally let loose a bunch of them until they destroyed the town. It was black and white and the special effects were horrible. The dragons were highly magnified iguanas. I think the idea of a dragon being something else is really cool, that it could transform. Maybe were-dragons."

"What the hell, Newt?"

I hand him the tablet. "This is the answer to the question. You see, you get total internal reflection. There's no refraction at angles greater than the critical angle."

I lean back, arching as I stretch my hands over my head, certain my explanation has made it perfectly clear to him. That's when I notice the two brothers, Jarod and Lucas, have left the basketball court and are now leaning against the broad trunk of a black walnut tree, watching us.

Once they know I've seen them, they come over. Jarod plops down beside me while Lucas looms over my shoulder. I'm pretty sure they're here for no reason other than to start crap.

"You figure it out, Mutant?" Lucas asks.

Jarod peers over Elliot's shoulder. He says, "Snell's Law," like it's some kind of wise pronouncement.

Elliot nods and for some reason flushes. "Why's everybody know this but me?"

"Cause you're just a jock," Jarod says.

"You know it, too?" Elliot asks Lucas.

"Yeah, it's not that hard."

Elliot slams the book shut and puts it on top of his tablet. He's got that congenial smile on his face, but his eyes are hard. "Why don't you guys get the hell outta here? I gotta get this done."

Lucas picks up the basketball and repeatedly tosses it into the air. "God, stop being a baby. We'll go."

Before they leave, Lucas leans over Elliot. "Hey, we're going to Vancouver. You should come. It'll be kickass."

"I dunno," Elliot says.

"We got a car we can use whenever we want. We're going to stock it with weed and drive out to the ferry."

They're not including me in the discussion. I'm invisible. If I got up and walked away, would they even notice? What if I transformed into a dragon? They'd probably still say I was a freak and tell me to get lost.

"What about your dad?"

"Old man's gone for a couple weeks. Some GERI business."

"Yeah," Lucas says. "You've got to come. This place sucks. We need to get high and find us some women."

"I talked to Maude today," I blurt. God, why can't I keep my mouth shut?

Lucas clamps the basketball in both hands, then drops it on the ground. "What? Why the hell would we care? She's just another mutant, but with a chest flat as a surfboard."

"She's kinda cute," Jarod says.

"She has a boy's body," Lucas says. "And she's weird as hell. You know, she's the kind who likes to stand out but gets pissed when you notice her."

The brothers laugh and I feel my face twist in irritation before I see the sparrows in the closest tree building a nest. The male has a feather stuck to his beak. He can't shake it off.

"So, what about it, Elliot?" Jarod says. "We need you with us."

Lucas, Jarod, Jarod, Lucas. How do they tell themselves apart? A sound grabs my attention. A small plane is coming; one of the vertical lift Bells that GERI is using.

"Wish we had that to travel in," Lucas says. "I want to learn to fly. It'd get us off this island and to Vancouver a hell of a lot faster."

"Did you see the heavy equipment coming in all day yesterday?" Jarod asks.

"I bet they're going to generate a containment shell," Lucas says.

We all stare at him.

"For what?" Elliot asks.

"For the anomaly."

"They're not even finished mapping it," I protest. "You don't know what you're saying."

"The hell do you know," Lucas says. He punches my arm, and it hurts like crazy. I wince and rub the spot.

"I wanna take out a mini-sub," Jarod says.

Elliot raises an eyebrow. "You'll kill yourself."

"I could handle it," Jarod objects. "I wanna take out one of those underwater scooters, too."

I think about that thing in the water; the spray coming off a hand punching up through the waves.

"I saw something strange in the water yesterday," I say and instantly regret it.

"Yeah?" Jarod says? "What'd you see?"

"Nothing." What the hell can I say? *I saw a hand made out of water.* Yeah, that's the way to get punched in my stupid, impulsive mouth.

"Don't be a dick," Jarod says. "What'd you see? A mermaid?"

"I'd like to see a mermaid." Lucas puts his hands in front of his chest as he mimes holding large breasts.

"Oarfish." Sometimes I can keep it together and use my filter. Better late than never, right?

"Oarfish? What the hell? Who cares? Shut the hell up." Jarod looks like a pissed-off ferret.

He punches me again. This time I jerk back and Elliot's tablet goes flying. It hits the ground at an odd angle. When Elliot reclaims it, I see little spiderweb cracks spreading out from one corner.

"Look what you did, Mutant." Jarod pushes me backward. I tumble off the bench and land hard on my back, the wind knocked out of me.

Elliot isn't laughing; he watches me with what might be concern. But he doesn't get up, or even say anything. I wish he would do something, tell the brothers to screw off, or help me up or something. But he just sits there.

I stand and slowly turn, hoping they don't see the tears in my eyes or the flush of my cheeks.

Lucas is ready to uncoil. I think he might take a swing at me. "What? You going to do something? Do it."

I imagine swinging back, sending Lucas on a trajectory that would land him right in the middle of that sparrow's nest. Instead, I step away.

"That's right, you're not going to do anything. Don't be all tough if you're not going to follow through."

Elliot finally stands and moves between us. "Stop. Act your age for once."

Jarod laughs. "You act your age."

His brother finds this hilarious and for some reason Elliot laughs with them.

"Let's shoot pool," Elliot says.

The brothers love pool. I'm ridiculously good at it, I suppose because I can see the angles in my head and figure out impact and outcome. Maybe Elliot's trying to play peacemaker.

Jarod nods. "Sounds like a plan. Come on, Luke."

Elliot picks up his cracked tablet and I see him in the reflection, the mirror man, his fractured face staring out at me, until Elliot shoves the tablet into his backpack.

They set off for the short, drab building. It's a minute before he turns around and realizes I'm not with them.

I've climbed onto the picnic table, breathing hard, trying to keep the anxiety down.

Elliot gives me a look of pity. I hang my head.

I notice powdered bird crap on my pants. I have no idea how it got there.

I don't want Elliot to come back. Partly because I'm ashamed, but mostly I don't want him to notice my panic attack. If he asks what's wrong, I can't tell him.

I might tell him.

Because I don't always control my impulsive mouth.

Access Denied

Jennifer

G ETTING THE DATA SHOULDN'T have been a big deal, but the classified designation told Dr. Jennifer Newton otherwise.

Jennifer frowned, leaned back in her chair, and tried another request, sure she had entered something incorrectly. Submitting the form again, she waited for computer authorization.

A flashing red rejection icon from GERI popped up. She moaned.

Why block the data?

If some control freak protecting turf turned out to be responsible, and never mind that she had top clearance or that she worked on a project that should've automatically opened such doors, she'd see that asshole busted.

Bureaucracy empowered a paranoid and secretive mindset, and it didn't help that this bureaucracy was not only multinational but tied into the private sector as well.

Everyone had something to hide; that gave them the illusion of value.

She needed the data on the electromagnetic field around the Earth. Sure, GERI regularly published that information, but the public information wasn't precise enough. She needed more detail, and they had it.

She could make a call, but stopped herself, electing instead to work within the chain of command. At least for the present.

Sorting through the personnel roster, she found the name. She sent off a message letting that person know what she wanted and why with a deadline for a response. If she didn't hear by that time, then she'd blow her cool.

Jennifer stood and rolled her hips, then leaned farther back to ease lumbar pain. Too much sitting. She used to run daily and go to the gym three times a week. She used to do a lot of things.

Three other people worked nearby, all of them bent over a desk as they spoke into a headset or typed something onto their computer screens. She took the next half hour checking in with each of them, offering encouragement or giving suggestions.

"Hey, Jennifer, have a look at this." Dr. Herschel Alfredson, head of the research team, waved her over.

On his computer, a web-shaped image based on statistical modeling took up most of the screen. It was a graphic representation of the energy readings they continuously collected, which showed the area surrounding the anomaly they'd come here to study.

Right now, it displayed a green blip she hadn't seen before.

"Time stamp?" she asked.

"Just happened. I froze it."

"That's in the water near the beach."

"Not more than a couple yards out."

"Duration?"

"A few seconds."

It could be anything. The anomaly gave off strange emanations from time to time and produced unpredictable aberrations. Another thing to put down and study. Still.

She called to Alex Schwedt, a nearby tech, to replay video of the beach area around the time of the stamp. Ten minutes before, and ten minutes after. They had cameras placed throughout the compound, surveillance drones, and three more cameras floating on buoys near the anomaly.

He pulled up the video feed from the beach, the time of the recording running in the lower right-hand corner. As she watched, it occurred to her how strange it was to study something in such a detached way. She hadn't seen the anomaly with her own eyes. Couldn't. Because it wasn't safe.

Her current work was so hands-off. Not like when she did lab experiments in college, using a Geiger counter to measure the radiation from samples of petroleum-immersed Barium.

When was the last time she'd gone down to the beach? She was on a gorgeous coastal island in a dramatic northwest paradise, and she couldn't recall strolling along the water more than a couple times since arriving nearly six months ago.

The timestamp on the video showed seven minutes before the blip when Spencer came walking into view of the beach camera. Jennifer grinned. He squatted, looking at something in the water. Soon, another figure appeared. The Faradays' kid, Maude. Funny. Smart.

The two soon started talking. Jennifer wished she could read lips. Not that she would ever invade Spencer's privacy. But she hoped they'd become friends.

"There's your boy," Herschel said. "He's a sharp guy."

"Very sharp," Jennifer agreed.

"If he were working with us, he'd probably be the one to make the breakthrough on what the data means."

The statement was only half in jest. Jennifer had overheard several scientists making hushed comments about Spencer's observations with patronizing amusement about her "*crazy*" son. Give him another five years and he would run a project like this.

"I'm having a hard enough time keeping him from looking over my shoulder as it is."

"If you were his age, you'd have your nose pressed against the window."

They shared a laugh as Jennifer remembered her own ambitions entering college. Damn straight. She would have found a way into the middle of it all.

"Thank God he hasn't connected the project to his advanced schoolwork," she said. "But I think he has suspicions."

"It's tricky with him. I'm giving him enough to be creative so he doesn't get bored. It would be so much easier if I could give him the initial conditions that caused the anomaly. He's in the dark trying to find an underlying pattern among chaos. Still, he's finding seemingly random solutions more often than he should, statistically speaking. Isn't it nice to know your boy has such outstanding abilities?"

Jennifer smiled, but her eyes felt so tired, weighed down with years of worry about her son. "I wish he had them for making friends."

"Right now, we don't need him to make friends." Herschel put a hand on her arm, an awkward gesture. They weren't close. Not outside the lab. The act was that of a leader offering necessary support to keep an employee working. "Spencer gave me a prospectus to look at last week," Herschel said. "He's delving into hydrocarbon molecules for quantum computing. He wants my permission to run some experiments."

"He didn't mention that to me," Jennifer said, but she wasn't surprised.

On the screen, Spencer was more animated than usual, smiling often, waving his hands about. He liked that girl.

"I didn't know your boy and Maude were friends," Herschel said.

She leaned in closer to the monitor. "I don't think they are. But maybe they will be."

"She's a good kid. A little rebellious."

"Maude? Rebellious?"

"You watch. In another few months, Fran will have her hands full." Herschel raised an eyebrow. "She has them full now. Maude won't want to stick around here much longer. She'll probably end up in New York where she belongs. Not on an island surrounded by statistics-loving people like us."

An idea crept into her mind that Maude would tire of the compound, but Spencer wouldn't. Immediately, she resented it.

Spencer was adventurous. He was a non-conformist, too. But perhaps that wasn't true rebellion. To him the rules often didn't seem to exist. She wasn't sure if he was unaware, or too aware.

The numbers running on the screen showed that the time when the blip should appear was coming up. Maude left Spencer, running off screen. Spencer watched her, then turned his attention to the ocean.

There. The blip. At that moment, something disturbed the surface of the water. She couldn't make it out, but Spencer responded. He almost fell, his arms shooting out for balance.

"Did you see?" Jennifer asked.

Herschel stopped the video, ran it over several times, freezing it. Then he tried zooming in on the surface of the water and enhancing the image.

She couldn't see clearly. It looked like a fish or something, but that shouldn't cause changes in the energy.

She considered asking Spencer what he'd seen, but she didn't want him to think they spied upon him. Even though they did. Such was the nature of their work. And if they forgot about Big Brother GERI keeping eyes on them, the military presence in the compound served as a solid reminder. Not that she minded them, not after living through the chaos of the quakes.

"I'm going to compare the new reading to the other irregularities we registered in the last month," she said.

Herschel nodded. "Good idea."

As she went back to her desk, a stupid thought scratched the back of her mind: that there were too many recent coincidences.

When she sat down and brought her computer out of sleep mode, a new email alert popped up. It was a reply from GERI stating that the requested data on the Earth's magnetic field was "unavailable."

She pinched her throat, a quick pulse beating beneath her fingers.

She had questions, but would anyone give answers?

Another Spencer

Spencer

B EFORE THE EARTHQUAKES. B.E. Another time. I have memories, and some are real, and some may be, or maybe they were, but aren't now. Another life. Another Spencer.

One of these Spencers, ten-years-old, heard a cracking, ripping sound, like whatever was breaking was hollow inside.

It shook me out of sleep. I shot up, struggling to orient myself, my heart beating too fast. A dream, maybe? The panic receded with each second until it released me. I fell back on the mattress, breathing hard and pressing my palms against my eyes.

Some dream. Some nightmare.

Predawn light filtered through the window. From downstairs came the sounds of my dad in the kitchen, opening and closing drawers and clanking utensils. The smell of strong coffee wafted upstairs.

It was a Saturday. No school. I could go back to bed, but the uneasiness continued.

My attention wandered until I finally noticed the mirror. I watched the crack from the corner of my eye. I'd broken it last night, slamming the closet door too hard after a fight with my mom.

The crack shifted.

No, it didn't. The light played tricks. But I felt compelled to look.

I turned my head away instead. If I didn't look, it wasn't real.

My heart skated up and down my throat and I couldn't swallow.

I inched over, keeping my back to it, counting my heart beats.

I spun around.

My fractured image stared back at me, but it had a wrongness to it that was more than the distortion caused by the damage.

I moved closer to the glass, watching myself advance like cautious prey. My shadow moved in the distance, running along the wall inside the mirror, well-defined despite the diffused light coming through the blinds. I stopped, but the shadow kept moving.

I stepped away from the wall and screamed, but my voice caught no sound. I whirled around, imagining myself fleeing, sprinting to the door and charging through the hallway.

Nothing. No shadow behind me except the one where you would expect it to be. A blurry smear along the wall.

My eyes darted, flicking back and forth between my room and the world inside the mirror. Blood rushed past my ears, muffling the sounds of the morning routine; the rustling of papers, the sliding of chair legs. My heartbeat quickened.

I stretched my arm out slowly, straightened my elbow, uncurled my fingers, the heat of my fingertips fogging up tiny spots on the glass.

The shadow remained several feet beyond. I didn't blink, even though my eyes watered. I didn't want to miss anything.

"Go," I said, with no idea why the word came to my lips. My voice, but not me. "It's getting late. It may be too late."

A grainy patch flickered in the mirror. It reminded me of sand vibrating on a metal surface. It had order to it, like a picture slowly resolving on a computer screen, assembling byte by byte.

Again, I scanned the bedroom, but it was empty. I returned to the mirror. The image continued to organize and expand until it took on a shape about my height. It could have been me.

"Spencer, don't be afraid."

That was my voice, only deeper. Heavier. And, what made it worse, I wasn't sure if I was afraid of what I was seeing or something else, a vast presence that had piggybacked onto the image, lurking somewhere out of sight. It was so empty. I felt I could tumble into it, let it suck me in. Stretch out that moment, until time smeared and it threatened the meaning of my current existence.

I looked over my shoulder again, then back at the glass. I swallowed hard. My legs wouldn't move.

"You know what I am?" The question came in a whisper, the voice uncertain, hesitant. "No, you have no idea. But I need you to know something."

Another voice spoke, this one younger and angrier. I couldn't make out what it said, but the figure in the mirror turned away for a moment.

"If you come through, you'll end us both." This time the words were clear. The voice sounded like me.

"You can't get through, can you?" This voice was younger. It sounded like me, too.

From the hall, our black cat Spithead yowled. I saw him over my shoulder, back arched, ears flat against his head.

Then the mirror shattered. Tiny shards shot everywhere. Glass sliced my forehead and cheeks and stung the exposed flesh of my arms. I staggered back, half-blinded, falling against the wall on the other side of the room before I dropped to my knees. I cried out, but not because I was hurt.

That's when I heard the name for the first time.

"Tha!"

The shout ripped through my brain. I gasped as it gripped me with a meaning I didn't understand, as if I'd known the word my whole life. "What?"

My dad stood in the doorway, out of breath. He stared at the ruined mirror for a second, then rushed in, helping me to my feet. When he touched my cheek, he pulled back bloodstained fingers.

"Your face." His voice broke. "What happened?"

"The mirror exploded." My answer was so absurd I laughed until I hiccupped.

God. Six years ago. And a thousand years into the future and the past.

Get A Grip, Spencer

Spencer

VANCOUVER ISLAND and...

Mom is at her computer, super focused. She's been at it for a while. She's still wearing her fluffy bathrobe, the one that feels like baby lambs, and she smells like white soap.

An outsider looking in on us might think she doesn't notice my presence, but her eyes show too much white as she slides papers she wants to keep from me into a desk drawer. She waves as I approach, then returns to the laptop, instantly engrossed.

I wish I had focus like that. Yeah, I can problem-solve, but I'm always thinking about something else. My mind jumps between a million things at once.

I don't spend a lot of time on homework, but I don't have to. I work in bursts, then bug the rest of the universe. I've beaten all my video games, and every security guard in the compound has begged me to leave them alone, although I think they get a kick out of me.

"What are you working on?" I rub my belly, counting my scrawny six-pack.

I hate my bellybutton. Is it possible to not have a bellybutton? I should have mine surgically removed.

Mom taps the desk; a sign she's mentally arranging stuff. I wait, hoping she'll finish and pay me some attention. I'm bored.

"I saw these fish, you know, and I think their behavior is being affected by the anomaly. It's possible to have brain waves affected by changes in electromagnetic fields, right? I read that some people have hypersensitivity to them. Which probably explains a lot, if you stop to think about it."

No response, but the corners of her mouth shift into a frown. She's heard me. My mom's hair is graying, but it looks cool with silver strands. Right now, it's a pile of messy waves because she forgot to dry it.

"What are you working on?" I ask.

She clicks her tongue and gives me that look. "Spencer, you're driving me bananas."

"I want to know."

"I can't talk about it."

"Come on, I'm not stupid."

"I never said you were stupid, I said I can't talk about it."

She leans back in her office chair, stretching. I pull open the desk drawer and peer at the top article.

"Magnetic reconnection and solar flares." I try to keep my tone light, to keep her annoyance from turning into furious yelling for me to get the hell out of there.

She shuts the drawer, so I shut my mouth. That look intensifies.

"Dr. Alfredson gave me some problems to do with solar flares a few days ago," I say.

Hard stuff. Mostly because the data is incomplete. Sure, the theoretics were solid, but the figures he came at me with didn't match my calculations.

I know I didn't make a mistake, so his data must be flawed. When I asked him about it, he laughed it off, saying it was a just an exercise. Only now I'm looking at the stuff my mom is working on, and I wonder.

"You're a field theorist," I say.

I'm trying to understand what her approach might be. Truth is, I want to show off. And I also can't help wanting to needle her a little, but only a little.

My poor mom. She's so patient. I know it's been hard since Dad died. She's disconnected from people, and her work doesn't encourage social activity.

My mom reaches for my hand. I instinctively back away. I wish I hadn't, so I step closer, but the moment is gone.

"You think solar flares have something to do with the anomaly?" I ask.

"I'm trying to look at different ideas and see what I can piece together."

"Yeah, but solar flares?" I can't imagine.

"Maybe not solar flares, but I'm examining some properties of solar flares. I'm looking for possible causes." She rolls her shoulders, working out the tension. She lets a little smile break through the exhaustion.

"Solar flares can cause electrical malfunctions. Maybe that's why my calculations and your data don't match. Maybe your equipment's flawed."

"Spencer, why are you torturing me? I don't have time."

Talking to her about her work is a dice throw. Sometimes mom will open up and play along, but sometimes, like now, she shuts down entirely. She seems to shut down more often when I bring up the anomaly.

Some people say the anomaly is a recent phenomenon. Others insist it's been there a long time, maybe decades, only now discovered. I find that hard to believe.

Marine biologists were the first to notice; they said the fish were behaving strangely. EcoCanada requested government funding. Their research findings sparked other studies until a satellite picked up odd readings.

That was at least a year ago. Six months ago, my mom dragged me here.

I step closer and hug my mom. I always feel like such a kid when I do.

Over her shoulder, I see a computer model of a solar flare along with a stream of numbers running down the side of the screen. All those particles accelerated by magnetic forces, converted into X-rays and gamma rays. Maybe the particles stream in patterns, or maybe their movements are chaotic.

When we separate, I say, "You're not thinking the quakes caused the anomaly, are you?"

Her smile fades, and she turns back to her computer. I don't look at her because I sense her eyes tearing up. She's in that mood, but so am I. We don't need to fuel one another. I hate when I'm this way. Get a grip, Spencer.

Mirror Man

Spencer

SEATTLE... back in Middle School

My dad walking reminded me of someone on stilts. His legs were crazy long, and he wore his pants loose so the way his legs bent looked artificial. I took two steps for each one of his.

It usually took me twenty minutes to walk to school. Trying to keep up with him that day, I knew it would take under fifteen.

Most kids got rides from their parents. My dad made me walk, no matter what the weather was like. At least he wasn't a hypocrite.

It rained that day. We slanted against the wind, heads down, as people rushed for eaves, flattening themselves against the sides of buildings. Others wrestled with umbrellas. Lightning stretched above us for a second. I stopped and lifted my face.

"Not now." Dad gave me a gentle shove, but I heard the irritation in his voice.

He was pissed. He had been since last night, when he got the call from school.   ·

I kept walking.

By the time we reached the gates to the Tahoma Middle School, the rain had stopped, but the air still felt dense. We cut across the blacktop, past playground equipment and climbing structures.

The birds had come out from the trees to arc across the sky, but they avoided one spot, as if sensing a trace of the storm that hadn't dissipated. I turned my head down and avoided a large puddle, my reflection stepping as I stepped.

We headed through the front doors of the school. The bell sounded for the end of the period. Kids rushed by, gray uniforms flapping, as they pushed through the halls to get to the next class. Some stared at us. Probably most did. The giant and his monkey. A couple of them smirked. A few more gave me that look, and I hoped my dad didn't see it. I didn't respond.

We weaved among the crowd, heading down the corridor. You had to go through the secretary to get to the principal.

The secretary's office had shiny floor tiles that the custodian waxed pretty much every night. Pictures lined the wall behind her desk, several with cheesy inspirational sayings like: "What lies behind us and what lies before us are tiny matters compared to what lies within us," and, "Be faithful to that which exists in yourself."

She sat behind her desk with a stack of yellow papers that she worked on while talking into a headpiece. Opposite her, there were plastic bucket chairs with metal legs. I sat in one. My dad sat beside me. A round wall clock ticked above us.

The secretary, Ms. Leigh, looked our way, holding up an index finger to show it would be a minute. She was very young for a grownup; a favorite of the students. Her eyes were expressive, especially when she laughed.

My dad didn't look at me that whole time, but I saw tension in his face. I sank lower in my seat, feeling awful he had to be here on my account.

After a little while, a buzzer sounded on the secretary's desk. She nodded to my dad. "You can go in now."

I stood up, but my dad put an arm across me that told me to sit back down.

Shit. Not good.

Without a word, Dad headed into Mr. Kaminski's office. I watched him shut the big wooden door, then let out a loud sigh that caused the secretary to frown.

"It's not as bad as all that, Spencer," she said.

How could you not love Ms. Leigh? She gave an encouraging smile, then answered an incoming phone call with such warmth, it bolstered hope that it really would be a, "Good morning!" A few minutes later, she hung up and smiled at me again.

The clock ticked and ticked. I stared open-mouthed at the flaking plaster ceiling until, ages later, Mr. Kaminski opened the door. The students all called him Commander, but not to his face.

I don't know why they called him that. Maybe it was because of his size and the vaguely military cut to his blazers. Maybe because he ruled the school and accepted no challenge to authority.

He smiled with yellow teeth, pointed a thick finger in my direction, and then crooked it.

"See, that wasn't long," Ms. Leigh said.

I rose and headed in, surprised by a third person in the office besides my dad and Mr. Kaminski. He was small, with watery blue eyes and gray hair. He had a neat beard, and wore oval glasses, with a nylon cord attached to the earpieces, so they could hang around the neck.

The small man whispered something to Mr. Kaminski, who nodded solemnly. He turned his gaze my way, his eyes softening.

"Hello, Spencer. I want you to meet Mr. Schreiber, our special education coordinator."

"Hullo," I said.

"Nice to meet you," Mr. Schreiber said. "Come have a seat and join us."

It sounded like I was being invited to a cookout.

Mr. Kaminski took a seat behind an antique desk that looked too small for him, while Mr. Schreiber sat on a leather chair, flipping through his notebook. He tugged his beard while he read whatever was written there. I sat on the couch next to my dad.

"We've been talking about the difficulties you've been having with the other students, about how they pick on you," Mr. Kaminski said.

Yeah, the other kids picked on me, but I didn't rat them out. They already thought I was weird enough. Getting them into trouble with the grownups would've only made them hate me more.

"You almost got into a fight with a few boys yesterday."

"I threw their football on the roof," I offered. "I didn't mean to."

I did. They were playing ball and wouldn't let me play. Then they started saying things about me and someone threw the ball to hit me.

Mr. Kaminski nodded. "What happened with Jeremy Dunkel?"

"He kicked me."

"In your private area?"

I didn't respond at first, so Mr. Kaminski repeated the question.

My dad was staring at me, so of course the tears started. My cheeks got hot, and my stomach contracted. I made myself answer, keeping my voice low, so they couldn't hear the tremble in it.

"He was fooling around. It was an accident."

Defending him was the best option. Because telling the truth would've been the worst. I didn't want any more trouble. Drag another kid into it, especially that kid, and instead of one bad episode, it became a series of bad episodes spread out over the rest of the school year. If not from him, then from his friends.

"This has been going on for a while, Spencer. The staff have tried to keep an eye on it, but it seems to be escalating."

My dad looked like he was about to say something. Judging from the sternness in his face, it wouldn't be pleasant. Mr. Schreiber must have seen it too, because he gestured for attention.

"I'm going to say something and it's going to be hard to hear," Mr. Schreiber said.

"What?" My father's question came across as a challenge.

Mr. Schreiber hesitated. He looked at Mr. Kaminski, as if getting permission to continue.

When the principal nodded, Mr. Schreiber said, "I know that Spencer is being bullied. We're doing what we can. We're working with the other parents, we're educating the student body about the need to treat one another with respect and to be sensitive to feelings, but there's more to bullying than that. People don't like it, but the person being picked on sometimes contributes to the situation without realizing it. That doesn't excuse the person doing the bullying, but—"

"You're saying the victim should shoulder some of the blame?" My dad turned redder. The vein that ran up the side of his neck throbbed.

"I'm not blaming anyone; I'm trying to problem-solve ways we can make Spencer's life easier. The medication's made a significant difference. We can see he's having an easier time concentrating and staying in his seat, but there are still things we can work on to help him. What are your thoughts, Spencer?"

I heard my name, but it was far away, coming at me from another universe.

I'd caught sight of a picture across the room. An old ship, maybe the Santa Maria, under glass. In it I saw our reflection: my father all tense and about to lose it, the principal sitting with the cast of a soldier, the meek special education coordinator, my own face—mouth open, eyes wide.

And there was someone else. Behind me. Reaching out in the picture's reflection.

"I've got a couple other students signing behavior action plans," the principal was saying. "And I have their parents coming in. But in Spencer's case, I'd like to make a plan that helps him deal with these issues in a more positive and appropriate manner."

I let my head drop, staying quiet, but I couldn't help stealing a glance at the thing in the reflection. Almost a year since I heard the name, Tha, but I still couldn't figure out the pattern; when the mirror man would show up. Infrequent, random, sporadic.

I wanted to draw attention to it. I wanted someone else to notice besides me.

The special education coordinator saw my gaze, responding with a puzzled expression. He turned toward the picture, then back to me. He obviously saw nothing out of the ordinary.

I felt like I might cry.

And then I did.

Through the blur of tears, I couldn't tell if the mirror man cried, too.

Secret Military Conspiracy

Maude

M AUDE WALKED WITH LONG strides through the north end of the compound. She couldn't shake the outrage.

The Wheelers hadn't touched her. They'd called her a surfboard. Made a few other stupid comments as she walked by the basketball court. No big deal. But she couldn't put it out of her mind.

She headed southwest, down a path toward the ocean, moving with deliberate grace, weaving through a copse of red cedars, the old lurking giants blanketing her in green shadows, soothing her with their fragrance.

Maude stopped and pressed a palm against the rough cedar bark. If only she could climb one of these ancient guardians; imagine stretching out above the ground, hidden in the leaves, escaping civilization in feral bliss.

Ok, maybe that was too far.

Maude took a deep breath, exploring the texture beneath her hand, the soft spots where moss covered the bark, and the dry, abrasive patches. Putting her mindfulness lessons into practice, she tried letting go of the anger and stress.

No judgement. Let the stupid Wheelers go. Put the jerkwad asshats out of her mind.

Screw them all. Even Elliot. Well, maybe not Elliot. She could kill the Wheelers slowly and never twitch, but maybe she could salvage Elliot, although it might take a lobotomy.

Elliot was hot. No, make that smoldering, an important difference. When he played basketball, Maude watched his strong, effortless movements, until she thought about how the other girls in the compound appreciated his assets, too.

And that's when the spell broke. Because she wasn't the kind of girl someone like Elliot ended up with. Also, he'd bore her long before it got serious. Still. Definitely hot.

Maude left the cool shade of the cedars and cut across the grass, along a well-worn path that took her between the dwellings and the lab. Cascading rock fountains and log benches gave the area a Zen atmosphere. Willows slumped down, their leaves shivering with the breeze, too depressed to reach for the sun.

She spotted Spencer and Elliot loafing under one of the weeping trees. Maude hadn't seen Spencer since that day at the beach, when he'd sat on the sand as if in a trance and accepted her like they'd known each other for a long time.

There was something about him. His features were rough and asymmetrical, but she liked them. And when he smiled, it seemed like he had something funny, or at least offbeat, to say. He was too cute.

"Maudie," Elliot hailed her like a long-lost friend.

She compared the two of them, standing side-by-side. Elliot, lean-muscled, powerful, confident. Spencer, tall, skinny, unsure of himself, with gangly arms and legs, and a neck that went on forever.

She played it cool.

"We're going to the rec center," Elliot said. "Shoot pool or something. Want to come?"

"Maybe in a minute," she said.

Maude nodded at Spencer. He rewarded her with a broad, crooked grin. Goofy and adorable.

She kicked the ground by Elliot's feet. "What are you doing here? I thought you were hanging with the Wheeler beasts. What are they destroying now?"

"Forget about earlier," he said. "No reason to be mad, Maudie, they're assholes. Don't let them get to you."

"Don't call me Maudie."

"You got it, *Maude*."

She turned her face skyward and said, "Anyway, I don't want to go indoors. It's too perfect today. I'm going strolling, then heading over to the cliffs."

"What for?" Elliot asked.

She shrugged, not sure how to translate her feelings into words. Because the sea was beautiful; because the water rushing up on the rocks, and the sound of the seabirds, and the smell of the salt made her feel like the quakes never happened, and there was no such thing as the anomaly.

She realized Spencer was staring at her and made eye contact. He blushed and turned away.

"Want to come with?" she said, then started walking down the path to the beach. Spencer and Elliot fell in beside her.

"How's everything, Spencer?" she asked.

"Good. It's good."

The sound of a helicopter arriving from inland made Maude look up. She watched it head for a landing pad at the far south end of the compound.

"Second one today," Elliot said.

"Yeah," Spencer said. "The first was a monster. It was carrying this huge metal frame for the offshore work they're doing."

"This one's military. See the markings?" Elliot said.

"Something's going on," Spencer said, then paused. For a few moments, his gaze tracked a squirrel making an impossible jump between two branches. "The faculty's all on edge," he said, as if he hadn't stopped talking.

Maude watched the helicopter drop out of sight, though the whirring of its blades stayed loud. "I didn't see any weapons on it," she said.

"Lots of military shit coming in," Elliot said.

"What branch of military?" Maude said.

Elliot cocked an eyebrow. "Top secret," he said. "I'd tell you, but then these guys in white would come from the bushes and they'd have to drug you and wipe your memory."

"And yet, I'm not intimidated," Maude said.

"She's a hardass," Elliot said.

Spencer didn't jump in. She wanted him to, but he wasn't paying attention. Where was he now? She tried guessing, tracking his gaze, but the buzz of a small motor interrupted.

A sleek burgundy golf cart sped toward them, horn blaring.

Dr. Alfredson, the compound's coordinator in charge of research, waved for them to get out of the way.

He was a rotund guy, a big shot from GERI, the group started by the United Nations, with a shiny bald patch who wore a white-collared shirt with straining buttons. He was the one who sent for Maude's parents to work on this project no one talked about.

Elliot and Maude stepped aside for the golf cart, but Spencer held his ground. The golf cart veered at the last moment, and Alfredson glowered.

"Goddamn, Newt," Elliot said. "You do that on purpose?"

Spencer looked after the cart as though seeing it for the first time. "Huh," was all he had to say.

"How're you still alive?" Elliot teased.

They took a shortcut down a steep incline, ending up near the beach, not too far from where the helicopter came down. Alfredson's souped-up golf cart parked short of the cement landing pad near the storage units the military had built.

The doors of the helicopter opened. Several soldiers exited, followed by General Dawes. Alfredson left the golf cart and the two men hugged like old friends.

"Military. Told you," Elliot said.

General Dawes and Dr. Alfredson's words were lost to the deafening roar of the helicopter.

Another group of soldiers exited the aircraft, transferring equipment to a waiting truck. They moved with grim efficiency.

Two soldiers stood near the general. They wore sidearms and carried rifles. One soldier noticed the three of them, and his eyes locked on, making Maude feel recorded and catalogued.

The soldier stepped close to the general and said something. Dawes peered their way as well, and then Alfredson.

"Shit," Spencer said.

"What?" Elliot said. "These guys act all secret military conspiracy, and *we* look suspicious? I say chill."

The scientist turned back to the general, saying something that caused the other man to laugh as they both got into the golf cart.

"See," Elliot said. "No reason to panic."

Maude agreed with Elliot, but sometimes authority gave you something to panic about for no good reason.

Maude watched the golf cart fly back up the trail. She and Elliot waved. Either the general didn't see them, or deliberately ignored them. Alfredson tilted his head, a brief acknowledgement.

Elliot slapped Spencer on the shoulder. "Don't know about you, but I want to see what they're offloading down there. I'm thinking we take a peek."

"Bad idea," Maude said. "It's not like we'd know what we're looking at, anyway. Well, maybe Spencer would."

"All that equipment is still in the crates, unassembled," Spencer said. "I don't think we'd know what they have down there. Unless we asked. Even then."

"Thought you knew everything, Newt," Elliot said.

Spencer ignored him. "They're bumping up the military presence. I don't think it's related to the anomaly. Interesting."

Maude considered her mother's work. Lately, she'd heard the phrase "mandatory security protocol" often repeated. She suspected the increased number of soldiers had to do with that.

"What do you think they're working on?" she asked Spencer, but he didn't answer. She asked again without response, then let it go before his lack of attention drove her nuts.

Maude watched the area around the helicopter, where soldiers manipulated large sections of opaque plastic into a screen for something.

"I'm bored," Elliot announced. "Time for the rec center."

Two soldiers passed by on the path, heading toward the administrative area. Their posture was more relaxed now, with the general out of sight.

Spencer watched them, his eyes following their shadows. There was a lot going on in that head. Maude nudged him.

His eyes snapped to hers. "What if shadows are really souls?"

"What?"

"You're really pretty," he said.

Her cheeks became hot. She never knew what he was going to say, and he probably didn't either.

Maude could tell Spencer regretted his words as red blotches appeared on his cheeks, his brows knitting together. She was flattered but didn't know what to say.

"What about me?" Elliot asked.

"You're pretty, too," Maude said. And he was, the asshole. He was prettier than her.

Elliot smirked, and Maude was sure he wouldn't leave it alone.

Spencer walked away with his head down.

He was a bird who got inside the house and kept flying around. You were scared he'd hurt himself, but too afraid to help him for the same reason.

Maude caught up to him, and Elliot matched pace.

They made an awkward parade.

Talking To A Puddle

Jennifer

A CHEERFUL ELECTRONIC DING notified Jennifer she had new email. She rolled her office chair closer to her work computer.

> *Jenn,*
> *Landing at the compound shortly. I need to get up to speed on where we're at with lab findings. Let's meet soon.*
> *Drew*
> *Sent from my cell phone*

So, he'd returned to the compound after six weeks on the mainland. Jennifer grinned and admitted she missed him. General Andrew Dawes and Dr. Jennifer Newton kept their relationship under the radar; she bet few people realized their closeness.

When she was with Drew, she felt permitted to both miss her husband, to grieve his passing, but also think about the present and a future without him. Drew was the reason she came here.

She wanted to say something to Spencer about the relationship, but worried about how he'd react. Maybe Spencer already knew, or suspected, but he hadn't said anything. Yet.

If he took the news badly, she might have to call it off. And she didn't know if she could. She certainly didn't want to. But the relationship could send Spencer into a tailspin.

He still had so much repressed grief about his dad. Her moving on could break something loose inside him. At sixteen years old. she couldn't force him into counselling or hide meds in his apple sauce.

From across the lab, Dr. Mitchell Plumber called out to her, "What's with all this stuff!"

Mitch loved doing that. He would drop sentences and expect people would know what he was referring to.

"What, Mitch?" she asked in a patient tone, holding in a sigh.

"Look at the beach. What's all that crap they're setting up?"

"They're putting in a sensor grid and monitoring station."

The sensor grid would warn them of any dramatic changes in the electromagnetic field. If extreme enough, an alarm system would sound throughout the compound, sending everyone to their designated spots. Worse than extreme, and there was an evacuation plan, if they could hold on until the mainland helicopters came. If the choppers didn't come, there were underwater scooters so they could take their chances against the elements.

Mitch cleared his throat. "That doesn't look like a sensor grid."

She counted to three. "What's it look like, Mitch?"

"It looks like shielding."

Jennifer clicked on her monitor controls, calling up the beach. They were using machinery to move equipment to a large metallic platform. Radiation shielding? The labs had shielding against electromagnetic pulses or other radiation issues brought on by possible changes in the anomaly, but why did they need shielding on the beach?

Too many unanswered questions in the last couple weeks. Too much secrecy. She recalled the raw data GERI denied her. She didn't like feeling paranoid.

She'd see Drew tonight. She hoped he didn't use her lack of security clearance as a reason to hide the answers.

Spencer

My mother came back late last night from "catching up on things" with General Dawes. That's fine. Seriously. She's an adult, right? I get that. She can come and go as she pleases. Yet it still bothers me, and I hate that it does.

When she got up in the morning, I didn't say anything about her and Dawes. I played it nice, then headed outside. We don't talk much, at least not about things that make either of us uncomfortable.

I pick up a stone and toss it into the ocean. There's rain in the air. A storm feels heavier when you're right by the shore. I peer across at the stretch of greenish gray toward the distant mountains on the mainland.

General Dawes. He's okay, I guess. I don't know him well, though he's friendly enough. For some reason, I can't generate the same response in return. When we talk, I think he tries too hard, but then I'm sure I'm imagining things, that I'm throwing up my defenses.

When I check in with myself, I'm not sure how I feel or what he's putting out. Talking to me must be like jumping into the middle of a foreign film but without subtitles.

Heading along the beach, I walk with my head down, hoping I'm not approached by anyone. Being alone sounds good. And then I remember the army guys who invaded my spot, setting up their equipment by the water.

I keep going though, seeing them still there, voices lost to the sounds of the waves slapping the shore. They've spent two days erecting whatever it is they're putting in place. It's piqued my curiosity.

One guy stands with his olive drab shirt off, tucked into his waistband. He's short, but solid, with a webbed neck that makes him look like a bullfrog.

All the military folk I've run into so far are American. The political and geographical borders relaxed after the earthquake, but for the US to have a presence here, the UN must expect trouble. Or maybe they want to make sure we don't run off with all the expensive equipment that's being installed.

"When do you want to start tests?" he says into a headset. There's a pause before he speaks again. "Above my pay grade, buddy. It's not my Lego set."

That makes me chuckle. He turns and gives me a quick glance. He actually smiles. I can't help smiling back.

"Hey kid," the guy says.

Judging from the shape of his nose and the scars along the side of his face, he's had his share of fights.

"Hey," I say back.

He takes a few steps toward me. I sense he'd rather be hanging out on the sand, watching the others work, instead of busting his butt on something he has no real investment in. That's how I'd be.

"What's your name?" he asks.

"Spencer Newton."

"Newton?" He nods, weighing my name, giving me a once over. "I'm Cal Johnson."

Cal digs into a pocket, pulling out an energy bar of the military MRE variety. He peels away some of the green foil and pops a square into his mouth. He offers me some, but I shake my head.

"How come you guys are building shielding?" I ask.

"I don't know, Spence. I'm only inserting tab A into slot B." He laughs at his own joke.

I like his laid-back manner and sense of humor. He pulls the shirt from his waistband, slipping it on over his head.

Fish break the surface of the ocean. They jump with gleaming wings, hang in the air for a moment, then crash back down. I've never seen anything like it. The soldier turns to watch as well.

"Would you look at that? Too bad we're not out there with a reel." He laughs and turns back to me. A frown pulls at his face. His voice changes tone as he says, "Solar batteries. Yeah, I'll get it taken care of. Are you coming down now?"

It takes me a second to realize he's back on the headset.

"How many?" he asks. "Well, I'm glad I won't be one of them. Just come on down."

Cal's frown disappears. He once more stares seaward.

When he speaks, he sounds genuinely regretful, but there's an edge to his voice that allows no argument. "Spence, I have to ask you to go. We've got a bunch of stuff happening around here today, and we're supposed to keep the area clear."

I lean past him to glimpse what's happening inside the still partially open shelter. Two men in beige jackets wrestle with an expensive-looking piece of equipment; an enormous circular plate they lower onto a silver frame.

I'm certain it's germanium, a substance used in solar panels and optical fiber. I learned about it in my introductory electrical engineering class.

"You guys are getting ready to string out a sensor grid, right?"

"Spencer, seriously."

The words spill out; I can't help saying it. Maybe I want him to know I'm not some stupid kid. "Are you guys coordinating this with the lab, or is this something independent?"

The friendliness disappears from Cal's face. "Mr. Newton, I have to go."

"Yeah, but—"

"Shoo, buddy. You shouldn't be this close to what we're doing. I could get in trouble, and you wouldn't want that."

I raise my arms in surrender and turn. Idiot. I should've kept my mouth shut. The guy tried being decent, but I always have to be an asshole. And he has my name. If he really wants to be a dick, all he has to do is report me, and my mom will be all over me. She's way scarier than the military when she's mad.

I walk away without looking back. Being kicked out of here doesn't surprise me. I'm used to being kicked out of places.

My path slants away from the ocean, passing the cliff Maude scaled. The grains of sand are bigger here, more like miniature rocks. It's nowhere near as comfortable as my usual spot. The water is calm today, in stark contrast to all the commotion going on with the army guys.

I close my eyes, shivering as the brisk air tickles my cheeks and the back of my neck. When I open them again, there's something reflecting in the pool of water gathered in the rocks by my feet. The old feeling comes back, the uneasiness that I keep hoping will go away.

I check the area behind me, but there's nothing there to be reflected in the water. When I look back at the windswept surface of the pool, a man's face is visible at my shoulder.

I touch a finger to the water's surface, setting off concentric circles from the point of contact.

"Spencer."

I haven't heard from him since the earthquake. I don't want to hear him again. "There's no mirror here," I protest.

"There are millions of them on the water," he says.

This isn't real, it's some part of me I refuse to deal with. That's what my doctor would say, although I never told him about the thing in the mirror. I don't want to be as damaged as everyone believes I am. Maybe I'm not. Maybe I'm worse.

"Spencer?" It's the voice again, sounding like a far away echo.

"Water doesn't count," I say, and wish I hadn't. Responding gives a thing credibility. I should get the hell out of here. Go home, blast music through my headphones until my eardrums melt.

"Stop, Spencer," he says. "You're always flying to extremes. Black and white. Calm down."

A voice tells me to calm down. I almost laugh at that, but people laughing at disembodied voices that talk to them are obviously crazy. I decide to laugh anyway.

"I have a unique form of ADHD," I say. I'm calming myself. "Maybe they'll name it after me."

"There's nothing wrong with you, Spencer."

"My brain works differently."

"I know."

Talking to whomever it is, or whatever it is, makes me want to cry. I run my hand through my hair, fighting a sudden sickness. I fight the urge to throw up.

My foot comes down in the shallow pool of sea water, splashing the rocks and upsetting a couple of nearby gulls.

The voice is almost a whisper, but I can't shut it out. "I don't want you to be scared, and I don't want you to think you're crazy. You're not. You're stronger than you give yourself credit for being."

"I'm not," I say.

The reflection speaks in a low tone. I can sense its urgency. "I don't have much time, but I have to tell you. Everything is about to change, but I don't know how it's going to turn out. I thought there were certainties, but there aren't."

"I don't know if I want to hear this," I say.

"I promise you, you don't. I wish I could spare you this, but Spencer, people are going to die."

They're Coming

Spencer

I DON'T WANT THIS. Whatever the thing has to say, it's going to be bad, and who will I be able to tell?

"You're going to have to trust me," it says.

Tears sting my eyes. I had put this behind me, forced myself into believing what the doctors said, that I suffered from post-traumatic stress from my dad dying in the quake.

One doctor suggested to my mother that I had PTSD with dissociative symptoms. Depersonalization. Derealization. They could call it what they wanted as long as it had a name.

The image in the water crackled for a moment, like a signal breaking up from interference. It came back in mid-sentence: "... and things are coming to a head, but I don't know the result. All I can say is that the time may arrive when you and I face the danger of coming together. I don't know if it's possible, but if it is, you should turn and run."

I fear, for a moment, that he's gone again, leaving me with puzzling statements.

"Why?" I ask.

"Because I don't think either of us would survive."

The sound of an engine startles me. Further down the beach the soldiers start up a generator or some other large piece of machinery. I turn, taking in the whitecaps along the ocean's endless surface.

"Spencer."

The image in the pool sharpens. I see the usual suggestion of a face but, as always, I can't make out its features.

"Spencer!" This time his voice is angry, bitter. "Look for patterns. Look at how things fit together. I can't tell you anything other than that, because it will make no sense. But when the time comes, you follow Maude. You follow her."

"I don't know what you're talking about. Who are you? What are you?" I'm screaming now, my legs apart, my arms at my side, hands curled into fists.

"I'm the Molecule Thief," he says at last, like that should make everything clear.

"I'm not doing this," I say, more to myself than whatever's communicating with me.

"Stay with me, Spencer. Just for a second longer. What I know is limited; I can't see it all. I only know that you're going to have to make a choice, and it won't be a good one. You look for me though, you'll know when the time comes. You look for me. But keep your distance."

"That makes no sense."

"It will."

The image fades, then returns. "One more thing. The anomaly. It's there, right?"

I don't answer, so he shouts my name.

"Yeah!" I counter. "It's here."

"This is the day and time. I want you to leave the beach now. Run back to the compound as fast as you can. You've got to this time."

"That doesn't make sense, either."

"It's about to happen. They're coming. They're almost here. I'm not sure why or how, but you can die."

There's a difference to the pool; the surface looks less like water and more like a puddle of blackness. The face is clearer than it's ever been.

I have a wild urge and give in. I reach down to touch the thing in the water. As I move, there's resistance. The air pushes back.

The pain hits as I break through, touching the blackness. My forehead explodes.

I'm falling into myself, dropping through white and black static as bits of me detach, molecules flying into a void. There's a threshold where, when enough pieces break away, I'll fall apart like a million Legos scattering across the floor.

"SPENCER!"

Maybe I passed out, or maybe I'm having a seizure. My eyes are squeezed shut, and I'm keeping them that way, because I'm horrified that if I open them, I won't see the ocean, or the beach, or the sky. If I open my eyes, I'm afraid that whatever I see will be real, and everything else illusion.

But in a minute, or maybe it's a millisecond, or an hour, things shift. I can smell the ocean again. I feel the breeze against my cheeks.

Cold runs up my arms, settling around my shoulders, then works its way to the edge of my mind. I'm always afraid. Always.

I think I'll shut my eyes, and when I open them again, I'll be back in the old house, falling to the floor as the ground shakes and growls. Or I'll be a hundred-year-old man, blinking rapidly, thinking about everything I've missed. Or I'll be stretched out along the horizon until I snap into thousands and thousands of me.

I have questions, but I can't ask them.

"Spencer." The voice is at it again, but it sounds different. I almost think my dad is here, expecting to turn and see his static-wild hair and enigmatic smile. I miss him bad.

"What now?"

"I want to say how sorry I am."

"For what?"

"For what I've done to you all this time."

That makes me panic. For an instant, I lose control. Bits of me slip away, and the man from the other side of the mirror drinks them in.

My stomach contracts. I throw up my breakfast and see chunks of egg flecked with blood.

Since the quakes, since leaving Seattle behind and coming here, I've been sick a lot.

I wipe my mouth. The pool is still there, but not the Molecule Thief, or whatever he is. He's gone. I hope he never returns.

I peer behind me, studying the shadows in the pines, the places where the trees crowd together, competing with one another for soil and water, starving one another even though there are enough nutrients and room to grow.

As soon as my head clears, I'm getting out of here.

"Molecule Thief," I whisper. "Up yours."

I burrow into the sand with the tip of my shoe. My mind zips all over the place because I can't stop his words from echoing through my thoughts.

It's scary as hell because there's a truthfulness about him. Even though sometimes it seems like he lies, there's something intimate when we interact.

I scan the horizon, peering at the stark difference between the gray sea and lighter gray sky. A line divides two worlds. I reach out, tracing the horizon with my finger. I know it's not really a straight line. I want to erase it. I want to rub it free and let the grays merge.

Something is there.

I watch the ocean. I imagine the energy fields around the anomaly shifting, sliding, and something pushing through.

They're coming.

Pissed Myself

Spencer

I'M STUCK AT AN intersection where time both exists in its entirety and doesn't exist at all. A noise startles me. I whip around.

Maude stands there, mid-step, hands raised like she's surrendering to the cops, mouth open in a perfect oval shape.

"How long have you been there?" I demand.

She blinks quickly, looking a little startled. I'm about to apologize, but she sets her mouth in a hard line. She moves closer, hands at her sides.

"It's nice to see you, too," she says, matching my tone. "Who were you talking to?"

"No one." The words are unconvincing.

Maude arches an over-plucked eyebrow at me. She doesn't respond, but I know she won't go gossiping about strange Spencer sitting by the shore talking to imaginary friends.

"You said Molecule Thief?"

"I'm just crazy," I offer, but it sounds awful.

She looks into the pool, really looks into it. She even bends forward slightly, placing her hands on her thighs for support.

"How did you get here?" I ask. "Did you walk by the soldiers?"

"Yeah, I watched them for a minute. I kept waiting for them to shoo me away."

"They didn't shoo you away?"

"No."

"Apparently, they don't mind being watched by a pretty girl. They kicked me out."

"And here I thought I'd dazzled them with my shining wit."

"You have that, too. I didn't mean—"

"Why do you hang out with them?" she asks.

"Who?"

"You know, Elliot and the Wheelers. They're such assholes."

She's right about the Wheelers, but not so much about Elliot. I think she knows it, too. As much as she declares Elliot's a jerk, her demeanor around him says otherwise. She gets into banter in a way that's almost flirtatious.

Elliot's okay, not always, but most times. Elliot is different when he's with them than when we're alone. That's the way it always is with people. We're always different with someone else. We're a thousand other people and ourselves at the same time.

"What do you mean?" Maude asks.

Shit, I said that out loud. "I mean, Elliot isn't that bad."

"You let them pick on you, you know."

"I don't let anybody pick on me." The words ring false, making me cringe.

I wish she hadn't come by, but I don't want her to go. The warning of the thing in the pool is still there, pressing me. I don't trust myself.

We fall silent. The ocean again draws my attention. After a few moments, I shut my eyes hard, then open them again.

The surface is wrong. Maybe a hundred and fifty yards out, the water in one area looks different.

Along the beach there's constant wave activity, foam splashing hard against the rocks, then receding with a rush. Out a little further, there are lazy swells. But in that one spot, the gray greens darken into a dull purple.

"What's out there?" she asks.

"Maybe a whale by the surface, or a big school of fish." I keep my attention on it.

"I don't think so," she responds.

"Then you tell me." I immediately hate myself for sounding snotty.

The water rounds upward, like the back of a gigantic tortoise, then drops. It happens a second time.

Could the military be doing this from down the beach? I doubt it. They only had sensor grids and things like that. I didn't see anything capable of displacing a large amount of water.

Maude's got a phone in her hand. She holds it up, taking a video. She glances my way with an excited smile.

I don't share her enthusiasm. I'm freezing inside. All I want to do is run like hell.

"We have to go," I say.

Light pulses on the water in impossible fractals. It's hypnotic. I watch, standing there like a fish gulping air, but not getting oxygen.

"Maude, listen to me."

"What is that out there?"

"I don't know, but we need to run."

"Maybe there's some sort of blasting going on," she offers. "You know?"

"I don't think so."

"Then what?"

They're coming.

I stare at her, then back at the ocean. It's like I'm standing outside myself, in another place, in another time, looking at this frozen moment. It's hard to breathe.

It would be so easy to stay stuck in this fraction of time, to never take another breath. But in a snap the world catches up to me and I'm watching Maude. She stands with her hands on the side of her head, her teeth clenched.

"What's wrong?" I nearly shout the words.

"Do you hear that? Oh, it hurts!"

I hear the ocean, the waves that run up on the beach and crawl back down. I hear the wind pick up, and my heart as it drives the blood through my neck and past my ears.

"I don't hear anything."

"God, how can you *not* hear it? It's like the worst kind of high-pitched feedback at a heavy metal concert."

The mound disappears from the surface, but now the water churns near the shore, spraying us with salt water, dampening my hair and exposed skin. I back up, watching the ocean.

I don't have time to explain. She wouldn't believe me. I don't want her to laugh at me, or worse. I can't stand that thought. She's been the coolest person I've met in this place since I got here. I've let her matter.

Run, just run. Get out of here. If I bolt, she'll follow. I wouldn't have to explain then.

The thing in the water is closer. Maude doesn't seem to see it; she shakes her head, pressing one ear, then the other, like someone coming out of a swimming pool.

I grab her hand, half-dragging her for several steps. I don't usually touch people, girls, boys, anyone. It feels good, but strange. I don't let go.

Her eyes are wide and indignant. She's a tough one. I can imagine her taking a swing at me. I don't want that, so I stop.

She pulls away. "What the hell, Spencer?"

I reach for her hand again, but she snatches it back.

Why did I just grab her? Stupid. No time for apologies. The air hums with energy. I see lines in the spray. Is that what she hears?

"We have to go," I say.

Forced calm is horrible. As soon as I stand still and straighten my posture, I feel exposed. I don't want to look over her shoulder. I don't know how many more seconds I can hold it together.

"What's happening?" Maude says.

My mom uses that tone when she tries to calm me.

I can't put it into words. "Something," I start. "It's..."

The frustration is so great tears roll down my face. I cry in front of her. Not a loud wail. Silent tears, but I still don't believe I'm crying in front of Maude.

"There's something coming," I manage to say. "I don't know what it is, but we have to go. Can't you feel it?"

Having said what I said should be enough, but not for Maude. She waits for more. There's a look of determination on her face that shows she won't move until she gets it.

I back away from her. She tentatively follows.

It's a weird dance. I take a step. She takes a step. We've moved maybe ten feet when I fall over a half-buried rock. Maude stops too late, tumbling over me, landing hard on her knees.

She has sand on the side of her face. In the last few seconds, I've done everything I could to convince her I'm truly insane.

"Shit." She sits there, rubbing a scrape through a new hole in her pants.

I stare beyond her, watching the surf, waiting for something, but I don't know what.

I want to punch myself.

The military shelter is about a hundred yards away. Two soldiers stand in front of it, one of them is Cal Johnson. I stand, grabbing Maude's hand and pulling her to her feet. That stops her protests.

Maybe there's something about my appearance that finally convinces her to take me seriously. That's when I catch movement from where we stood a few minutes ago.

Sand kicks up on the beach and it's not the wind. She falls in next to me, following my gaze, her entire body tensing.

"What is that?" There's fear in her voice. Finally.

"Shit."

I wave at Cal and the other soldier. They're facing us, talking to each other, but neither moves in our direction.

Maude and I run the rest of the way to the military structure. As we arrive, more soldiers come out of it to stop us. Cal waves them off.

"Spencer," he calls out.

He smiles, but it's the sort of smile you give someone to try to calm them down when you think they're bat shit crazy. What am I going to say? My mind is blank. Any words that spill out are going to be ridiculous.

Chaos fills my head. Relax. Take a breath. Get control.

"You two shouldn't be here." There's a note of regret and warning in his statement. "I'm sorry."

Two men step past us. At first I think they see something and they're heading to confront it. Then I realize they're getting in position. We're being surrounded? They're taking us in?

"Something's coming," I finally say, struggling for breath.

Cal exchanges looks with the others. "I don't see anything."

"Maude, tell him."

"He's right."

Only when Maude says this do I realize she believes me. We're all watching the beach now.

I'm glad I'm standing alongside soldiers with powerful firearms because my mind is in low-power mode. I can't fathom it, but I'm shutting down. I'm losing it. Next, I'll find a wall to lean against because that's what I do when the world threatens to fall away.

"Wait," one soldier says.

He studies the beach, looking over my shoulder. I don't know what he sees, and I don't want to.

That's when a string of green lights near the sensor grid suddenly goes red.

"We've got code red," one soldier comments into a microphone. "Repeat, we have code red on the beach."

The compound's alarm system activates. Sirens shriek through the treetops and down the beach, like they do during the drills we have to endure. But now they sound different, more urgent.

I stagger back, my heart jack hammering in my chest. Maude's mouth is wide open. She might be screaming, but the sirens are so loud I can't tell.

Cal grips my shoulder, shouting into my ear. It's almost impossible to hear him. "Get the hell out of here!"

He gives me a nudge, gesturing up the hill toward the compound. When I don't respond right away, he shoves me, then pushes Maude, too.

She runs. I freeze. I don't know why, but I do, and then vertigo hits me.

Maude is several yards ahead. She makes it to where patches of tall grass intersperse the sand when she stops, realizing I'm standing like a pathetic marionette with cut strings.

She comes back for me. As she takes my hand, pulling me along, I'm both ashamed and grateful.

Trees crowd us from the east, but to our left the western view of the ocean is unobstructed. I can't help looking.

What I see makes me pivot, yanking against Maude's pull. She tugs right back in the opposite direction, toward the foot-worn path that leads up the hill.

"What are you doing?" she shouts.

We both strain in different directions, rendering us motionless. Back where we came from, a lone figure approaches the sensor grid. Its strides are long, its legs rigid, as if it's having trouble bending its knees.

It looks like a soldier, but where did it come from? Even though we're yards away, I can tell something's wrong.

Maude lets me go. We both stumble a few steps as we regain our balance. Maude's face goes from puzzlement to horror.

One man from the grid steps forward and the stranger shudders.

"That's what we were running from," I manage.

A soldier comes out from the ugly rectangular structure, his rifle at the ready. Cal and two others stand with sidearms aimed at the stranger.

Cal's face darkens as he barks out orders we're too far away to hear over the cacophony still blasting from the loudspeakers. By the way he gestures with his weapon, it's clear he's ordering the intruder down on the ground.

One soldier moves closer to the newcomer. He keeps his gun trained on the man, but his hand shakes. The stranger turns and they stare at one another.

"What's going on?" Maude asks.

Time to go. Time to hide. I'm losing my nerve. I'm dropping, dropping, dropping. I gulp air, tasting bile at the back of my throat.

"Spencer?" Maude says.

She presses a hand to my shoulder. I don't want her, or anybody, to see me this way. Run, Spencer. I can't.

"I'm okay," I whisper.

There's commotion on the beach. One soldier kicks the back of the stranger's knee. It doesn't budge, so he kicks again. Another man prods the stranger with a rifle butt.

The soldier with the quivering hand fires, the weapon barely moving in his grasp.

The shot is a killing one to the head. Cal and the other soldiers yell at him, and among themselves. The stranger stands still as if a bullet hadn't blasted into his skull.

"Oh my God," Maude says.

Cal and the others fire their sidearms.

Maude forces me into cover behind a rock. She pulls me against her, one hand on the side of my head, hugging me close. The contact overwhelms me. My first instinct is to fight it, but I choose to surrender and stay put.

Crouched behind the shelter of the boulder, there's nothing but alarms. It's like the gunfire happened somewhere and somewhen else. Not seeing what's going on is horrible.

I rise, breaking free from the safety of Maude's arms, peeking over the rock as a burst of light comes from the beach. It's the same color I saw in the oarfish scale.

In an infinitesimal fraction of time, the air around the stranger fluctuates. The man stutters, his jerky figure at odds with the fluid lines of everything around him.

And then he disappears. One minute there, the next minute gone.

The soldier who fired the first shot is rigid. His mouth is open in a scream. He falls straight back; a statue tipped over. The other soldiers fire their weapons at empty air, shooting the place where the stranger should be.

One of the three remaining men drops to his knees to attend to his fallen comrade. He's going to find it's too late. I'm not sure what's been done to him, but I know he's dead.

Cal still shouts orders, but his attention is on the ocean. I don't think he really sees it.

Maybe he's trying to get control of the situation, or maybe he's trying to make sense of it all, trying to connect bits of information that don't want to connect. Welcome to my world.

His gaze turns our way.

I realize my pants are slightly wet. I'm a sixteen-year-old boy genius, and I've pissed myself.

Fractured

Spencer

A S THE MINUTES TICK by, I keep sitting, stiff and unmoving. I could believe I imagined everything, but Maude is next to me, eyes wild.

Her hands shake, so I look away, focusing on the ground. I study a nearby swaying bed of eelgrass.

I've seen geese there before, small black geese with white tails. They were there when Mom and I first came here, but I haven't seen them since. Birds always know something.

The sirens keep sounding, but the volume is more tolerable. Maybe I've gotten used to it.

"I'm going to be sick." Maude drops her head, slowly drawing in air.

I have to say something, anything, to fill in the awful emptiness. My arms are frozen at my side, my mouth sealed shut.

I resist the urge to cover my damp crotch with my hand. I don't want to be here. I don't want to be anywhere.

A piece of poplar fluff catches the breeze and is drawn up over our heads until it vanishes from sight. That's me someday.

"Are you okay?" she says.

Oh God, I should be the one who asked her. I'm a thousand miles away from Maude. A million. If only I could say something.

She's got that look I've seen on my mom's face when she's afraid she's done something to drive me outside myself. It's never her fault, and it's not Maude's fault. I need to say something. Anything. Say it.

"I didn't pee my pants."

Maude's eyebrows shoot up. A trace of a smile appears. "No? Well I sure did."

I feel like I'm running, tearing across the sand, speeding along the whitecaps on the ocean, trying to catch the horizon. Maude laughs and cries and hiccups. She moves closer and throws her arms around me.

I can't return the gesture. I can only sit here until my mind slows, and the fear recedes. Maude's cheek is moist against my neck, and hot. I can feel her eyelashes. I don't mind it so much.

Eventually, I pull away from Maude, peeking over the rock. Maude eases up beside me and I take in the scene at the beach. Our breathing synchronizes.

The soldiers are still standing with rifles ready. One calls into his radio. Maybe numbers. Maybe words. Nothing else happens.

Maude says, "I can't believe we watched someone die."

Don't talk about it. Let it go. The smell of blood fills my nostrils, along with charred flesh and ozone.

I'm hearing the crackle of a downed power line. I know people are dead. I haven't seen them yet, but they are all around me, scattered under the rubble left by the quake.

Here and now, Spencer. Come back. Forget the past. What's Maude saying? Am I afraid? She repeats herself.

"Aren't you afraid?"

I only nod. She leans forward, as if expecting me to elaborate. What's to elaborate, right? Nothing's changed. A second ago she tried making me feel safe. Now she's asking if I'm afraid?

"We should get out of here." Her voice has an edge now.

"Yeah." She means location. I mean everything.

She moves first, and I have the horrible feeling of being left behind. I scramble onto the path, staying with her as we race toward the compound's center.

Hardly any civilians are around. Soldiers have taken over, running here and there with a sense of urgency. The sirens keep up their constant wail.

"We're going to be in trouble," Maude says.

I agree but don't say anything. My hands shake. Calm down. A soldier sees us and pauses.

I think "here we go," but then he turns away, like he knows he should say or do something, but doesn't want to be bothered.

I reach for Maude's hand to pull her toward cover, then catch myself. Instead, I step toward the main path.

It's not as cool here as at the beach. Not as windy. I almost feel normal, except I know better. Nothing's ever going to be normal again. Not really. The world is barely holding together.

Maude walks faster, so I pick up my pace, too. I pass Maude and then she tries to pass me until we're almost jogging.

Stupid sand sliding down my back. Small grains made up of smaller grains, made up of particles and between them are these spaces that are actually enormous and filled with quantum foam.

"Stop," Maude says.

I almost bump into her. She breathes hard, moisture beading on her forehead.

"Sorry." I take a deep breath, like my therapist made me do when a session became too emotional. Calm down. Calm down. Inhale. Exhale.

"I'm going to head to the basement," Maude says.

We're at the rec center. I didn't realize we'd come so far.

"God, I hope the doors aren't locked," she says. "We're going to be in such shit."

She scans the surrounding area, biting her lower lip. There's something dangerous about her, like she's going to explode.

She studies me, and I ask myself what Spencer she sees. Here I am. The dweeby baby with my hands in my pocket, and a drying pee stain on my crotch.

"It'll be okay," I promise.

Stupid. No, it won't. We both know it. That's when I see in her eyes that she's more like me than I thought. She notices things too, things she shouldn't. Maybe not like I do. I hope not for her sake, but she does. Holy shit.

"I'm going home," I say.

"Don't."

"Why?" I ask. "What's the difference?"

Maude stares at me until I feel uncomfortable. I look away.

She takes my hand, holding it tight even as I start to pull free. I force myself to accept the contact, to surrender control. I drop my face so she can't see how hard this is for me.

Maude lifts my chin and presses her mouth against mine, her lips cold, her cheeks warm. She's kissing me, and then she isn't. It's over before I can wrap my head around it.

The intimacy of that second disturbs me, yet I want more. But the moment is over. All that's left is the flush in my cheeks and the tingling in my stomach.

"You okay?" she asks.

I nod, and she turns. A thousand unsaid responses fill my head and die on my lips. Maude heads off for her station.

When she's out of sight, I head home. I'm all over the place, seeing the grass around me as if through an electron microscope, following it down to a spectrum of infinitesimal green and up across various densities of water vapors in the sky. I inhale and pick through competing molecules from juniper plants, steak from the cafeteria, and salt from ocean spray.

I'm outside myself, looking in, looking back. This moment is shared, and I'm almost fractured by the number of observers.

Drone Eating Anomaly

Jennifer

T HE ALARM AND SERIES of lights over Jennifer's equipment told her this wasn't a drill.

She turned around, checking the nearby video feeds. She ticked off the possible scenarios, the most likely being a radical change in the anomaly; hopefully not a dangerous one. All the monitors started shutting down.

"Herschel?" she called out.

Dr. Alfredson wasn't there. Several people were fidgeting with equipment while talking to one another over their headsets. She put on her own, listening.

"It's not an EMP," Alex, the tech, said. "If it were that, our other stuff out there wouldn't be giving us data."

"Maybe someone pulled a plug." That was Fran Faraday's voice.

Several people laughed.

"I'm trying to get General Dawes online," Alex said.

"I don't see any evidence it's an automatic alert, so..." As usual, Mitch left the sentence unfinished.

"The system didn't trip it?" Fran said.

"Anyone know where Dr. Alfredson is?" she said.

"I think he went to the hospital," Mitch said, referring to the old tuberculosis hospital that stood concealed on the south side of the compound near the beach.

"I phoned, but they aren't accepting calls," Alex said.

"You mean communications are down?" Fran asked.

"I got hold of the communications officer, but he won't put anything through to anyone," Alex said. "I called several times. He just promises to take messages or redirects me to voicemail."

Jennifer bit the inside of her cheek, leaning forward. She studied the recording of the energy emanating from the anomaly.

Some fluctuations, but nothing dramatic. Maybe this wasn't about the anomaly. Solar flares could have set the alarm off, or some other atmospheric disturbance. Not that she had any basis for comparison. This had never happened before.

She didn't know what to make of it.

The alarms ended. Several people in the labs cheered. Some applauded.

"We're still under lockdown," Mitch called out, and the mood in the lab quieted.

Jennifer collapsed into her chair. The inability to make outside contact or see what was going on through the compound frustrated her, and the data coming from their sensor array was insufficient. They needed raw data from the satellite, along with approval for the mini-subs to explore first hand.

They'd used an underwater drone, but at the edge of the anomaly it stopped transmitting. They searched the area, but it had obviously gone into whatever was behind the patch of energy twenty feet below the surface of the ocean, then lost contact.

"We received some strange readings right before the alarms went off," Fran said.

"Let's see." Jennifer stepped over to Fran's station.

Fran was a tall woman with a dancer's body and legs. Stunning, with a strong chin and round eyes accentuated by natural heavy lashes. She looked much like her daughter, but Maude was in that awkward stage where she held her body so she collapsed in on herself, hiding her beauty.

"Here." Fran hit a button and a strip of data scrolled across the screen.

Jennifer stopped the readout. It was like the blip, the one that had occurred off shore the other day when Spencer was at the beach and she'd seen video feed of a disturbance in the water. Only this spike was bigger and lasted longer.

"We should run all the information we've gathered since we started monitoring the area through the computer," Jennifer said. "Let's see if there's a pattern, or if there is some sort of corresponding atmospheric or geological activity."

"I'll set it up," Fran said.

Three short blasts made her head jerk up. She frowned, exchanging looks with Fran, who shrugged.

"I hate feeling like I'm being shut out of everything," Jennifer said.

She understood her place in the hierarchy, but she didn't like the idea of the military, or anyone else changing the rules. Why hadn't someone given them some indication of what was going on?

A few people in the labs made preparations to leave. She watched them, debating ordering them back to their stations, but maybe they were onto something.

She considered heading out herself. There wasn't much she could do here until someone gave them more information to work from. Besides, she wanted to make sure Spencer was okay.

She sat back in her chair, struggling with her duty to stay. It wouldn't be too long. Maybe an hour to check out the data Fran called up.

It made little sense to start a project and leave before its completion. It set a poor example for everyone else. And it wasn't fair to Fran, who had Maude to worry about. But Fran had a husband who was there to help.

Jennifer promised herself that once they did a precursory run through the information she would head out, no matter what.

Maude

Maude looked down at her feet as she walked; a little kid pose she couldn't help.

She'd kissed him. With everything going on, she'd kissed him. She hadn't meant to, but he'd looked so shaken and vulnerable. And it had broken her heart to see him that way. Worse, she sensed that being so lost hurt him.

Moisture from Spencer's mouth still clung to her lips, now cooling in the air. Her mouth suddenly felt cold, even though the weather was pleasant. She lifted a hand to rub the feeling away, but then lowered it. She wanted the kiss to stay. It lingered in a slightly uncomfortable way.

The scene on the beach replayed in her mind as a series of distorted images. Maude stopped, squeezing her eyes shut.

It really happened.

The high-pitched whine from the water ran through her head, a metal bow scraping the strings of a rusty violin. Even over the sirens, she'd heard it.

Maude collected herself, opening her eyes and tugging open the rec center door. She stepped into an impossibly silent room.

Usually boisterous with life, the vacant space of the long, narrow cafeteria with its low drop-ceiling suddenly felt like a vast cavern.

Her sneakers squeaked as her feet rolled over the linoleum. She hurried, rushing to get away from the thoughts bouncing through her mind.

Maude took the concrete steps to the basement two at a time but stopped before the bottom, where a soldier watched her with harsh eyes.

Get it together. They always posted a sentry during the drills. But Maude couldn't meet his gaze without seeing the soldiers they ran to for help on the beach.

They shouldn't have gone that way. They had led the thing right to the sensor rig. But where else were they supposed to go?

Maude dug in her pocket for the badge they carried everywhere and were supposed to wear during drills. Thank God she actually had it on her.

She hung the lanyard around her neck and approached the door. He leaned closer to read her name.

"Maude Faraday, you're in a shitload of trouble."

"I got held up."

"Yeah. You know your station?"

Maude nodded, and he let her pass.

He couldn't know what had happened. Not yet. Few on the compound would. She wished she wasn't one of them.

Maude stepped into a storage area where maybe twenty people gathered, most of them students. She didn't make eye contact with anyone as she turned her back to the wall and slid into a sitting position.

The Wheelers were on the far side of the room. They sat at a table, making their warped version of origami out of some poor kid's homework, folding stupid stick figures in exaggerated sexual positions.

The paper people seemed horrible to Maude, each one a series of stiff lines.

At a nearby desk, Elliot poked his head out from behind a math text. He grinned, then walked over to her.

"Maudie, where you been? How come you make a guy wait all day?"

"Oh, am I late?" she said, working to keep it together.

"According to the guys in green, you are. You missed all the fun drills, flopping face first on the concrete and hiding under furniture. I'm surprised they let you in."

Maude shrugged and gnawed a fingernail.

"What's wrong?" Elliot asked.

When she didn't answer, Elliot slid down next to her, giving her hand a quick squeeze.

"Drill should be over in a minute," he said.

"It's not a drill," Maude whispered.

Three short horn blasts sounded. Not an all clear, but a signal to go straight home to wait for further instruction.

Maybe the danger was over, or the military had neutralized the threat. Everyone rose, lining up at the door while soldiers marked their names off. There was a red check mark next to hers. Great.

Leaving the basement area, Maude quickly made for the nearest exit, her arms rigid at her side.

"Hey, Maudie, wait up. Why'd you really come late? And what did you mean it's not a drill?"

"I don't know what I meant."

"So where were you?"

"I was fooling around by the rocks. Took me a while to get down."

Elliot stepped in her way, forcing Maude to stop in the middle of the cafeteria.

"Where's Newt?" he asked.

She hoped he was home, or at least somewhere safe. Maude affected a casual shrug, feigning disinterest.

"You were on the beach with him," Elliot said. "What happened?"

Elliot might have been nowhere near the top of his class, but sometimes his street smarts made him seem more intelligent than even he knew.

"I don't want to talk about it."

Elliot touched her shoulder, but she moved back.

"Something happened. You don't want to tell me, that's cool. I just hate seeing you upset."

Elliot slipped a cigarette from his pocket. He scanned the cafeteria, then lit up.

"This isn't a designated smoking area," she said.

"Nope."

Maude took the cigarette from his lips and took a long draw. She exhaled and resisted the urge to cough.

The smoke made her a little dizzy. She liked the way she looked with a cigarette in her hand, but hated the feeling of smoke in her lungs.

"Look who's smoking," Jarod said, as he and his brother caught up to them. "Hey ass wipe, that's my cigarette."

Jarod offered Maude two lewd paper figures.

"Whore-igami," he said.

"Christ, they've named it," Elliot said.

Maude slapped Jarod's hand away, and the paper fell to the ground. She stepped on it. Lucas' mouth rounded in surprise.

"What the hell," Jarod said. "It's just a joke."

Maude realized the action had been irrational, but she wasn't in the mood to deal with anything right now.

"You guys should go ahead," Elliot said.

"Aw. You taking care of her?" Jarod said.

Lucas appeared amused. "You're going to make Mutant Boy jealous."

"Hey, Maudie," Jarod said, "next time I'll make you a whole diorama of the Kama Sutra. It will give you and Mutant Boy something to practice to."

"Lay off," Elliot said.

"I don't need you sticking up for me," she said.

The twins moved around Elliot, heading for the compound's center.

"She's got more balls than you, Born," Jarod sang out.

"No, she *has* Elliot's balls," Lucas said.

The brothers laughed at this final taunt as they departed.

While Elliot waved his middle fingers at the Wheelers, Maude left, walking across the grass to the main path.

Depending which direction you went, it led either to the beach or to the neighborhood; a paved circle where many families lived.

Elliot followed her; a surprise. He caught up to her, moving in close enough that she sensed his body heat.

"Sorry about those jerks," he said. "I can tell something's up. That you're not okay."

Maude stopped, blinking rapidly. He put an arm around her. She leaned into him, not caring what the few people walking by thought.

"Spencer saw it first." She had to say it, had to hear it.

Elliot waited, and she guessed he was determined to stay silent until she shared something more with him.

"I don't really know," she said. "We both saw something strange in the water and felt something chasing us. And that's when the noise started."

"The alarms?"

"No." She couldn't say anything else, couldn't talk about the soldier that wasn't a soldier without reliving the experience. She wasn't ready for that.

Elliot held her tighter and Maude let him, even though she was used to being the rescuer, not the other way around. She didn't need Elliot taking care of her or defending her, but it was nice that he did.

"What happened then?" he asked.

Maude shrugged, reciting a Katharine Hepburn quote: "*Never complain, never explain.*"

Elliot stepped back. She saw the look, a momentary flicker of uncertainty or judgement. People did that when she said something overly dramatic.

"I'm okay, but I can't talk about it anymore," she said. "If you want more details, ask someone else. Ask Spencer. He knew it was coming before anyone else."

A Summons From The General

Spencer

A<small>T HOME, I WATCH</small> the door, waiting for my mom, trying not to think about what happened at the beach. Of course, by deliberately not thinking about it, all I can do is think about it. And I worry about my mom, but I know with all the stuff happening, the likelihood of her coming home anytime soon isn't great.

That sucks for me, because being alone right now is torture. I can't sit still, and I don't have enough focus to do anything productive.

I go into the kitchen and yank open the refrigerator door. Nothing grabs my attention. I shut it, then open it again, then shut it.

Maybe I can work on a school project or something. I keep thinking about the model Alfredson gave me to study. It's hard to wrap my mind around it.

He wants me to look at John Wheeler's "delayed choice thought experiment" and some math from the Australian National University that possibly proves the idea "measurement is everything, and reality doesn't exist if you're not looking at it."

Here's the thing. Newtonian physics, the old world of "for every action there is an equal and opposite reaction," breaks down at the frighteningly tiny level of electrons within an atom; the quantum level.

For example, is light a wave, or a particle? Some scientists say it's both, that reality is determined by what's being observed. Until then, light's in a state of superposition and will "choose" its state depending on whether someone looks at it.

Maybe that's a thought that people can deal with but try to picture it in your mind. Try to really see it.

I can almost feel my brain stretching, struggling to visualize a concept that goes beyond our hard wiring to think in three dimensions. What does something look like in four dimensions? In five?

Anyway, the idea is that reality is fluid and subject to external influence.

Mathematician Étienne Ghys claimed he could visualize four-dimensional structures. I've watched videos he made, trying to help others do the same.

I can almost hold the images in my mind, almost. But they're slippery, always slightly beyond my grasp.

Letting my mind wander through this maze calms me. Mostly because it gives me something to focus on, rather than allowing my thoughts free rein to bounce all over the place.

That's good, because it distracts me now, helping me not think about the beach, or the other destructive thoughts I think when life slaps me around.

I stop and stare at the wall. It's something I do. When I'm deep into an idea, I find a fixed point. Right now, I visualize the wave patterns I've seen from the Australian experiments. They remind me of something.

"Water is made up of millions of mirrors." The Molecule Thief was playing with me.

Everything is a mirror. It's how we see reality.

Our eyes perceive light bouncing off an object at different frequencies. It's not really the world, but a representation of the world that we interpret. We're always looking at mirrors.

Maybe the Molecule Thief isn't the one on the wrong side of the mirror. Maybe both sides are wrong. Until they aren't.

I hear the front door open. "Spencer," my mom calls.

Hearing her voice, my shoulders loosen. "Here."

I come back to the moment. She breathes heavily, like maybe she was running. Her face is flushed. My mom brushes hair from my face, peering at me. I don't know what to say.

"Did you go to your station?" she asks.

I hear the edge in her voice, the worry. Did she see what happened on the beach?

"No," I say.

Her mouth forms a hard line. "This wasn't a drill. You can't be irresponsible."

"I know."

Mom moves closer, and her face lightens. She usually looks younger than her age, but when she's near exhaustion, her face betrays her. Like now, little wrinkles pull at the corners of her eyes and the sides of her mouth.

From her college pictures, she hasn't changed much. Maybe we never change. Maybe we stay the same forever, moving from one minute to the next, so it only appears we change.

"Where were you?" she asks. "When the alarms went off?"

I don't want to answer, but I can't help myself. "Down at the beach. Where the soldiers are." I know I need to say more. "Something came out of the ocean."

Mom's face crinkles into deeper worry. She puts a hand on my shoulder, and it's probably the only thing that keeps my feet on the ground.

"What came out of the ocean?" She's accepted my statement and now maybe she fights to keep herself under control, or maybe she's trying to parse out what I'm saying so she can separate what's important versus what's my usual rambling.

"I don't know," I say.

"Concentrate," she says. "Tell me what happened."

Her tone suggests she doesn't really want an answer, but knows more than she's saying. She's the scientist now. The scientist always has her shit together. She may not have all the answers, but the questions show she's in charge.

I tell her. All the time I stare at the floor, noticing the newness of the carpet, and how the fibers show where most foot traffic passes.

When I was little, I'd rub my shoe along the carpeting, then touch metal to ignite a static spark.

In school a teacher had a Van de Graff ball, and when you pressed your palm against it, the hair along your body and on your head would rise as the electrons repelled one another. And when you interacted with a plasma ball, the coolest thing ever, the blue-white electrical tendrils within the glass responded to your touch, like they were alive.

I hold out my hand as I remember, wiggling my fingers while I think it through.

My mother taps my wrist and brings me back, but I'd rather be where I was.

"Spencer, what were you saying?" she asks.

I start over. This time she hears everything. Except, I'm not really there, I'm already in my bedroom, throwing myself onto my bed, reaching out to play with the electricity within the ball.

Glancing at the mirror, waiting for the inevitable.

I must have fallen asleep, because there's a knock at the bedroom door. I sit bolt upright in my bed. Sweat trickles down my back and my mouth tastes like old milk.

"Spencer," my mom says. She sounds funny. "Wake up."

I shake away the confusion and stand. The clock on my nightstand says I've been asleep for an hour.

"Come on," she says.

I follow her, freezing at the sight of two soldiers in the living room. One of them tenses as they study me.

The name embroidered on his uniform says Papineau, and he has three stripes on the collar of his fatigues. He's impossibly tall, with a long giraffe neck and a high forehead. His fingers twitch. He introduces himself as Jeff.

It's weird thinking of military guys with first names. It almost seems they should order them to give them up when they start their service.

The other guy has two stripes on his collar and his chest pocket says Hernandez. He introduces himself as Rod. He looks like a Rod or an Al or Pete. A tough guy name to go along with his angular face and wrestler build.

"Spencer Newton?" Jeff asks. Hearing him pronounce my name makes my intestines twist.

"Yeah?"

"General Dawes wants to see us." The nervousness in my mom's voice puts another knot in my guts.

"Why?" I ask.

"I don't know," she says.

"I'm sorry, Dr. Newton," Jeff says. "We're just following orders."

"No need to apologize."

I don't want to see the general. I don't want to talk about things with him, not now.

I don't understand his relationship with my mother, and I'm uncomfortable trying to frame it. Shrugging on a frayed mantle of self-confidence, I walk to the door.

We climb into the back of one of those souped-up golf carts the military here favor. Rod gestures for my mother to come up front.

Worry makes her look older again as she shrugs and climbs forward. Jeff slides in beside me. I feel his weight.

The golf cart takes off with a little jerk. We bounce through the compound at a pace that would have gotten me grounded for a week had I tried it. Not that I ever would; I've never been a fan of amusement rides.

The only people visible are military. There's at least a dozen of them scattered about on guard. The compound is normally quiet, but it feels unnaturally so now.

"How long are they going to keep everyone on lockdown?" I ask.

The soldier shrugs. Just as I think he's giving me the cold shoulder, he says, "They don't discuss that stuff with me, kid."

"What about the thing on the beach?"

He looks at me, the twitching in his fingers more pronounced, like he's nervous. He shrugs again, then turns away.

"They're going to helicopter in more equipment though, right?" I ask.

Nothing.

"They'll want a buffer between us and the beach. That's the idea, isn't it?"

"Is that what you'd do?" he asks.

No, I would get us all the hell out of here, as far away as possible. I don't say that. Instead, I slouch down a little, focusing on my surroundings.

We pass the rec center. I wonder how Maude is, and if she's pissed at me for not following her into the shelter. She shouldn't be. She didn't seem upset with me.

I should have gone with her, though. That would have been the right thing to do, right?

I wonder if she's told everyone what happened at the beach. Maybe that's why the soldiers are here. Or maybe she's said nothing and the compound is hunkered down, praying the sensors aren't predicting another quake.

That's something we're all nervous about, although we seldom talk about it. Most of us from the West Coast have lost people in the quakes; my dad, grandparents, uncles and aunts, cousins.

Mom glances back at me with worry in her eyes. I want to make her feel better, but what can I say? Instead, I squirm. I do that.

Jeff raises an eyebrow, like maybe he thinks I'm having a seizure. "You okay?"

"I'm fine," I say. I'm not. I'm all over the place. I make another effort to relax, to shut out all the chaos pouring through my thoughts. It doesn't work.

I'm watching the burst of light and the stranger at the beach suddenly vanishing. The soldier is opening his mouth wide. It keeps opening until his head is cracking like an egg and he's falling back and shattering into a thousand little pieces.

The world spins, and I imagine tipping forward, crashing to the pavement. It takes everything I have not to scream.

Loose Molecules

Spencer

"**S**PENCER?" MY MOM SAYS.

The golf cart has stopped, but I'm still pitching inside. She has an arm around my shoulders, and I know she's supporting me because my head hangs forward.

Rod is at my other side, helping me out of the cart. Jeff has a bottle of water he got from somewhere, and that makes me wonder how long I spaced out.

"We can take him to the medic," Rod offers.

"No." I stand on my own. "I'm okay, no big deal. I'm fine."

"Are you sure?" he asks.

"I'm sure!"

My mother scrutinizes me. I keep my expression the same. If the soldiers weren't here, she'd be all over me, pushing until I opened up and told her what was wrong. It's like what Maude used to do.

That last thought throws me. *What Maude used to do?*

"I'm okay," I lie. "Let's go see the general."

What Maude used to do? Like when she and I were kids? We were never kids together. Like Maude will do?

Oh God, I can't start hallucinating, or thinking my daydreams are real. I shove the thoughts aside, not wanting to deal with anything that's going to rattle me further.

Jeff stands with his arms crossed, watching me with a flat expression. I take my time moving away from the cart. One leg, then the other, then an exaggerated stretch followed by a checking of my surroundings with a cool eye.

My mother's not amused. And I don't think Jeff is, either.

"This way," he says.

The hospital is old and dark. Once it was a private facility where they shipped kids and their families suffering from tuberculosis.

The military were here on the island first. They used it as their center, and still do; most of the new buildings erected north of the area are set up as research facilities, with equipment able to accommodate the sizable power demands.

We've always joked about it being haunted, but it really is, by soldiers who look out of place, no matter how hard they try to fit in.

We enter the lobby. It's cooler in here, and it's quiet. The ceiling is high, with wood beams coming together in the center and ornate plaster around them.

I hold up my arm, wiggling my fingers. If I could fly, I would reach the shadows there and touch the wood. I would shove aside the dust particles and find a hiding place.

"Elevator?" Jeff asks.

"They shut them off when the alarms were on," Rod says.

We move up the broad steps to the next floor. On the landing is a large stained-glass window. A nun dressed in a yellow habit stands in a multicolor bed of roses. She looks down at us with pity.

What about the soldier on the beach? Did she pity him?

On a plaque beneath the window is the legend, "St. Therese of Lisieux, of the Little Flower of Jesus," with the years of her birth and death. And below that information about her being the patron saint of tuberculosis, which is a shitty assignment, if you ask me.

"Spencer?" My mother's voice.

She's getting angry, but I can't pull myself away from all those colors in the glass coming together, bouncing off one another, forming lines that strike and veer off in other directions until there's no up or down.

"I'm fine."

I brush past her. The soldiers fall into step on either side of me, as if they think I'm going to get violent. Maybe I am.

Past some desks, abstract artwork, and a water cooler, is an office door with a gold plate that says, "General Andrew Dawes." Jeff knocks and a voice booms, "Enter."

The inside reminds me of Principal Kaminski's old office, except someone's set up a metal frame along one wall with a bunch of flat screens showing a view from over the labs. One is from the center of the compound, one from the rec area, and one from the end of the main street where most of the residential housing is set up.

Our house is visible. I wonder if he was watching us the entire way.

Another monitor is from the sea, maybe from a buoy. They even have a satellite image.

Encroaching on an antique wooden desk is General Dawes. He's muscular, with luminescent skin that doesn't camouflage its roughness. He has short black hair that's graying at the temples.

I see him watch my mom. Something in his expression softens. He leans forward, gesturing for us to sit in two leather chairs opposite him.

"Dismissed," he says.

The soldiers salute him.

Then we're alone with him. He smiles. My mother smiles back, the friendly exchange between them appearing sincere.

"I hope my men didn't make you nervous."

"No," she says, and there's a tone in her voice that says she's pissed. "I would've brought him myself if you'd answered your calls."

"Protocol."

My mom makes a disdainful sound that surprises me, but what grabs me more is the discomfort her attitude seems to bring to the general. He places his hands flat on the desk, avoiding her stare.

"And the monitors all shutting down, that's protocol, too?" she asks.

"Maybe Spencer should leave the room for a moment," he says.

"No. Spencer, stay where you are. Dammit, Drew, GERI is responsible for operations here. Cutting us off from everything isn't part of the arrangement," she says.

"I'm afraid it is," he says.

"Since when?"

"You'll have to discuss that with Herschel. I'm not saying anything else. I've been generous discussing as much as I have."

"But—"

"That's it," he says.

My mother sits back and fumes. I should be pissed at the asshole for talking to my mom this way, but to be honest, he scares me.

They make eye contact, communicating at a different level. I suddenly wish I'd listened to him and gotten the hell out of the room when I had the chance.

He pushes a tissue box along the surface of the desk as if to brush it clean. Then he shifts in his chair, fixing his gaze on me.

"You're not in trouble, Spencer. I'm looking for information. I'm hoping you can fill in the blanks for me. That's okay, isn't it?"

"I guess."

My mom's shoulders loosen a fraction. The general nods and once again meets Mom's gaze.

"He told me something came out of the ocean," she says.

I don't like that. She's suddenly not my mother but an informant. The skin on my arms is itchy. I try to scratch my forearm in a way that doesn't attract attention.

The general faces me again, offering a sympathetic glance. "This must have shaken you up, son."

"I'm okay."

I scratch harder, then realize he's noticed, so I force my arms down and ignore the itch. I'm standing, giving everyone a last scornful glare, and walking out of here.

"I'm going to start by asking some questions," he says.

And if I refuse?

"Before all this began, just before the sensor grid set off the alarms, you came running up and told one of the men we were under attack. Were those the words you used?"

I don't remember what I said. I shrug and inspect my surroundings.

Some people have died here. Maybe in this room. I don't know much about tuberculosis, but I don't think it's a pleasant way to go. It's one of those lingering illnesses, isn't it? I don't want to linger. I want to leave now.

I keep my eyes steady on him, willing myself not to look away. Instead, I'm seeing the dead man and smelling the salt on the breeze and something burning. There's a color I can't identify because I've never seen anything like it before.

Focus, Spencer. Focus.

"Why did you say that, Spencer?" he asks.

I keep my breathing steady as I answer. "I know things."

Like the general is wiggling his toe inside of his shoe. Like how my mom switched brands of soap this morning. Like the windows are streaked and there's a spider asleep in the ceiling's apex.

Like there are twenty-eight leaves on the emblem of the blue and white flag of the United Nations that stands in the corner. Like the other flag here, the black and blue banner for the Global Energy Research Initiative, is hiding a framed photograph of the general shaking hands with the Canadian Prime Minister.

Focus, dammit.

The general's eyebrows pinch as he leans forward, placing his elbows on the desk. I want to say something, but I'm terrified how I'll sound. I'm scared, and when I'm scared, I get stupid. I want him to take me seriously, not see me as a mutant.

"What things?" he asks.

My mouth won't work. If you say something, it's real. Think it all you want, but say it and it takes flight. It's too late now, though. Fantasies have become real and they have consequences.

My mom watches me, her eyes encouraging, but she also rubs her ring finger, something I've seen her do when agitated but trying to hold on to self-control.

"What things?" he asks again.

His voice is kind, his face patient. He's sincere, and that surprises me. You don't expect that from someone in such a position of authority.

"Spencer." My mother's voice is a whisper.

Her hand flinches as she struggles not to touch my face. She wants to. She touches me all the time; it's how she reassures herself while assuming she's reassuring me.

"Tell him what you told me."

When my mom says that it's as though I'm suddenly stripped naked. It's a horrible betrayal. It sounds petty. Like she's coaxing me in the psychiatrist's office, trying to get me to say what he wants me to hear. I know I'll tell him, we all do, but I have to do it in my own way.

The general is a man used to giving orders and having them obeyed. The chair creaks as he shifts in it. He still smiles, he's still patient, but maybe that's coming to an end.

"Maybe I should start," he says. "That might help. Jennifer, let me show you what I have. You would have seen this soon, anyway."

General Dawes leans to the side, pressing a button on what looks like a video game controller. The monitors all blackout, except for a larger one that dominates the others.

The image there is of the beach and ocean. At the bottom, numbers roll by, marking time. The soldiers are working, dragging equipment until it's out of view under the large tarp.

I suddenly enter the frame with Maude close behind me. We're running like maniacs.

I'm all arms and legs, looking like I might pitch face-first into the sand at any moment. Maude, on the other hand, is graceful. Her strides are easy.

The soldiers wave for us to stop. We do, but we're gesticulating. The soldiers look over our shoulders at something out of frame.

Maude and I start running again. In a moment, a figure materializes on screen. It looks like it springs up from the sand. The general pauses the video.

My mother turns from the monitor. "What is it?"

General Dawes advances the video a bit until the image is clearer. A soldier stands with his weapon raised, facing the stranger. The stranger's features are wrong, fuzzy, as if draped in gauze.

Then, the general zooms in on the two figures, and the features on the stranger's face crystalize until they're a reflection of the other soldier's. Same eyes, same nose, same mouth.

Even if I hadn't seen it change appearance, I'd have known it wasn't human, but a horrible doppelganger. At least, I think I would have. Its wrongness is sickening.

What if it had caught up with us? Don't let your mind go there, Spencer. Not there.

My mind goes there. The thing is touching me, and my molecules are loosening; spreading far apart.

Depressions In The Sand

Spencer

W HEN I SNAP OUT of my freak out, two identical forms stare out of the screen at me. If the general zooms in more, the scene will explode into microscopic particles, and closer in, dancing inside the molecules, the atoms.

"Spencer?" The general leans back until his head almost touches the wall.

My mom's cheeks redden as she makes sporadic eye contact with him. Her stomach gurgles, and there's a hint of bile on her breath.

The general eyes me again. I have to look away.

Dawes will never believe it. He won't believe me if I lie, either. I'm in a bad spot, but it's not my doing, which makes me angry, giving me the courage I need to lift my head and look back at him.

I don't say anything. I can't. I don't know what to say. And that's when my smiling starts.

It's a nervous thing. I'm not even aware I'm doing it until I see his gaze harden, eyes narrowing into slits.

"Answer him," my mom says.

I force the smile from my lips. "I don't know what it is. Honest. I only know it came from the other side of the mirror."

He raps his desk and there's disappointment in his face. My mother appears on the verge of tears.

"From the other side of the mirror," he says. He purses his lips, like he's giving something deep consideration.

The next words slip. "Sometimes I see things in mirrors."

He grunts, picking up a tablet and tapping its screen a few times. I can't see what he's looking at.

He says, "I went through your school files before calling you up here. You're one hell of a smart kid. And imaginative. You're a pretty good coder, from my understanding. And you've been doing some interesting work with Dr. Alfredson. He's impressed."

Dawes puts down the tablet, face down, resting his elbows on the desk. His eyes burrow into mine.

"Tell me, have you tapped into your mother's computer? Maybe accessed her files? I need the truth, son. You won't be in trouble."

No, of course not. Whenever adults have said to me, *you won't be in trouble* in the past, the phrase has usually meant the opposite, or had at least been an attempt to lull me into lowering my defenses. And, for a kid with impulse control issues, it's always been irresistible.

"No, I haven't." I can see by my mother's posture she believes me.

The general gives me another stare, and I sense he's a person who's good at figuring people out. He keeps his sights trained on me. "Has your mother talked to you about any of her projects?"

"No. Not really."

"But you've asked."

"I've asked."

"You know what her area of knowledge is in, and you know what GERI is doing here. If you had to guess, what would you say she's working on?"

The smart thing to do is shrug, or give him only a little, enough to show I'm not a total idiot, enough to satisfy him that maybe I just put a few things together in my head.

"I think GERI is here because of the energy anomaly. It should have dissipated by now because there's no reason for it to exist. My mom was working with the people who were doing experiments with the giant particle accelerator, the one that they're using to conduct tests on massless particles. So maybe the two are connected."

That should have been enough, but I'm Spencer Newton. So, of course, I continue, "She's helping to see if the collider experiments, and maybe some other GERI projects, have had anything to do with the weird energy readings in the ocean. And then, there's always the question of manipulating the electromagnetic fields around the Earth, but I think that's more a thought exercise than a serious activity, at least for now."

I manage not to mention the earthquakes and their possible connection to the electromagnetic fields, or my suspicions that both have something to do with the anomaly.

"Spencer!" My mom's eyes widen, her mouth hanging open.

The general has a shit-eating grin all of a sudden. "And you're telling me you haven't tapped into your mother's computer?"

"That's what I'm telling you. I wouldn't do that to her." I'm pissed at myself for how hard I'm protesting, pissed at Dawes' accusation, and scared as hell about how all of this is going down and whether soldiers will suddenly swoop in, lock me up, and throw away the key.

"Okay," he says, tapping the video game controller on his desk.

The video resumes. The soldier fires his gun and his replica appears unaffected. A flash blanks the screen for a second, then the soldier stiffens and falls over.

All this time the general isn't watching the video, but keeping his eyes trained on me. I'm not sure how to react. Look appalled? Start crying?

I want to cry. I keep thinking about that poor guy on the beach; how shocked he must have been when his mirror image didn't drop. He's dead now. Should I be, too?

"Let me slow this down," he says.

When the rate of replay slows, the video remains surprisingly clear. As the soldier fires, prior to the flash of his gun, the duplicate blurs slightly and seems to move a couple inches, like an image jumping on the TV. For a millisecond, brightness engulfs the replica, and then, almost simultaneously, the soldier.

As the soldier falls, the replica vanishes. Snap. Empty beach. At least that must be what it looks like to the general and my mom.

They don't see what I see; the wrongness in the air. They can't tell that the thing hasn't disappeared, that it's still there.

I didn't see it the first time, but magnified like this, I notice small depressions as they appear in the sand, stuttering toward the ocean.

The general shuts off the video and closes his eyes. He's affected by this. I feel bad for not seeing that before. When he opens his eyes again, he looks tired.

"Jennifer, just prior to this happening, we saw a fluctuation in the field, enough to trigger the alarm. And before that Spencer tried to warn us. He knew."

I drop my head, studying my hands. I rub my palms together until they're hot. When I raise my head again, the general and my mother are both watching me.

"Was it from the anomaly?" the general asks. "That's the other side of the mirror, isn't it, Spencer?"

Maybe. Or maybe only a pit stop on the way to the other side of the mirror. I don't say this.

"What do you know about this thing, Spencer? I need to hear it all."

I see the scene play out again in my mind. The entity follows us because we draw attention to ourselves. We kick up sand and pebbles as we charge down the beach, shouting like banshees.

The thing sees the soldiers, but the soldiers don't run. They stand still, giving the entity the chance to study them before choosing one of their forms. It mimics the soldier, and I think of a toddler who learns something by imitating an adult's action.

"Well, Spencer?" he asks.

"I'm sorry he died." I lower my gaze, trying not to get sick. "We were afraid. We weren't trying to lead it toward the soldiers, we just wanted to get away. Maude and me. It came from the sea, and it wanted information about us. The soldier fired first. It couldn't do anything else once it killed the soldier. It spent the rest of its energy and had to return."

I cry. Tears roll down my cheeks, and I have snot in my nose. I wipe it with my sleeve, trying to stop, but I can't now. I'm embarrassed and relieved at the same time.

The general will write me off as a lunatic, but I don't care. I slump back and continue my breakdown as my mom watches me like I'm someone she doesn't know.

"You're not being up front with me," the general says. "You're still not saying how you know all this."

Confession

Spencer

I'M UP RUNNING OUT the door, down the hall, down the stairs, outside. But I'm not. I sit here crying and terrified.

Mom reaches across General Dawes' desk, handing me a tissue from the box. I blow my nose, trying to pull it together.

"Are you okay, Spencer?" Dawes's voice is gentle in a manner I hadn't expected.

I nod, but he gives me a couple more minutes.

"What's happened is terrible," he says. "I can't imagine how frightening it must have been for you. But I need your help now. I want you to tell me everything you know. I don't care how strange it sounds, or how unbelievable. I want you to tell me everything that might even remotely relate to what happened on the beach. Do you understand? You might have noticed something that can give us a clue."

I know I can't avoid talking about it, but telling him I'm insane and letting my mom know is unforgivable. I can't. But I keep seeing the scene at the beach and I'm compelled to share what I experienced.

I open up with the general, going on about seeing so many things that other people don't, not because I'm crazy, but because I notice them. I explain I hear things, too. Not in my head, but from the mirror. Not things, but a person, or at least a personality reflected in any mirror.

General Dawes doesn't laugh at me. He doesn't show any expression at all, just listens. Maybe because he's got a dead soldier to account for.

My mom grips the arms of her chair, maybe to keep from cringing at how ridiculous I sound as I stutter and twist my words around as my attention darts.

There's a mirror on the sidewall and I turn to look in it, really look in it, hoping the fuzzy static will congeal and give me some guidance.

I talk again, now about the hole. The general jots down notes, stopping me occasionally to ask questions.

I'm not used to people listening like this. It's at once liberating and troublesome. I want to caution him to take what I'm saying with a grain of salt.

"I'm crazy," I want to add as a qualifier. *"You know that, right? Certifiable."*

Instead, I keep going.

"I don't know what they want," I say. "I mean the entities. Only I don't think they want to be here. It's hard on them. It takes up energy, and it hurts. I'm sure it hurts them."

I don't know where that comes from, but I know it's true.

"The Molecule Thief? Is he one of them?" Dawes asks. "Tha? That's what they call him?"

"No."

The general follows my gaze and we both stare at ourselves in the mirror. He's deep in thought.

Maybe he's forgotten my mom and I are here. He rubs his neck, kneads a scar there. That's when I notice another along the back of his hand.

My mother once mentioned that he'd fought in a war. Maybe it's changed his way of looking at things so the rational and irrational dance together in unison. He's lonely.

The machinery in his head clicks away, accessing past data banks and applying them to current logarithms.

He transforms what's happened into terms of military threat.

"I don't know what else to say," I explain.

I wish I did. Passing this information off to someone else has exhilarated me at some level. He smiles, his face warming. I can't help liking him.

"You've said a lot," he says. "I need time with it. Either you think what you've said is true, or every word out of your mouth is gospel. My mind is open."

He sounds more like a scientist than a general.

"I wish we knew more about what we're dealing with," he adds.

"You mean, what are they really like? They're completely different from us," I offer. "They don't exist like us."

He waits for me to elaborate, but I can't. Words fail me. It's hard to stay focused. My mind wanders, following that statement along dark paths.

"They exist though," he says. "They have substance."

"They can," I say.

The general is in my mind, capturing bits of reality and fitting them together.

"Is this from the entity you've been talking to?"

"Partly. And partly because things fall together, and I know they're true."

The last statement brings him up short. I see him mouth the words "things fall together," as if repeating them gives him some sort of special insight. He turns back to my file, then looks at me.

General Dawes stands, striding to the window. His hands are behind his back. I imagine him posing for a sculpture.

He talks without turning around. "My son, Scott, has ADHD," he says. "He's in college now. Massachusetts. He's a genius, works almost independently. He contributes to research. Incredible young man."

"Spencer's pretty incredible," my mother chimes in.

I'm both pleased and embarrassed.

Why do people do that? Why do they take an affliction like ADHD and identify it with some family member? If my face burned off would the general say, "You know, I have a son who's horribly burned, too."

Okay, I'm not being fair.

"Scott finds it hard communicating with people," Dawes says. "He sees things differently, maybe, and has trouble finding a reference point sometimes. He adapts, though, that's the important thing. He finds his place in the world."

Dawes returns to his desk, sitting down. "Spencer, do you own a cell phone?" he asks.

"Who would I call?"

The general laughs and leans back in his chair. He's quiet for some time, but I'm at my limit.

I've sat here forever, although part of me is running down the stairs and slamming into the heavy wood door of the old sanitarium. I'm racing along the path, touching the flimsy light poles, and talking to myself, not really talking, but making sounds, because it feels good.

"I want to give you something." Dawes reaches for the coffee that's been on his desk the entire time and slowly brings it to his lips.

It must have gone cold some time ago. I hear the liquid sloshing down his throat. I see the old scar jump.

My mother gives him a nod. He opens a drawer, taking out a cell phone. He slides it toward me.

"Spencer, sometimes when we relax, after something has occurred, details come back to us, or we think of things we might not have at first. I want you to take this phone as a gift. It's yours. I'll have an account generated in your name and make sure it's paid up for the next year."

"Thank you." I don't reach for the phone yet, meeting the general's eyes. They study me, and I note how the pupils widen.

He blinks. "All I ask is that you call me if you think of anything else. Or even if you just need someone to talk to. The number's pre-programmed."

I take the phone now. It's a new one. Expensive.

"And Spencer, can you do one more thing for me? I'd appreciate it if we could keep this conversation between us for now. People might ask what we talked about, maybe your friends, but for my own reasons, I'd rather limit the number of people who know about this."

"Ok."

"Good. If you wouldn't mind waiting outside, I want to have a few words with your mother."

I give my mom a last look. She slouches in her chair, the curve of her spine shrinking her a few centimeters. She exhales slowly.

I head out, closing the door behind me. The secretary looks up, giving me the briefest smile. I take a seat in a chair by her desk.

She ignores me as she peers over the top of her rimless glasses, working on her laptop. I feel him nearby, the Molecule Thief. I sweep the waiting room for reflective surfaces. There are none.

I try to peek around at the screen of the laptop, but the secretary shoots me angry eyebrows. I play it off like I only needed to stretch, backing it up with a wide yawn.

"Why me?" I once asked the Molecule Thief. He never responded.

It's because I'm special, but for all the wrong reasons. Standing out at a party is one thing, but standing out because of an open zipper, or because everyone knows you're about to become the target of some prank is a special I can do without.

Now I'm special because I can see and talk to the Molecule Thief. What a name. What kind of weirdo calls himself that, anyway?

Every Mirror, A Door

Jennifer

S HE WAITED UNTIL SPENCER closed the door behind him before looking up at Drew. He studied her face, maybe looking for a tell about how he should react. In the end, he shrugged and placed both hands flat on the desk.

Jennifer didn't trust herself to start talking, not yet, so she tried putting things in perspective, finding a way to empathize with this man whom she had feelings for. She had to separate him from his uniform, and understand he had a duty. So did she.

"You sent a military escort?" The anger in her voice came through. "What the hell?"

"By the book, Jenn. People would expect it."

"You couldn't have warned me?"

Drew shook his head. He stood, then stepped around the desk, slipping into the seat Spencer had occupied. He held out a hand. She took it. Reluctantly at first, but then she squeezed it.

"I'm sorry, but we need to keep a distance and remain professional. That's what I was doing."

"I know," she said. "I know."

They sat for a moment before Jennifer asked the question that hurt the most. "Do you believe him?"

Drew shrugged. "At least it gives me somewhere to start. I can't tell you the shit that has come down on me in the last few hours. And I don't know what to say other than we're looking into it and hope to have something substantial to report in the next twenty-four hours."

"What were you building on the beach?" she asked.

He frowned at the question. "We were told to create a separate data station."

"Why?"

"I don't know. Orders from GERI, and per military orders, right now GERI is running this show."

And who was running GERI? They'd been a research group, a non-political organization funded by different countries and by the private sector, with the idea that the threat of climate change made it necessary to forgo the usual territorial disputes fueled by greed and suspicion. Too idealistic? Apparently.

"You know they shut off my access to different data feeds," she said.

His expression told her he didn't know. "Sounds like they're shutting you out and getting ready to transfer responsibility."

"Why?"

He blew out a long breath. "It could be they recognized they were entering another phase in dealing with the anomaly. If that's the case they might be changing personnel, opening up a new book of regulations. It's possible it's harmless, and you're simply walking through a shit field of bureaucracy. Talk to Alfredson."

Alfredson. Dear, annoying man. If he knew anything, she would have to pry it from him, feeling the entire time as if she was taking away bits of his ego with every byte.

But if he knew anything, he would have told her so. Maybe not told her exact details, but told her enough to warn her away.

Jennifer remembered Spencer. She didn't want to leave him waiting too long.

"Thanks for how you handled him, by the way," she said.

Drew nodded in a self-effacing manner. "I like him. I know he's going through a lot. That he has gone through a lot."

Jennifer didn't respond, recalling her son's voice when he spoke about the Molecule Thief. The name frightened her; she couldn't think of it without seeing that entity at the beach.

How many years had Spencer been fixated by mirrors? Before the quakes, for sure. Before the death of his father.

She always assumed it was part of his focus difficulties. That the mirror gave him something to fixate on to help clear his thoughts. How could he see something there?

Jennifer leaned back, covering her face with her hands. Oh, God. The stress made her dizzy.

Poor Spencer. He didn't need any of this. It was hard enough for him coping with being a social misfit, with having his father stolen away, with just *everything*.

If GERI wanted to push her and others out for another team, one more loyal to their agenda, then fine. She could get Spencer away from here, move closer to her sister, get a better job, start a different life. Probably that was anger talking.

And Drew?

That wasn't a real thing, was it? It could be. She didn't want to let go of that.

Jennifer rose and stepped behind where Drew sat, leaning forward until her lips pressed against the crown of his head. He pulled her lower, turning his face so they could kiss. It was a gentle one; intimate, and comforting.

"Jennifer, we should talk about us," he said, as though he had read her mind.

"I can't. Not now. I need to get to Spencer."

"With all this craziness going on around us, we need one another," Drew said.

"I know," she said, fighting back tears.

"Keep a low profile while all this is going on, if you can," he said. "Spencer, too."

She nodded. Without saying anything else, she left.

Spencer

I'm screwing around learning how to use my new phone when an irritating whine buzzes at the edge of my consciousness. I shake my head clear, but the sound continues. He's back. God, that sounds like something from a bad horror film.

I toss my phone onto the bed and reluctantly approach the mirror. I can't stay away.

It's not just that being the only person who can see or talk to him makes me feel special, but I have a genuine connection with him. I don't understand that. When he's around I'm scared to death, but I also have more confidence and focus.

My palms are sweaty, and I rub them on my pants legs. My image is in the mirror, watching me. I smile. The mirror-Spencer smiles. I wave my fingers. The mirror-Spencer waves his fingers.

He's there, too. I know it. I move closer to the mirror, turning first one way, then the other, searching for the right perspective.

The surface of the mirror shows me a dot on a light blue horizon. Darker blue lines zigzag back and forth like netting. I concentrate until my forehead hurts, and I see him, a grainy person-shape.

The fuzz of hair that covers my skin stands straight up, crackling with electricity, as he siphons my energy.

"Molecule Thief," I muse. "Sounds like the name of a superhero."

He laughs at my joke, and I smile.

"That was close, Spencer," he says. "Down at the beach, I mean."

"Yeah." Why do I feel he qualified his statement because more close calls are on the way?

"It's not going to get any easier for you, Spencer. Your life is about to change again."

"We lost our home, and I lost my dad. You think that was easy?"

"I didn't mean it like that. We always say the wrong things when we're nervous, don't we? You're not going to see me again. We can't. That's not why I'm here, but I thought you should know."

That disappoints me.

"Where are you going?" I ask.

"I'm not going anywhere, but we won't be able to talk anymore."

"Why?"

"I can't say."

"You won't say."

"I won't say."

The Contained

Spencer

"I'M AFRAID FOR YOU," the Molecule Thief says.

"Why do you care what happens to me?"

I feel betrayed by his refusal to tell me what's going on. I turn from the mirror and the room looks wrong. After staring in the mirror, the real world always does.

The Molecule Thief speaks again, and his voice is tinny. It sounds desperate, and it scares me. "Such is the power of love in gentle mind, that it can alter all the course of kind."

I look back at the mirror, and I swear his grainy outline is sucking in clusters of dots, syphoning them from energy streams. Why does he need to steal matter? Curiosity taps my forehead.

"What would happen if you weren't grabbing molecules?" I ask.

"I'd only exist in one state," he says. "Probably Oklahoma."

His voice changed timber. He sounds young; he almost sounds like me.

"First awareness," he says. "A moment of revelation. A sudden state of being. And then, then you start fighting to stay aware. A universal law: Everything wants to exist."

Artificial intelligence? No.

Spontaneous intelligence? Is that even a thing? I can't imagine.

"You're in the anomaly," I say.

"Yes, and no."

"I want a straight answer for once."

What connects us? Why am I the only one who can see him, or am I the only one he'll show himself to? He's involved with those monsters from the anomaly, but he's not one of them, that's for sure. So why me?

Because of my stupid ADHD? Is that why I see him? Is there meaning behind it, or is our relationship a random accident, like being born with an extra chromosome? I don't believe that.

The questions and answers form a Mobius strip, a surface with only one side, non-orientable. I'm on the wrong side of the mirror.

"You never tell me anything," I shout. "You just give me these stupid half answers. I don't work that way. I have to know stuff."

"If I tell you what you want, we run the risk of messing it all up. Knowing changes everything, and in ways that could be dangerous to all of us."

"Then what's the point of coming here?"

"Seeing you gives me hope."

I fake laugh and refrain from punching the mirror. Hope?

Molecule Thief's voice changes again. "Angels come to learn frail minds. You frame my thoughts, and fashion me within. You stop my tongue, and teach me to talk."

"You're no angel."

"Neither are you, kid."

In a flash I'm on his side of the mirror, peering back at myself. There's awkward Spencer, the kid with uncombed hair over jug-handle ears. He and I sharing a second in time when everything's possible. Everything. Don't look, or it all collapses into one path.

Except I haven't moved. I'm still on my side. None of that makes sense, but it's true.

The poem he recited kicks me. "You were quoting Spenser," I say. "Not me. The poet."

Molecule Thief jerks his head, appearing to listen to something or someone I can't hear. He grimaces, moving away before sitting on the bed, which doesn't bow under his weight. I'm afraid to turn around, afraid that if I do, I'll be the reflection and not my real self.

I can't imagine what would happen if he stepped through the mirror. Probably nothing good. Being on opposite sides of a mirror is as close as we can get to one another without the world exploding.

Yeah, my mind is off and running. The lines of energy grow frenetic. I won't see them if I turn around, but I know what I'm seeing is real.

"What would happen if we were together in the same place at the same time?" I ask.

"There he is. There's my Spencer. A stern discipline pervades all nature, which is a little cruel that it may be very kind. Do you understand that? Or am I talking to myself again?"

He's struggling with something. His laughter rings out, shrill, and annoying, and I hear myself in it. I don't know if he's mocking me, or if I'm listening to something that should terrify me.

"They're coming," he says.

The statement is off-handed, as if he's telling me my shoelace is untied, or I have something in my teeth.

But, then I picture movement in the water, something solid pushing through the waves. They'll leave the anomaly, slipping through the rift, fighting through to the surf until they stir the sandy beach.

The alarm will go off again. Not one scout this time, but hundreds of intruders. Maybe thousands.

"Who are they?" I ask.

He looks over his shoulder, turning back again with a grim smile. He nods. "They're not the ones you should be worried about. The Contained just want out. The ones you should worry about are those on your side of the mirror. Frankly, it's safer in the anomaly."

"Why can't you just say what you mean?"

"I can't."

"Because by saying it, it becomes real. That's nonsense."

"By knowing it, it becomes real. That's physics."

The Molecule Thief phases in and out, a grainy phantom in the mirror. He's older, with his jaw well-defined and eyes arresting in their intensity. I look over my shoulder at the empty room, then back at the mirror as he stands up from the bed.

I'm frightened, frustrated, and nearly in tears. "Who are The Contained? They're after you, aren't they?"

"They are. I'm stuck in the middle. Both sides want me. The Contained and the ones who want to keep them contained," he says. "And Spencer, here's the part I'm sorry for, but if they're after me, then they're after you."

I can't trust him. I know I can't. He's stronger than before, so I get a better sense of who he is, though I don't know what he is.

He's playing me, right? Or maybe this is the one time he's being genuine?

"Spencer, snap out of it," he says. "Get your phone. Call the general."

"And say what? Say I've finally completely lost it?"

"Say that he's about to be attacked."

"He won't believe me."

"Oh, he will."

I reach for the cell phone General Dawes gave me, taking my eyes off Molecule Thief for a second. I expect when I look back he'll be gone. But he's still there. I get an idea then. I don't know why it's never occurred to me before.

An eternity passes as I unlock the phone and activate the camera app.

I take the picture, sure that when I check it, all I'll see is some skinny goofball with uncombed hair and heavy freckles on both sides of his nose holding up a phone.

When I look at the result, I can't believe it. There I am, a nerd in a mirror selfie, and behind me...a grainy image of the Molecule Thief. Holy shit!

I take several more pictures.

"Spencer," he says. He sounds far away.

Mom's never going to believe this. I have his picture, don't I? Yeah, but.

"Spencer!" Our eyes meet. In a younger voice he says, "You have to get Mom now. Okay?"

Energy lines slice through the other side of the mirror. And then he's gone.

I grip the phone tighter, checking the room. I have his picture. I know I need to call Dawes, but first I have to show this to Mom.

I run out of the room, down the stairs.

Wait until she sees this. I'm afraid to let the phone shut off, concerned that if I do that when I turn it on again the picture will be different. I'll be alone.

"What?" Mom comes shooting from her office.

"I got him," I say. "I got him."

I put the picture up and watch her. She stares hard but doesn't say anything. I'm terrified the picture's changed. I look, but no, he's still there.

"You see him?" I ask.

"You just take this?" she asks.

I show her the time stamp. It's been four minutes.

She takes the phone from me, clicking it again. The Molecule Thief is still there. Before I can say anything, she taps the picture. I lean over in time to see her send it to her own phone.

"I want General Dawes to see this," she says.

"Me, too." What will Dawes make of this? He'll want his phone back, want to give it to his people and maybe have them go over it to see if I somehow faked the image.

But what if he doesn't see the same thing I see? How come Mom can see the photo, but sees nothing in the mirror?

What if it's superposition? What if he exists in multiple states at one time and, by snapping a picture, I fix him in place, forcing him into one state, making him observable to everyone?

This isn't the time to spiral down a rabbit hole of thought.

I remember what the Molecule Thief told me. "Mom?"

"What?"

"We should take it to the general ourselves. Or we should go to the lab."

I didn't mean to speak in a worried tone, but she stops and stares at me. She reaches for the hair at the side of my face, but I pull away.

"What aren't you telling me?" Mom gives me back the phone.

"He said something was about to happen."

"What?"

"He means like what happened on the beach. We should get someplace safe."

They're Here

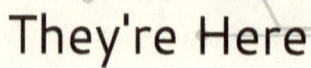

Maude

"**C**RAP," MAUDE MUTTERED.

Depending on the situation, some words worked better than others, and this one wouldn't stop rolling through her mind. Crap, crap, crap.

She couldn't stop thinking about Spencer and what happened on the beach. No matter how hard she tried seeing it in her head, she couldn't make it feel real.

How could she? How could anyone? Though she liked Spencer, his connection to those things frightened her.

She sat at the piano in the front room, unhesitatingly tackling Liszt's *Feux Follets*. She didn't have the sheet music for it, but after hearing the recording a couple times, she didn't need it.

The piece appeared in her brain as a series of equations and sequences. They flowed through her fingers.

A tech once said, *"She's scary."* He didn't think she'd heard. *"She looks and acts normal, though."*

Another commented, *"Not so much,"* and the two of them laughed.

"Jesus. Wouldn't you like to know what's going on in that head?"

No, really, you wouldn't.

She played the piece as fast as she could, fingers racing over the keys, striking them hard and decisively. The urgency of the work became manic. When she made it to the end, she did it again, then again, until her fingers hurt, and her palms were slick with sweat.

Then she stopped, sitting in the emptiness that came when the music ceased. She blew a lock of multicolored hair away from the corner of her mouth. Rolled her shoulders. Massaged a knot at the base of her neck before hopping over to the ultra-modern armchair with the cheap cotton slipcover.

She wished she could speak with Spencer, process with him what happened, and what they were going to do about it. She'd messaged him on the compound's student social media site even though it showed he hadn't been online since late last night.

She tapped her foot, then rose, retrieving a sketch pad and pencil from her backpack. She drew without focus, letting the graphite smear lines across the paper.

When finished, she had dozens of lines flowing over the paper, projecting chaos on first inspection, yet filling the page with an organization that she gathered didn't translate to two-dimensions.

Without knowing why, she made a dot on one line. The dot, an anomaly. Or a person.

She heard her father enter through the front door, and her mother greeting him. They spoke in low voices, making it difficult for her to understand them, but the worry in their tone made her concentrate on eavesdropping.

"... I pushed for the helicopters," her father said. "They won't give approval. They're not calling it a quarantine, but that's what it is."

"I could make a few calls," her mother said.

"This is a military situation."

"That's not the plan. We have a protocol."

"Well, they've circumnavigated those plans. I knew the increasing military presence didn't bode well."

Maude leaned against the wall and slid down. She chewed her lip, swallowing the lump in her throat as she tried to keep the rising panic from exploding, but the phone dinged, offering a moment of distraction. She checked the message from Elliot.

Elliot: *Wzup???*

She considered a few responses before settling on: *Terrified. Have you heard from Spencer?*

Elliot: *No he barely uses that phone. U no thats his 1st*

Maude: *I'm worried.*

Elliot: *Me 2. Hear choppers?*

Maude: *Yeah.*

Elliot: *Somethings going on. Meet me. Lets sneak over & C if Newts home*

Maude scrunched her mouth to one side. She wanted to get out of the house but didn't like the idea of pushing lockdown. If they got caught, her parents would scream. Or worse, she and Elliot might be the ones in an army truck.

Elliot: *U there?*

Maude: *I'm here.*

Elliot: *Come on lockdown making me crazy lets go C Newt*

Maude: *I don't know.*

Elliot: *Did U no some army guys picked him up?*

Her stomach suddenly felt like someone punched her. She looked at the door, thinking about her parents' whispered conversation. If they picked Spencer up, then why hadn't they picked her up as well? They both went to the beach against orders, right?

Maude: *Because of the beach.*

Elliot: *IDK Maudie lets go C him & C wat happened*

Maude: *We get caught during lockdown and they'll throw away the key.*

Elliot: *Theres other people out.*

She stared at her phone, then again at the sky outside her window. She wanted to see Spencer, especially if what Elliot said about him being carted away by the military was true.

Maude: *Fine. I'll meet you. I'll be by the birches.*

There was a patch of birches in the yard behind their house, a strange white spot against the dark green. Since

Elliot lived only a few houses away, he must know the place.

He apparently did, because he typed: *Cya in a few*

It occurred to her a face-to-face conversation with Elliot wasn't much different from a text conversation with him. She hoped to find more depth, but he'd given no evidence so far. Why did they hang out together?

Now she just needed a little luck sneaking out. If her parents caught her, she wouldn't be going anywhere for a long time.

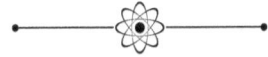

Spencer

I step through the front door first, my mother right behind. We stand on the porch, scanning the street for anything unusual.

The private residences, homely looking prefab units thrown down along a hastily set street, look harsh and unfamiliar with their backs pressed against the dark greens of the spruce woods.

Mom grips my hand and squeezes. Her jaw muscles work as she grinds her teeth.

Across the way, Lisa Sharone, an acoustic researcher Mom's lab, sees us and gives a quick wave. Mom heads toward her, still holding onto me.

Lisa's smile does a poor job masking her worry. "Another alarm," she shouts.

"Yeah," Mom says.

"I hate these."

Without further conversation, we head toward the labs. I pull loose of Mom's death grip, dashing ahead, hurrying them along with an impatient wave. My pulse thuds in my ears.

Lisa stops, taking a step back as if slapped across the face. I follow her gaze and stiffen. A handful of people run in our direction.

My mom grabs me again, above the elbow, her nails digging into my bicep.

A thin man wearing a t-shirt and shorts stumbles. He lands hard, then rolls once before remaining still.

His body twitches, reminding me of someone being tazed. Little spots of energy run along his body.

I make out uniforms behind the people, a group of soldiers moving in an awkward mechanical fashion, arms raised as if gripping weapons, only their arms are empty. Something else is there, too. It's hard to make out, but I see moments of blurring that shouldn't be there.

The phone's camera has a zoom function. I click on it and play with the app for a second. The phone screen picks up detail I can't see with my eye, like the mirror catches things for me I can't see directly. The blurs have shape.

"Those aren't soldiers," I say.

I'm hot and cold at the same time. The cell phone nearly slips through my fingers.

My mom pulls me along, heading between two prefab units. As we move into the shadow of a house, I shake loose again, fiddling with the camera.

"Put that down." Mom shouts to be heard over the alarm.

"It's sort of like a mirror," I explain.

Lisa peeks around the corner, then jerks back. "They're coming."

"How many?" Mom asks.

"Maybe four."

"There were five."

"We can't stay here," Mom says. "We have to keep moving. Get to the lab."

I kneel on one leg at the corner of the house, holding the phone out, angling it to see the street.

"They got another one," I say. "Mary Greenwald."

"Sal and Kit's kid," Lisa says. "Oh God. Jesus."

"Shit," Mom says.

I pocket the phone, then grab mom's purse and unzip the pocket where she keeps her makeup. She shakes her head at me, but before she can snatch it back, I find what I'm looking for—a small mirror.

I angle it at the approaching commotion.

"Let me just take another look."

At the same time, Mom and Lisa say, "No."

"Just for a second. I need to see something."

Mom grabs one arm, Lisa the other, pulling me along. I finally submit. We keep low, trotting along the back of the yards, staying in shadow where we can.

At each residence we stop, checking to make sure nothing comes up the side of the house to surprise us. Then we rush through the grass and repeat the process.

"They all have the same face," I say.

Mom inhales, catching her breath as she makes eye contact with Lisa, who doesn't appear as winded.

"They all have the same face," I say again.

"You mean they look alike?" Mom says.

When I get flustered, it's hard to talk. I start in the middle of a sentence. Or say something assuming others know what I'm referring to.

I should use my strategies. Take ten deep breaths, counting each one. Wait for my brain to calm so my words will make sense again. But we have no time for that.

"What are those things?" Lisa asks.

"They're sharing," I manage, but that's not what I meant to say. I take one long inhale, then try again. "They're copying the one from the beach."

I mean the soldier in the video. Mom's face pales, so I guess she gets my meaning.

I hold up the mirror again, checking the area. Lisa and Mom peer over my shoulder at the reflection.

"Do they look different in that?" Mom asks.

"When I see them..." I struggle to get out the words. When they don't come, I give up.

I start moving.

Mom and Lisa follow. We come to the next unit, but as I peek around the corner, a soldier appears.

He stands a few feet away from us, eyes without emotion as he fixates on me. It tilts its head to one side. What's it doing?

The soldier extends an arm, as if it wants to reach out and touch me. Maybe I should be afraid, but I sense it's more curious than malicious.

Mom springs forward, ramming a shoulder into the creature's chest. Maybe she hoped it would stumble back, giving us a chance to power past it into the next yard, and around the side of the neighboring house.

But the body yields on impact. It looks as though she's smacked into something flexible.

And then she falls.

She hits the ground hard on her hands and knees, looking dazed. The soldier's form blurs, then corrects, solid again. Its arms move.

I rush forward. Lisa and I each grab an elbow and yank her to her feet. Together, we bolt.

We get about ten yards when I feel an energy buildup; tiny electric jolts crawling over my skin. I throw myself against them, knocking both to one side.

As Mom shouts, I look over my shoulder.

"He's gone," Mom says.

"What happened to him?" Lisa asks.

I look in the mirror. A form steps from the shadow of a tree. No, that's not right. It stepped through the tree. Through the freaking tree!

"He's still there," I breathe.

I hold up the mirror but, by their perplexed looks, they can't see him.

The entity is almost six feet tall. This is what I saw at the beach before it adopted the soldier's likeness. This is what chased us.

I extend the mirror to my mother, and she looks, but I can tell she can't see what I do. Ms. Sharone's expression remains fixed, like she's waiting for something to materialize.

The figure stands there, stuttering like a bad video fighting pixel distortion. Its strength fluctuates, as if stuck in a door, struggling to get from one side to the next.

The surrounding air seems charged. I don't know which is worse, mimicking human form, or moving through the air almost invisible.

I don't know if it notices us. I don't know how it perceives the world. I freeze and thankfully my mom imitates my behavior.

"We don't have far to the path," Lisa says. "Don't stop and check between the houses. Just run."

"What's it doing?" Mom asks.

I watch it in the mirror. "It's calling for others."

Lisa shudders and retreats.

"What now?" There's panic in Lisa's voice.

Both look to me for direction. Me?

I don't want this responsibility. Sweat runs down the side of my face, but I don't wipe it away. I can't move. I'm too frightened, thinking about what happened when Maude and I left the beach, how I hunkered behind a rock and wet myself.

I've got to act. Don't think, just act.

"Run," I say.

Lisa takes off with a runner's grace. I hesitate, but mom yanks me into action.

Soon, we're following in Lisa's tracks, working hard to keep up.

My side hurts, my mouth gone dry. How much further? It can't be much.

Lisa shouts encouragement, picking up speed, arms pumping like mad, legs pounding the ground. And then stops quickly, fighting to keep her balance.

My mom cries out, grabbing me and jerking me back, almost pulling my arm from the socket.

Three soldiers, all with one face, stood between us and the labs.

Kindred

Spencer

T HE THREE SOLDIERS BLOCKING our way to the lab don't move.

"What now?" I ask.

"We can cut around them." Ms. Sharone's eyes are wide and wild. Her face is flushed, and there's a sheen of perspiration on her forehead.

"No," Mom says.

"We split up." Ms. Sharone dashes to the side. Two soldiers turn their heads, locking onto her with an eerie intensity. The third stares at me, and for an instant, we make mental contact.

Its presence is like the Molecule Thief's. I know it's come from the anomaly. The grainy images in the mirror, the limitless dots traveling along energy lines; I've seen them in the mirror, in the distance, over the Molecule Thief's shoulder.

But no, these differ from the others. These are The Contained. I know. They lack the sense of discipline and order of the beings in the mirror.

One of them raises its arms.

Ms. Sharone, so close to safety, is kissed by a shock of white. She falls forward, facedown, stiff as a board. Her body doesn't even tremble.

My mom sucks in a hitching breath.

One soldier has vanished.

I swallow down panic. Now's not the time to freak out.

I look at my mirror, checking the area. A cluster of geometric shapes, nearly imperceptible, reflect their surroundings, in almost, but not quite, perfect camouflage.

The mirror makes the distortions easier to see. It makes sense that, every time one of them hits someone, it releases energy. Right? But how long before it can recharge? Can it recharge?

"Spencer, move it!"

My mother screams at me, giving my shoulder a shake, then heads off. I watch one of the two remaining Contained approach Ms. Sharone and reach for her leg. The area between its hand and her ankle is suddenly blurry, the air fluctuating.

My mother runs to the left, hoping to succeed where Ms. Sharone failed. The remaining Contained hasn't moved, it's still watching me.

Maybe it's waiting for others. Maybe if it zaps me, it will disappear, like its mate, and then who would be there to collect me?

Why are they collecting us?

I run, faking in one direction, then bolting the other way, following Mom. And my mind is a step or two behind. I trip over a root half-buried in the grass and fall, sliding face first. The pain is stunning.

And I'm outside my grandparents' summer home in Oregon, sitting on the porch watching ants pour out from a hole in the damp earth. They're tumbling over each other on a single urgent mission.

I could be stomping them, God-like, and that's when I notice how they're avoiding my shadow, aware not only of my presence, but also of my alien thoughts.

Spencer Newton, Lord of the Ants.

In the mirror I see refractive masses, marching one way, then the next. And I understand why the entities vanish.

It's about energy. Everything is always about energy. The entities can mimic human form because of energy, and they can zap someone into a stupor because of energy, but they don't have enough energy to do both.

Once they hit you, they're forced into a form requiring less energy; one hard to see in three dimensions. In their lower energy state, they're naturally like the metamaterial used in stealth technology, refracting their surroundings, invisible.

Brilliant.

And my mother is yanking me into a standing position, and screaming, and pulling at me. We're going the wrong way. The lab is in the other direction, this way will take us back home.

I check the periphery. There are several of the Contained heading where we're going. If we don't stop, we'll run into them.

The creature following us is closing, still focused on me, but for some reason I don't feel threatened. I wonder; if they're using energy to mimic us, what do they look like when they're not?

"Spencer! Jesus."

My mom gives me a pull that almost has me on the ground again, but I find my feet and let her lead me. She talks to herself, her words almost incoherent, then another sound from above challenges her babbling.

A helicopter passes overhead. No, there are two choppers. They hover over the street beyond the units.

Different from the ones we're used to seeing, these are fully armed. Apaches. Holy crap. My head is up, my face tilted skyward, so I miss a dip in the ground and pain shoots up my leg.

I shout, and my mom turns. She has a panicked expression. When she sees our pursuer, still doggedly keeping pace, she lets out a cry of her own.

It feels impossible to move, but there's no choice. I limp, testing my ankle. It hurts like hell, but I can walk. At least the pain will keep me in the present. Mom takes my hand and pulls my arm over her shoulder.

"We're going the wrong way," I say.

Mom spits out an obscenity as the realization dawns on her. We turn, and she eyes the fake soldier in our path, the one pursuing us like a bloodhound.

Above, the roar of a gun blends with the thrumming of helicopter blades. A gunner works an automatic cannon that juts out from beneath the chopper, but I don't think it will do any good.

Even if he fires those missiles mounted on the side. Or the rocket launcher. What's there to hit?

These things don't have vital organs or flesh. I wish I could look between the housing units and see what was happening on the street.

Four people charge into the yard ahead of us. They've had the same idea about using a back way to the labs.

Six soldiers are in pursuit. If we go back, we'll head away from the labs. If we go forward, we'll end up in the middle of that mess.

There's no time to discuss options. As we try to flee from the closest soldier, the Contained that's been following us lashes out with its arm and touches me.

THA.

The word rips through me, and in that second, I'm shooting along a blue pathway, disembodied. My consciousness fragments into a million bits of me, all aware, all connected, then suddenly it collapses, back to the way I was a moment ago.

For this Contained, being here, outside the anomaly is horrifying, and painful. Stepping through the portal from the void broke its connection to the others of its kind. Here, potential grinds down, trapping it in a bleak linear present.

In me it sees comforting chaos. I'm Tha. I'm kindred.

We break the contact of a yoctosecond, of a millennium. I'm here, and the desperation of the chase returns. Mom shakes me, shouting, her eyes red and wild.

"You're okay," she says.

The fake soldier is gone. Vanished. Making contact cost The Contained energy, and it can't maintain the shell.

I'm still trying to figure out what happened, still struggling with the experience, but a scream locks me in place. The last of the four people I saw running not long ago now writhes on the ground, little sparks of blue light shooting from his body.

A strange noise makes me flinch. It's calypso music. I have the phone in my hand, and I stare at it like it's alive. It never occurred to me what type of sound it would make.

On the screen, I see the name: Gen. Dawes.

Soldiers In The Kitchen

Elliot

E LLIOT PREPPED HIMSELF TO slip past his mother, confident she'd never look up as she cleaned the kitchen.

When she needed a distraction, she scrubbed like a demon and wouldn't stop until she'd banished every speck of dust and every little smudge on the walls with Windex. You knew her level of anxiety based on the amount of cleanser in the air.

She'd twisted her long blonde hair into a loose bun at the nape of her neck. Wearing a yoga skirt and rubber gloves, her face bore an expression of intense concentration.

His father had ten years on her, and Elliot suspected she was too much for him sometimes. Too much energy, too much drive.

Elliot snuck by, stepping into the backyard. A cool breeze picked up, sending a chill down his back. He shook it off as he looked through the kitchen window at the top of his mother's head while she polished the sink.

A twig snapped nearby, and he scanned the trees. A raccoon emerged, stared at him, then darted back off into the forest. Elliot went back to watching the window, but he couldn't see his mother anymore.

Where was Maude? She should've been there by now. Why he thought checking up on Spencer warranted putting his balls on the line, he had no idea.

If the military busted him and Maude, they wouldn't fool around. They'd lose all privileges and have community service for months.

"Hey, Asshole."

Maude marched into the yard, waving in exasperation. Her attitude amused him.

"You were supposed to come to meet me," Maude said.

"No, you said you'd come here."

"What? No."

A helicopter roared nearby. Then another. They swept close to the tree-line, like the cop choppers in the city when they tracked criminals running away on foot.

Maude stepped closer to him, glancing left and right. She gnawed her thumbnail, winced, then dropped her hand.

"Instead of choppers, why don't they use the drones?" Maude asked. "If you ask me, they're compensating for something."

"Like what?" Elliot asked.

His mom approached the window again, leaning forward, maybe looking for the helicopter, maybe to see where he went. She had a wary expression on her face. Her lips moved; Elliot waited for his father to appear.

"Let's go," Maude said.

He wanted to say no, that he didn't think it a good idea right now. Elliot didn't know why, but he couldn't shake the nerves.

The siren screamed.

Maude stiffened, grabbed his arm, then let go.

His mom spun around. Light flashed, reflecting off the window glass. Then she vanished from sight.

"Shit," Elliot said.

He raced to the back door, Maude lagging. Elliot shoved the kitchen door open, jerking to a stop as his mother writhed on the linoleum.

Two soldiers stood over her. One of them glanced at him. The other stayed focused on his mom. Their faces were identical—and dead.

"Mom?"

Elliot shouted for his mother, reaching out. Maude tackled him from behind, her dead weight changing his center of gravity, so he stumbled to keep from falling.

A sizzling sound came from his left, followed by the acrid smell of burning paint. A blackened spot appeared on the wall near his head.

Only one soldier stood in the kitchen now. He didn't know where the other had gone.

"What'd you do to her?" Elliot shouted.

He shook free of Maude and lunged for the soldier, intending to shove him away from his mother, but at the moment of impact, the man's body yielded, stretching in response to the hit. The strangeness of the situation disoriented him, his legs gone to lead, his body clumsy.

Behind him, Maude gasped.

He half-turned as she barreled into him again. They both crashed to the floor as another flash illuminated the small kitchen. The soldier disappeared.

Elliot blinked, clearing his vision. What had just happened?

"Elliot, there's more of them. We've got to get out."

He didn't say anything, but crawled close to his mother, cupping the back of her head and partially lifting her into his arms.

"There's more," Maude said. "A lot more."

"Mom?" Elliot tried rousing her.

"She's in shock, I think. She's breathing."

"What do we do? Jesus. I dunno know what to do."

Maude touched his mother's face with long fingers, as graceful and strong as she was on the inside. Then she turned around, facing the front of the house. She ran to the window and stared out.

Elliot lowered his mother to the floor again, listening to her chest. He heard a faint heartbeat. Should he do compressions?

Maude returned, her eyes wild. "Do you hear that?" Her hands pressed against her ears. "It's them. We gotta go."

He turned from Maude and scanned the hall beyond the kitchen, searching for any sign of his father. They had to check the rest of the house; they had to get his mom somewhere safe, where she could get help.

He slipped one arm under her legs and another under her back. Her body threw off heat like a furnace. He cradled her as he stood.

Maude's eyes were frozen on the entrance to the kitchen with a grotesque twist to her face. Elliot followed her gaze.

Two more soldiers stuttered through the hall. Or maybe it was the same two.

They moved with intent and, before Elliot could do anything, the air snapped and a thousand daggers stabbed him. His mother writhed as silver bursts of energy passed over her. She went rigid, then rolled from his arms.

Elliot fell on his side, pain shooting through his limbs, rendering him helpless. He tried screaming, but nothing came out, and his vision darkened. The only thing real was the pain ripping him apart.

"Elliot!" someone called him from far away.

Anger roiled under his consciousness. He let it burst through his mind, and with dogged concentration, he broke the surface and opened his eyes.

The pain continued, but he battled it, breaking through the worst wave, and eking through the next, and the one after that, until he could move his fingers and toes. He lay on the linoleum, shouting unintelligibly as Maude held his hand, staring into his eyes.

"Stay with me," she said. "Elliot!"

When he sat up, she laughed and cried. Elliot gasped and fought through the haziness. His stomach clenched, and it took tremendous effort not to puke.

"We have to go," Maude said. "Elliot, look at me."

She gripped one of his arms with both hands and pulled him across the floor, talking the entire time, her words making little sense. He resisted her.

"Mom," he called again.

"She's gone," Maude cried.

Elliot forced himself to look. His mother lay at an odd angle, one arm thrown out from her body, the other under her chest. Elliot struggled to regain control of his arms, but managed to turn her over. Her eyes were empty.

Elliot had only partially absorbed whatever hit him. The shot had gone wide. His mother should be alive, too, but the first hit weakened her and the second proved fatal.

"Mom!"

Maude had her hands under his arms, helping him into a standing position. He staggered back.

One soldier remained. It watched them with a hollow stare.

What was it doing? He wished he had a gun.

"We gotta run," Maude said.

Elliot remembered his father and faced the doorway. The soldier raised its arm.

"No, no, no," Maude whispered.

He couldn't help his father; he couldn't make a stand against this thing. Elliot decided to trust Maude, letting her lead him away.

They made it out of the unit, Maude in command, yanking him along next to the short fence of the backyard. Elliot followed, his mind blank, denying that any of this was real. If he went back into the house, everything would be as it should be.

An older couple, hand-in-hand, ran from the front of the house. A spidery burst of energy slapped the man down, and the woman tripped over her husband. As she fell on her hands and knees, she was hit by the attack, too.

"Mr. and Dr. Hamilton," Maude said.

He stopped, jerking Maude to a halt. Through the space that separated his house from a neighbor's, he took in the scene of dozens of people in the street, running, heading for the woods at the end of the block.

Maybe ten soldiers followed close on their heels. Every few feet someone fell, and the number of uniformed men diminished by one.

"We need to go the other way," Elliot said.

"I have to go home. My parents will look for me."

"What about my parents?" he shouted. Tears flowed now. "I left my mom and dad."

Standing still, arms at his sides, he stared at the ground, jaw clenched, eyes shut. Maude touched his shoulder and spoke to him, but the sound of gunfire grabbed both of their attention.

A chopper held position over the roofs, the gun underneath spitting out rounds.

His Face A Bloody Cavern

Maude

MAUDE AND ELLIOT RAN in a crouch, avoiding the backs of houses, shrouding themselves in the shade of trees reaching over the fence line. Maude stayed in front of Elliot, picking their path.

The second helicopter loomed above the trees, almost directly over them. It moved past the birch patch behind her house, joining the first helicopter.

Elliot shouted, and she paused, but only for a second. She had to get home. He gripped her arm and pulled back, forcing her to the ground.

"Hold up," he hissed.

A little girl ran into the space between Maude's home and her neighbor's. Emily McGregor, the youngest child in the compound at eight-years-old.

A cute kid, on the skinny side, and at times a pest. In the past, Maude had to ditch her on several occasions to keep from being followed.

"Emily!" Maude gestured for the child's attention.

They briefly made eye contact before the too familiar sparks shot over the little girl's body. She landed hard, rolling along the ground.

"No!"

Three entities, as she now thought of them, approached. One stood next to Emily, touching her leg with its own. If it even was a leg underneath the guise of camouflage pants and combat boots. The other two glanced up at the helicopters, both still firing into the street.

Once it rubbed up against her, the girl momentarily hovered, then trailed behind them as the creatures moved away, floating on an invisible stretcher.

Pain lanced Maude's temples. She fell back against Elliot. He held her, his eyes wide.

A scream of energy chewed through her brain, building in intensity until she couldn't stand it. This wasn't from the nearby entities. This was something else, something more powerful.

"Do you feel that?" she shouted. "Oh my God, what is that?"

Sound built, screeching through the compound, louder in one spot, reaching a terrible volume. Too much.

And then it happened. The crescendo exploded in one gigantic pulse, the sound of a thousand rubber bands snapping.

The helicopter above them tilted, in danger of crashing through the trees. Its rotors clipped several large branches, causing the body to shudder.

Elliot scrambled back, dragging Maude with him. They both looked skyward.

Maude saw the determined but panicked faces of the men within the helicopter; one partially hanging out an open door, held back from falling only by a restraint that might have been a belt or a cord.

The other helicopter now dropped, careening one way, then spinning back around. It crashed into one of the houses. Her house.

It ripped through the roof, spitting debris into the air, caving in the front of the structure as the body of the machine dropped through the second floor to the first.

Flames came a moment after, followed by popping sounds. All the glass shattered. Maude screamed. Elliot held her tight, keeping her from running into the blaze.

She body-checked him and slipped from his grasp, running with abandon for her home. The sight of another body stopped her. Emily's mother lay on her back, bleeding profusely from a cut to the forehead.

Elliot knelt by the woman, but Maude ran on. A crash sounded behind them as the other helicopter fell into the yard, taking part of the fence down with it.

Elliot left Mrs. McGregor and joined Maude, who hugged the side of her house, swallowing hard.

Before Elliot could say anything, Maude darted past him, staying low and slipping into the side door.

Acrid smoke filled the house, assaulting her eyes and making her cough. She shouted for her parents as she felt her way through debris into the kitchen. There was no access to the front of the house.

Maude looked down and saw her mother's bloodied legs, the rest of her hidden under the downed helicopter. Maude's father lay close by, unmoving, his face a bloody cavern.

Maude covered her face, wracked by sobs. She coughed and dropped her hands, forcing herself to look.

Elliot touched her shoulder, but she shook him off.

"Sorry," he said, touching her again.

This time, she let him leave his hand there. Let the tears stream down her face. Elliot's eyes shone with tears, but he held them back. After a moment, he took her hand.

"We have to move," he urged.

"I'm not going anywhere." Maude sucked in a lungful of smoke. The pain felt right and necessary. She doubled over coughing it back up.

"Maude, let's go."

"I'm done. I'm not going anywhere. You go. Get to the labs."

He gaped at her, then his expression changed to fury. "I'm not letting you die," he yelled.

She pushed him. "Get out!"

Elliot surprised her by shoving back.

"I should have been here," she moaned. "I should have been with them."

"So, you could be dead, too?"

"That's right." Maude dropped beside her father's corpse and touched him. She stared up at Elliot, who shook his head and left, leaving her alone in a house burning around her.

Alone, Maude folded into a ball and wished herself dead. It wouldn't be long. She didn't have the courage to act. Not like Elliot. And not like Spencer.

The door opened again, and Elliot filled the frame. He stood with his arms folded, looking down at her with empathy.

"Both our parents are gone. You kept me alive. I'm returning the favor."

"I'm afraid," Maude confessed.

"Me, too."

"I can't stand that my parents died not knowing where I was, not knowing I was safe. My mom would have been crazy with worry."

She let out the pain and smoke in a long burst. When her throat ached with rawness, she swallowed hard.

Elliot offered his hand. She took it and rose. They both stared at the wreckage with blank faces.

"Your mom wouldn't have wanted you to die," Elliot said. "She would want you to keep moving."

Maude nodded, but remained rooted. The longer they stood here, the less likely they survived. She didn't care about herself, but couldn't expect Elliot to die with her.

She collapsed against him, but he didn't hold her or say anything else. With a last look around, Maude headed outside.

She and Elliot didn't talk. Instead, they headed back the way they had come.

"What are those things?" Elliot asked. "They can't be gone."

"I don't know. I think I can feel them, hear them."

"Jesus," he said.

He gave his big hands a shake and looked like he wanted to punch something. Maude didn't want to deal with his anger. Her own was hot enough.

If only Spencer were there. Maybe he could make sense of all this, or at least make it less devastating.

Maybe he couldn't do anything, but she wanted him there anyway.

"We need Spencer," she said. If he was even alive.

"Oh, sure. Newt."

Elliot paused and studied the surviving portion of fence. He pointed. "We should go through the woods, head for the other side of the island, wait for someone to get us."

She considered that. Her gaze went to the downed helicopter. They should check for survivors, shouldn't they?

"Sirens have stopped," Elliot said.

Maude nodded. The static still sounded from the sea, and she had some kind of premonition that more of those things were coming onto the beach.

Maybe Elliot was right about heading through the woods. They could try making it to the ferry to Vancouver, provided the ferry was there.

"So?" he asked.

"So we should check the helicopter."

She didn't wait for his argument as she started walking, hands at her side, muscles tense, ready for flight.

"Maude, no. We don't know how much time we have. More of those things could be on their way."

"They are," she acknowledged.

"Then let's keep moving."

"After we check the helicopter."

He sighed, keeping pace with her.

As they approached the crashed machine, they both paused. A soldier lay on the ground, a thickset man with heavy facial bones and a shaved skull.

Maude approached, then squatted beside him. She touched his throat and felt a pulse. He lived.

Another man lay on the other side of the fence. He didn't look good. One leg bent at an impossible position, blood covering his face and stomach.

"Help me," he said.

JPEG Easter Egg

Spencer

M Y MOTHER AND I press against the wall of a house as I kill the cell phone. Several fake soldiers approach people laying in the grass. I pray they didn't hear the ringtone, but I'm sure if they had, they'd be coming our way.

In a systematic manner, they touch a leg to the fallen and lift the person. In the mirror, there's a visible distortion where the two are connected.

My ankle kills. I experiment by putting some weight on it, then a little more. It'll be okay, but not for running.

The soldiers leave the yards, towing their prey behind them. I wait until they're out of sight, then hit the phone, calling the general back. He answers immediately.

"Are you okay, son?" The general's voice is gruff but tempered with concern.

"I'm okay."

"Where are you?"

I look around like I'm expecting to see a sign. "We're trying to get to the path leading to the labs. We're in the yards behind the houses."

"Are you safe?"

"I don't know. For now. They chased us."

"Like the beach?"

"Yes, sir." Then I add, "I can still see them after they disappear."

He anticipates me, and says, "In a mirror?"

"Yes, sir."

"Like the Molecule Man?"

"Thief. Molecule Thief."

"We need to get you to safety. Your mother's with you?"

"Yes, sir."

"Put her on the phone."

I hand the phone to my mom. While she talks to the general, I use the opportunity to scan the area again with my mirror.

It would be easy to miss them. They're a shimmer in the air. A sense of wrongness noticed out of the corner of my eye.

For the time being, we're all right, but I know they're out there. All over. What do they want with us?

Mom hangs up the phone and says, "We should get going."

"There's lots of them."

Fear in her eyes makes her look vulnerable. That upsets me. It's like something has shifted and it feels wrong.

She hands me the phone and we're off again, my mother supporting me as I sort of hop on my one good leg, putting light pressure when I step on the bad one. We don't make fast progress.

"They're everywhere," I say. "I think they went down the street and have started going into the houses looking for people."

A helicopter comes from over the tree line. It swoops down to roof level and a burst of gunfire cracks the air. My mom stops, her mouth opens, and then she looks back as if reconsidering the way we're going.

We're close to the path. Now isn't the time to second guess.

The helicopter flies on, firing off another round. And there's another helicopter at the north end of the compound, where the residential area backs up against the fencing that separates us from the woods. I can't help thinking they're in trouble, that all their conventional weapons are useless.

Something flashes in the mirror. It's as if I've turned it at the sun. The reflection half blinds me.

Then, there's a crash at the end of the block. The second helicopter drops into the trees, vanishing from sight.

My mother pulls me hard by the arm, on the verge of losing it here and now. I want to reassure her, but my vision is full of spots. I struggle to find the mirror that has somehow tumbled from my hands.

"What?" Mom asks, while dragging me.

"Mirror."

My mother shouts, "Leave it!"

I hesitate. She's right, but I can't. She knows I can't. It's so close. It will only take a second to locate where it's fallen.

I swipe it, see myself in the glass, thinking that if I had a larger mirror, I could step through and fall up. Fall somewhere else, tumble into an idea that's safe. Or an alternate place.

Mom pulls me again. I shouldn't slow down, shouldn't look, but I can't help it. I peek.

"I don't see them anymore."

"Keep running!" she shouts.

The ground ahead is scattered with little shining lumps.

"What are these?" I ask. "Is that metal?"

"I see them." She moves even faster. "No time for curiosity now, come on!"

I keep pace, but I'm desperate to pause and check out this new weirdness.

We push through a wall of bushes and burst onto the path. We made it. I can't believe it. We made it, goddamn it.

The quad is graveyard silent. I have no idea where the entities have gone.

"Hell," Mom says.

She sprints to the front of the labs and pauses in front of the biometric security pad beside the door. When the system refuses to recognize her iris, she punches in a code on the keypad.

"They knew we were on the way," she mutters.

I wave at the camera.

"Hand me the phone," Mom says.

I do, and she fiddles with it for a moment before handing it back.

"Dead," she pronounces.

"How? It had plenty of power. I don't understand."

As my brain grapples to find the answer, a Venn diagram forms, an overlap of the helicopters crashing, the unresponsive keypad, the dead cell phone, and the lumps of metal on the ground.

An electromagnetic pulse? It could explain why I can't see any of the entities.

I press my hand to a scorch mark on the door and find the spot still warm. I give Mom a worried look and scan the area, certain another radiation burst will occur any moment.

The emptiness, the quiet, is an illusion. It's like the time after the earthquake.

After it stopped, part of me felt like none of it had been real. But another part of me knew what I went through wasn't over, that an aftershock was on the way.

"Spencer, snap out of it!"

I face my mom, more frightened than when all hell was breaking loose around us only seconds ago. It's the eye of the storm. My hands are shaking. It's difficult to take deep breaths.

"There's another entrance around the back," Mom says.

She's trying to distract me.

"The cameras won't work there, and neither will the keypads. Anything outside the lab," I say.

"Why?"

"EMP."

She gives a slow nod as the data points converge for her, and she realizes I'm right. Then she steps away from the door, glancing down the path toward the ocean.

She turns, examining the area by the rec center. She's looking for them, considering everything I've told her about the entities and everything she's experienced first-hand, sorting through her observations, filing things away for later consideration.

I check the mirror. "I don't see them."

"Yet," she adds.

"Maybe we should keep running," I suggest.

Her eyes flick to my ankle for a moment. I'm slowing her down.

We're surprised by the door buzzing open. Mom pushes me through and follows immediately.

As soon as we cross the threshold, the door slams shut. We're between two solid metal doors, an inner and an outer. A hum sounds and I know we're being scanned.

When the inner door opens, we face three soldiers blocking the entryway, all aiming rifles at us. The main labs are through large double-doors beyond the entry area, and coming through those doors now is General Dawes.

"Stand down," he calls.

The general approaches and gestures at me. "You okay? You're limping there, Spencer."

That's all the greeting we're going to get. His face and voice are so stoic, he must be in crisis management mode. He nods at my mother, and something in his eyes softens, but I pretend not to notice.

"Let's get that ankle looked at," Dawes says.

He waves a soldier over. Giraffe Jeff—I recognize him from the last time they took me to see the general in that souped-up golf cart. But I'm not letting them take me anywhere today.

"I'm fine," I say.

Jeff looks to the general. Dawes gives him the slightest nod. Jeff steps back.

"We're still gathering data," the general says. "This happened so fast we lost a step before we knew what was going on. But we're setting things up, still coordinating our response. We're working out of the central lab for now."

As we leave the entry area, I try to keep the pain from my face. A set of doors opens for us and inside I glimpse a nearby table with a fume hood and all kinds of nozzles. Beyond that are gamma detectors, an ashing furnace, and a water system.

There's also a computer console. A man sits in there, scrutinizing a monitor with quiet intensity. The picture displayed on the screen makes me stop.

"That's the jpeg you sent us," Dawes says.

I stare at the screen, shaking my head.

"Dr. Alfredson enhanced it," Dawes says, like that explains everything.

It's me. Or rather it's me as I might look in twenty years. The Molecule Thief. Tha. It's me.

Pliable Bismuth

Maude

M AUDE CROUCHED BESIDE THE soldier nearest her. The man's camouflage pants had a hole in the shin area punched out by the jagged end of a broken fibula.

His skin was visible beneath; the bone protruding through. Bruising and swelling warped the left side of his face.

They must have a med kit. Maybe she could find it if she scrambled over the expelled cargo netting into the fallen helicopter.

The other soldier, further away from her, pushed himself up on his elbows. His light blue eyes were piercing.

"Everybody sound off," he called.

The man with the injured leg grunted, raising a hand. "Castro here," he said weakly.

The blue-eyed man found his legs and managed to stand. He glanced at Maude and Elliot, frowned, then moved slowly until he stood over his fallen comrade.

"I think you're in shock," the blue-eyed man said.

A third soldier crawled out from the overturned belly of the helicopter, a young man with a dark cloud of hair and thick glasses strapped to his head. Blood matted one of his sideburns, and a huge tear in his sleeve revealed several raw scrapes.

"Bailey here," he called. "I'm okay, First Sergeant."

"Castro is in shit shape," the blue-eyed First Sergeant said. "Anybody else in there?"

"Lieutenant Tunney's dead. So's Captain Campbell. Franken, too."

The First Sergeant's lips tightened. He shut his eyes, lowering his head. No one said anything.

The First Sergeant broke the silence. "Radio?"

"Not working. Everything's fried."

The First Sergeant stepped next to Elliot. He stood a head taller, and his build looked more imposing.

"I'm Maude," she said. "This is Elliot."

The First Sergeant stuck out a hand. She took it. His grip was firm but gentle.

"First Sergeant Martin."

"Our parents," she whispered. "Elliot's and mine."

He put a hand on her shoulder. "I'm sorry."

Maude nodded, biting her lip so hard she drew blood.

He looked to Castro. "How many rounds you got?"

"Three magazines."

"Bailey?"

"Five."

"Grab the tags of the fallen," Martin ordered. "Then grab the med kit and get back here."

"Yes, First Sergeant," Bailey said.

Martin gestured toward Maude and Elliot. "You two okay? Physically, I mean?"

They both nodded.

He pointed at the chopper. "Here, get that netting free."

Maude tugged at the clasps securing the canvas netting in place. Elliot turned to assist.

Bailey trotted over with the med kit and knelt beside Castro, using gauze and water to clean his face. While he did that, Martin cut the soldier's pants off with a pair of heavy scissors.

When Martin finished, Maude paled at the raw hamburger meat and dried blood that made up Castro's lower leg.

His face like a bloody cavern.

Maude gnawed her lip, probably doing permanent damage.

Castro moaned at his ruined shin. "What are you gonna do?"

Martin smiled for the first time. "Think I've got a hammer around here somewhere."

"Wha—" Castro went quiet as Martin plunged a syringe into his leg.

Bailey rubbed his face and scowled. "Shit. Oh, Jeez, Castro."

"Shut up," Castro said.

"Pour some rubbing alcohol on that wound and wrap it," Martin ordered Bailey.

"I'll get the splint," Martin said. "Bailey?"

"Yes, First Sergeant."

Once they wrapped Castro's leg, Elliot handed the netting to Bailey, who went back into the helicopter, retrieving two poles that looked as if they'd originally been attached to something inside. He tossed them on the ground.

He worked fast. When he finished making the litter, he and Elliot bent over Castro.

"On the count of three," Bailey said.

Castro screamed as they heaved him into place. Elliot stepped back, prowling like a nervous animal as he studied the area. He crept over to the fence, then came back.

"We need to get out of the compound," he said. "Cut through the woods, and up the hill until we make it where the ferry used to run."

"Why?" Martin asked.

"We'd be safer."

Martin shook his head.

Elliot paused in his pacing. "Why're you shaking your head?"

"We got a look around. The woods aren't safe. You'd do better to stick with us. We're heading to the beach to report."

"Oh yeah, the beach is real safe."

Bailey rolled his eyes. "Fucking civilians think they know it all."

"Stow it, soldier," Martin said.

Bailey shut his mouth, giving Elliot a broad, friendly smile that was as a good as an upturned middle finger.

"First Sergeant," Maude said, voice shaking. "I think we should go to the labs. Castro needs attention, and he can get it there. They have a full infirmary."

She didn't know what to do if he turned her down. In the safety of the labs, she could collapse and let the grief pounding inside her chest spill out.

Martin appeared to think this over.

"Like you said, he's in shock," she insisted.

"She's right," Bailey said.

Martin glanced at Castro, then back at the helicopter. Maude followed his gaze and guessed he was probably thinking about the dead men they were leaving behind.

He wasn't the only one.

"It's not far," she pleaded.

Maude prayed Elliot would keep his mouth zipped. Thankfully, he did this time.

Martin nodded. "You make a good point. Okay. We'll swing by there first to drop you two off along with Castro."

Maude let out a long exhale, stepping back so they could hoist up the litter. She gave Elliot a look telling him to help them out, but he ignored her and hung back.

They lifted the makeshift stretcher and started off. Maude fell into step behind them, elbowing Elliot in the ribs. "What the hell?" she hissed. "Seriously?"

Elliot glared. "What?"

She put her head down, staying silent, not wanting to set him off. They'd both been through too much. She supposed this was how he was dealing with it.

A high-pitched whine caused the hairs along Maude's arms to prick up. "I think those creatures are coming back," she said.

Martin and Bailey exchanged glances. The two of them scrutinized the surrounding area. "How do you know?" Martin asked.

"When they came last time, I kept hearing this annoying whine. It's like being able to hear a dog whistle. Right before the helicopters went down and everything stopped working, it was awful. It almost made me pass out."

"And that's what you hear now?"

Maude nodded.

"Shit," Bailey said. He readjusted his grip on the litter, looking as if he couldn't get out of there fast enough.

The First Sergeant released one corner of the stretcher, putting a hand on Castro's shoulder to reassure him.

Castro gripped his forearm. "I can't feel my legs."

"Are you in a lot of pain?"

"No."

"Liar."

Martin nodded, and they kept going, weaving between the houses before heading down the street. Several bodies lay sprawled on the ground.

At the sight of them, Maude stopped. She sucked in air, fighting to keep it together. Each step seemed enormous.

If she didn't know better, they could've been sleeping. She couldn't look at their faces. She knew most everyone on the compound and didn't want to remember them this way.

"They took a bunch of people," Elliot said.

Martin glanced back over his shoulder. He waited for Elliot to elaborate, then finally prompted him, "Tell me."

"It's why they're here, I think," Elliot said. "I don't know what they're taking them for. They knock them out. Not all of them. I don't think they all survive."

"The fuck?" Bailey said.

"Do you still hear something?" Martin asked Maude.

"Yes," she said. "It's louder."

Bailey let loose a string of obscenities, fear tightening his jaw.

"I was at the beach when they first came," Maude said.

"She was," Elliot said. He followed a few yards behind, head constantly in motion, eyes shifting from spot to spot, checking the lengthening shadows for threats.

"They try to shoot them?" Bailey said.

Maude nodded. "Yeah"

"They bleed?"

Maude shook her head, and he rolled his eyes.

"Shit," Bailey said.

"You scared?" Martin asked. It took a moment before Maude realized he was addressing her. "You got a right to be," he continued. "I'm terrified. Bailey there? I've never seen him this way."

"I'm scared," Maude answered. It took everything she had not to cry. If she did, she might never stop.

"Look," Bailey said, stopping.

They lowered the litter, then moved closer to something on the ground. Martin waved them back, crouching. He scratched the back of his neck.

"It's like metal," he said. "There's one here, a couple over there."

Maude couldn't believe they were stopping, not after what had happened, and not with what was surely coming. She forced the panic down and moved closer to Martin, peeking over his shoulder.

On the ground, there was a small block of metal with geometric crystals embedded in the top.

Maude crouched beside Martin. If they were going to survive, they needed to know everything they could about the intruders. She picked up a stick and poked it.

"Hey, don't do that! Jesus."

Maude poked it again. The cube stretched with the stick and stayed that way. "It's pretty pliable," Maude said. "I thought it would be brittle and snap off the way bismuth does, but this is something different."

"Brains," Martin grumbled. "I have no idea what bismuth is."

"It's an elemental metal," Maude said.

Martin raised an eyebrow in response.

"You know, like the periodic table? Anyway, I think the creatures dropped these nuggets."

"Then it's probably important," Martin said. "We should grab some. You can take them to the labs."

"They might be dangerous," Bailey objected.

"The kid just poked one of them," Martin countered.

"Kid, stop poking them."

The cool air made goosebumps run up and down her arms. She hugged herself, holding in a sudden wave of fear and grief. Maude needed a clear head. Like the First Sergeant said, she could lose it later.

"We need something to put it in," she said.

Bailey shrugged. "We don't have anything."

Martin reached into his belt and pulled out a cap. He handed it to Maude, who bent over and used the underside of the cap's brim like a dustpan, scraping the metal into the crown.

Then she folded it up and handed it to Elliot, who pinched it between his thumb and forefinger, holding the cap away from him like it might suddenly come alive and bite him.

"Put it in your cargo pocket," Maude said.

"Great."

Bailey and Martin picked Castro up again. Maude led the way while Elliot fell to the rear. A high-pitched whine cut through the air. Maude winced, covering her ears.

A group of soldiers appeared across the open area between their group and the labs. Eight of them. Mirror images of one another.

"That's them," Martin said.

"It's them," Maude confirmed.

"They're all the same."

Bailey lowered the litter, but Martin stopped him. Elliot stepped close to Maude, smelling of sweat.

"We're gonna run, right?" Elliot said. "Get back to the fence and do what I said we should've done in the first place?"

"We're not leaving Castro," Martin said.

"Then what?"

"What would Spencer do?" Maude asked, addressing the question to herself.

Think like Spencer. He could see things they couldn't; his mind put him closer to these creatures than any of them.

"Wait, what? Spencer?" Elliot said. "Oh my fucking God, we're dead."

Abduction

Elliot

E VERY INSTINCT TOLD ELLIOT to run. Get out while the getting was good.

"We should put Castro somewhere safe," Bailey said. The soldier gazed down at his comrade, eyebrows drawn together.

"Get your head on straight," Martin said.

"Yes, sir."

The soldiers from the chopper dropped back, finding a soft spot where they lowered Castro to the ground. They should've left him back at the chopper. He'd have been as well off. The guy was in and out of it. He looked like hell.

Elliot checked on Maude, who had surprised him with her sense of purpose. Until she mentioned Spencer.

"We're close to the labs," Martin said.

The big man glanced at Elliot with a curled lip. Elliot returned the toxic expression.

"Here's what I'm thinking," Martin said. "You kids sprint the rest of the way. We'll hold back, defend this ground, and give you a chance."

"You can't attack them," Maude said. Her voice sounded different, lower. Her eyes seemed empty. "Bullets have no effect."

"I wish I had a grenade," Bailey said beneath his breath, "that's what I wish."

Castro laughed, although his eyes stayed closed.

Elliot watched the advancing figures. They moved in a stiff, unhurried manner. They were coming directly for them.

"We could try communicating," Maude said.

Elliot gawked at her, fumbling for some way to express the stupidity of that statement. Communicate? Why would those things communicate?

Bailey had it right. They should blow them to bits. After what they did to his parents, how could Maude think like that? He kicked the ground.

"They haven't killed many people," Maude said. "They're taking them down to the beach. Probably to the anomaly."

"What for?" Elliot said loudly.

"I don't know."

"Jesus, Maude. Stop being stupid. Stop it!"

"Settle down," Bailey said.

Elliot hadn't meant to shout, but anger and frustration poured out of him. How could they waste time talking while the creatures advanced?

Maude looked at him with a coolness that fueled resentment. He looked to the others for support, but judgement shone in their eyes as well.

The First Sergeant said something to Bailey, then approached Maude in a way that reminded Elliot of a hunter moving in, trying not to startle a deer. The soldier established eye contact, then spoke calmly.

"Young lady, I need you to run. Get going."

She didn't say anything. Elliot had no clue if Maude heard him.

"You need to run," Martin said. "You and Elliot. Go around and head for the labs. Please, do this for me."

Her face softened, and Elliot's hope rose. He couldn't believe the First Sergeant had gotten through to her.

"Come on," Martin said.

Maude winced, then doubled over. Elliot took her hand. His alarm multiplied. Thank God he couldn't hear whatever signal those monsters sent out.

Regaining composure, Maude stood and did the unthinkable—she put her hands in the air and walked *toward* the oncoming figures.

"Maude, stop!" Elliot called.

"Fucking civilians." Martin held her back.

The sound of gunfire startled Elliot, and he almost took flight. Bailey stood over Castro in a protective stance while squeezing off several shots with a handgun.

As predicted, the shots had no effect on the advancing replicants.

Martin threw an arm around Maude's midsection, swinging her away, but their shouts ended as a web of silvery light exploded around the two of them.

Maude's mouth froze open, her eyes gone enormously wide. Next to her, Martin pressed his eyes shut, dropping slowly until his body touched the ground.

Maude landed beside him. Both lay paralyzed, ready to be abducted into the void.

An entity approach Maude, touching its leg to hers. Maude hovered on an invisible stretcher as the thing dragged her off.

Elliot heard himself scream. He couldn't do anything for Maude. Self-preservation mattered now; an impulse he should have obeyed before rather than lugging that doomed soldier across the compound.

Two paths lay open for him. Either bolt back the way they'd come, or sprint for the labs.

Elliot launched himself, keeping low to the ground, arms pumping at his sides. He broke stride, pushed off in one direction, then zigged the opposite way, hoping his movements were erratic enough to avoid getting hit by an energy blast.

He imagined the sudden jolt; the unbearable pain that would shoot through him. He'd shocked himself once while fixing an electrical cord. That'd only lasted a second. This would be a hundred times worse.

The labs were ahead. He took a chance and glanced over his shoulder. No one followed him. Elliot checked the path that led to the beach, expecting an incoming army. No one.

He didn't have whatever savant-thing Spencer had going on, and he couldn't hear them, like Maude claimed, but he knew when shit hit the fan. That's all that mattered.

He crossed the distance to the main building, hurdling over the two stairs to the door. He didn't know the entry code, but there was a black button on the pad that would call security.

He mashed it with his palm, then stepped back, tilting his face up at the camera, waiting to be recognized. Five seconds crawled by. He hit it again.

Elliot checked the path. Still empty.

He pounded the metal door with his fists, then went back to the keypad. He leaned on the black button. Why wasn't it working?

Elliot checked the path again, but now saw at least twenty creepy clone-zombie soldiers coming up from the beach. They didn't move in formation, but advanced in a horde.

Acting on instinct, he threw himself backward in time to avoid the energy strike where he'd been standing. He landed hard, but ignored the pain lancing through his ribs and forced himself to run top speed toward the bushes lining the path around the rec center.

On the other side of the bushes was a small picnic area by the basketball court. Elliot tore through, ignoring the sting of branches scratching his face and arms as he hurried across the pavement.

The smell of the sea hit him and he stopped. If he kept going, he would be near the small cliffs overlooking the beach. He didn't want that.

Elliot wished he'd gone the way he'd intended all along. He should have left Maude before this, said *see ya* to those army assholes, and gone with his original plan of making a break for the woods.

He still could. But not right now. He was better off hiding somewhere until it was completely dark. Or did those things see in the dark? Did they "see" at all? They might have other ways of finding someone. Elliot blocked all those questions from his mind.

He found a shady spot and dropped, pressing himself flat, hoping the tall grass would offer cover. If he saw the enemy near, he could run again.

For now, he'd gather strength and wait for the afternoon to end. And not think about his parents. Or about Maude and what was happening to her.

He dug the base of his palms into his eyes, rubbing away the wetness. When night fell, he'd take his chances across the compound and make for the woods.

What Did We Do?

Spencer

"**H**E CAN SEE THEM," General Dawes says.

"Sorta," I correct him.

Dr. Alfredson squints, rubbing his bald spot as he studies the image on his tablet. It's Tha. He glances up at me, then back down at the image, then up at me again.

I smile. He doesn't. My mother hasn't said much since seeing the enhanced picture.

I tap randomly and repeatedly on a nearby keyboard, but stop when I notice people staring at me. I lean back against the wall, jiggling my leg.

Alfredson pulls his seat closer. He's a serious man with a solemn expression, accentuated by deep lines that bracket his lips, as if he's constantly mulling over heavy problems.

His fingertips are colder in temperature than his head, and there's a spot near the back of his skull, on the highest point of the occipital bone, that's probably a good half a degree warmer.

"Is Spencer attuned to these things because of the connection with his friend in the mirror?" Alfredson asks. "If so, what's the nature of the connection? Are we talking about some sort of time fold? If this Tha is Spencer, how does he tie into the entities from the anomaly?"

"That's not Spencer," my mom says with conviction. "It's a trick. That thing's using Spencer for something. It chose his likeness because Spencer was the first one to make contact with it."

"A good theory," Alfredson says. "I can't disagree."

They haven't given us much room to breathe since we got here. My life has become a video game, and this is just the next level.

I've made it through the zombie apocalypse part, and now we're onto the cut scene, listening to exposition, giving us a reason to go into the upcoming part of the game.

"Spencer, can you describe again how you see them? The Contained?"

I explain that they're a blur, a difference in the environment, that I see them more clearly in a mirror, but my words come fast and jumbled. Everyone leans forward, trying hard to make sense out of what must sound senseless.

When I finish, Alfredson says, "Maybe it's some sort of refractive camouflage?" He sounds confused. "Maybe it's meant to hide them in three dimensions, but a mirror's two-dimensional limitations inhibit their abilities."

General Dawes laughs at that. I don't find much humor in it.

"Or it could be a matter of frequency. Maybe the boy's mind is more sensitive, more attuned to what some of us can't perceive. You see? More questions."

"We don't have time for questions."

We all sit in silence, but I talk, I muse to myself. I'm not even aware of what I'm saying until after I've said it because I'm scared and tired. The filter is even more off than usual.

"If it's a matter of frequency, then isn't there a way of making something that will let anyone see things visible at that frequency, or frequencies?" I say. "I mean, it can't be a single frequency, can it? We're talking about an entirely different spectrum, right? And that's not possible. Unless it's part of our spectrum, but just hidden in it. Maybe they use negative refraction, like a cloaking device."

People watch me, as if waiting for more. The scrutiny is unbearable. I scratch an earlobe, then run my hand over the top of my head.

"Spencer has an amazing intellect, doesn't he?" Alfredson says, as if he's talking about a pet rat that's made it through a maze for the first time.

"He's smart," Dawes agrees. "Doctor, is Spencer's suggestion possible?"

I can already see how we could do what they do, how we could hide in plain sight. A refractive invisibility suit, using graphene nanotechnology to make it dynamic.

I spin the idea around, turn it over, imagine the possibilities, but Alfredson's voice brings me back.

"It could be," he says. "We're dealing with a tremendous amount of information all at once. We need time to process it."

"How much time depends on the entities," my mom says.

"Maybe not," Dawes counters. "I'm waiting for permission to get us out of here as soon as possible. Right now I'm in a holding pattern."

There's something the general isn't telling us. I can tell by the tension in his shoulders and the way he averts his gaze.

My mom pressed her lips together in a straight line. She sits with both feet firm on the ground, her hands on her knees.

"Why?" she asks in a low voice. "They should at least be evacuating lower-level personnel. These entities have killed people and taken more for whatever reasons. We have no idea what they want."

No one talks. I wish I'd gotten a hold of Maude. Not that the opportunity arose as events went south. But I worry about where she is now and what might be happening. She's alive. I'm sure of that, but I don't know why.

"Who did you call?" Mom asks General Dawes.

The question makes him bristle. "I'm following protocol. You know that. And you know that given our status, I can't discuss that."

"Following protocol?" Mom says. "And what's the protocol now?"

The general flashes us a fixed smile, the sort that makes me nervous. "Protocol is we keep gathering information and wait for instructions. I'm sure the protocol on the outside is to keep this work apolitical. Nobody's going to loosen up on secrecy, especially considering what's happened."

"That's a bullshit answer," Mom says. "And I'm sick of being fed bullshit. Why don't we have access to the information we need to do our job? Why has the military been building shielded structures on the beach? Why do we keep getting the runaround?"

"Jennifer," the general says gently. "I'm not in charge of things, and, if I'm being honest, I'm glad I'm not the one who ultimately calls the shots."

"Dammit, Drew, that's not an answer."

My mom reaches for me. Although I don't want to be touched, I stay still as she squeezes my arm. She's holding back, there's something else she wants to say. I know it's coming. Maybe we all do.

"Maybe I can't get at the data GERI keeps moving around and denying me access to, but the holes it leaves are telling," she says. "If we opened the door to whatever is out there, we shouldn't sweep it under the rug. GERI should do everything in its power to help us deal with it."

"We don't know that we had anything to do with opening a portal to the anomaly, or anything else," Alfredson says, shifting position in his seat.

"Come on, Herschel. Come *on*!" My mom slaps the desk with an open palm.

"I've heard nothing but unsubstantiated ideas floated my way," Alfredson says. "Do you have any evidence our experiments with the magnetic fields caused it? Any shred of direct evidence?"

"You know I don't, and that's the point, isn't it?"

"The point of what?" Alfredson asked.

"Why GERI keeps us out of the loop. It's why they keep shuffling things around like a shell game. They won't give us enough information for a complete picture, and when we get close, they shift responsibility for on-site work to the military."

"We averted a second series of earthquakes with what we did," Alfredson says. "If that caused the anomaly, and I'm not admitting that, then I'd say it's a small price to pay for savings thousands of lives. Maybe tens of thousands."

I don't want to hear anymore, but I don't want them to stop, either. I knew they suspected opening the anomaly resulted from whatever project GERI had in the works, but hearing him talk about it makes my entire body freeze. I can't even blink.

"This argument is unproductive," Dawes says. "Let's focus on the situation at hand and not get sucked into politics."

He moves into position between Alfredson and my mother, playing peacemaker. I'm surprised. He struck me as someone who's used to getting his own way and bulldozing people opposing him. I would've expected him to shut them both down. Now I see him a little differently.

"GERI's playing damage control," my mom insists.

"Stop it." Alfredson's red now. He doesn't try to cover his anger. Or maybe his fear. "You always take the outsider's approach, don't you, Jennifer? That's why people have a problem taking you seriously."

That's my mother the asshole's talking about. If he wants me to cooperate with him, screw him. My face flushes, and I can move again. As I open my mouth, Dawes gestures for quiet.

"That's enough," he says. "I have too much on my plate without this. Look, Jennifer, keep working on mapping the anomaly, analyzing what data you have. Alfredson, assist her in whatever way possible. We need intel. The anomaly is obviously the key. If that's where the entities are from, which is a logical assumption, then maybe there's something we can direct the military to do to shut the damned thing down."

Dawes studies Tha's image. He rubs his jaw as he diverts his attention to me. He finally stands and gestures at a nearby soldier.

"I'm going to see what I can do about re-establishing contact with the outside," he says. "I need an estimate of the damage from this EMP, or whatever it was."

He leaves, and Mom turns to her desk. Dr. Alfredson doesn't move except for his eyes, which half close like a lizard's as he stares at the floor. I watch him, waiting for something to happen.

I'm eight years old again, listening and watching adults do things in their own sphere, leaving me to mine, certain it'll be fine. Except this time maybe it won't.

"Mom?" My voice is hushed.

She stops typing. I see how frightened she is by the set of her mouth and the way she blinks too fast. I put my hand over hers and squeeze it.

"What did we do?" I whisper.

Lights in the Dark

Elliot

E LLIOT WOKE IN A panic, rolling over and scrambling for cover. He rubbed his eyes. With so much shit running through his head, and all the flips going on in his gut, how the hell had he fallen asleep?

At least it was dark. Above him, heavy clouds blocked the moon. The air smelled like wet forest and saltwater.

He had to get going. Maybe hop the fence and cut through the woods. Or maybe stick to the base of the cliffs, then walk along the shoreline until he found someone, or some way to contact the mainland.

Vancouver wasn't far. He could go there once he was inland. He'd heard they'd mostly rebuilt it.

Or maybe he'd head straight to Washington. Either way, he had to get off this island. There had to be some small boats near the abandoned tourist area.

Elliot gave his head a shake. He was no hero. Never claimed to be. He ripped a chunk of grass from the ground and chucked it at the shadows.

The feeling of his mother twitching against his chest as he held her, then her dying as the second charge ravaged them, remained fresh in his mind. He couldn't shut it out.

What else could he have done? Nothing. What else should he have done? Something.

Elliot stood, taking cover in the bushes near the rec center. With no sign of movement, he pushed through and jogged across the basketball court.

Under the shadow of the rec center, Elliot peered down the path to the beach. That's where the tech shed was and, inside, three mini-subs.

He'd never driven one before, but if the Wheelers could handle it, how hard could it be? Unless they were lying, like usual.

The woods, or the beach, or the labs. Those were the choices. He went over pros and cons while he kept monitoring the surroundings for threats. Not that he could see far with no moon out.

The blackness gave him a false sense of safety, and at the same time made him feel very vulnerable. As a child, he didn't like the dark, same as most kids. But most kids grew out of the fear. He hadn't.

Go.

The decision to move almost felt external. Without making a solid commitment to any one path, Elliot headed back past the labs, stopping several times to listen, until he arrived at the spot where Maude dropped.

Now, the sky lightened as clouds moved away from the moon. He looked up at the stars.

"Kid," someone called.

Elliot leaned forward on the balls of his feet, fists up, ready to either run or start swinging. But then he remembered the wounded man they'd left on the ground and figured the moon was bright enough to give him away.

"Hey," Elliot said.

"Where are the others?" the man asked. Elliot struggled to remember his name. Castro?

Elliot squatted beside him. "Don't know. Those things came."

Castro's voice sounded weak. His hand found Elliot's and squeezed, the intimacy embarrassing, but Elliot didn't pull away.

"You think they're dead?" Castro asked.

With Castro looking to him for comfort, Elliot wasn't sure how to respond. "Don't know that either," Elliot said. "I don't think so. They probably took them to the beach."

"What are they doing with the people?" Castro asked. "What do they want from us?"

Elliot had asked himself the same question. He shrugged.

"I'm going to Vancouver," Elliot said. Why'd he say that?

"I've never been to Vancouver. I heard there's not much left of it," Castro said. "You think they're alive then?"

"Maybe."

"What should we do?" Castro asked.

"Are you in a lot of pain now?"

"It comes and goes. I can't move my fucking leg at all. My shoulder hurts like crazy."

Castro let go of Elliot, reaching with his good arm for a small knapsack resting on the litter beside him. He shook it open, pulled out a container, and offered it to Elliot.

"Thirsty?"

"No."

Elliot was parched, but didn't want to take the soldier's water. Castro took a sip himself, then fumbled for something else inside the pack.

He took out a military-issued candy bar, again offering it first to Elliot, who waved his hand in refusal.

"So, Vancouver," Castro said. It sounded so forced Elliot had to smile.

"Right."

"You think you can stay with me until morning. Just hang here a few hours? You think?"

Elliot didn't respond, and Castro didn't push it. The soldier peeled back the green foil wrapper and took a bite of chocolate.

"Anyone you know get taken? Or killed?"

"My parents," Elliot muttered.

Castro sighed and crossed himself. "I'm sorry. It's rough. I got nothing to say that can make you feel better, but I guess that's the way it is."

Elliot had been expecting a burst of sympathy. He found Castro's pragmatism unexpectedly reassuring.

"They say if you want to make God laugh, just tell him your plans," Castro said. "I wish I'd done more. You know what I mean? I wish I could go back and change things. I would've done it all differently. No, that's wrong. I would've done it all the same way, but it would've been different."

"So, it doesn't matter?" Elliot said.

"I'd still end up right here, but I would've ended up differently."

The way Castro worded it struck Elliot's sense of humor, and he laughed.

Castro shifted and groaned. Elliot wished he could do something besides sit there, but he didn't know how to help.

A sound stopped their chatting; like metal scratching on metal.

"The fuck," Castro whispered. He pushed up higher with his elbows, stretching his neck as if that would help him see in the dark.

A light appeared from the direction of the lab. It flickered upward before shifting along the ground, and then rising again.

"You think that's them?" Castro asked. "I mean the things."

"Yeah," Elliot said. The EMP would've knocked out all the military and science equipment, so it had to be the monsters. But did they even use technology? Elliot hadn't seen them carrying a weapon or anything else.

Elliot's stomach tightened, and he considered leaving, hightailing it out of there, heading away from the light. If those things were at the lab, then they might've brought something tech-like to help them force their way in.

Another light broke the darkness before they both disappeared around the side of the labs.

"I can sneak over there." Elliot regretted the words instantly.

"Don't," Castro said.

"What if it's not those things?" Elliot asked.

Castro didn't answer.

"I'll go check," Elliot said.

"No, wait."

They huddled in the darkness, watching the occasional appearance of light. Without further discussion, Elliot slipped off, moving in a crouch, ready to flee if necessary. He heard his heart in his ears, and each breath sounded too loud.

Around the corner of the labs, a man in jeans and a collared shirt stood on a ladder, illuminated by two spots of light. Two soldiers stood guard. Both held assault rifles with lights on them, both shining them toward the ladder.

The man climbed down, then dragged the ladder to another location. The soldiers followed him. He was replacing video equipment around the lab's perimeter.

Overwhelming relief almost caused Elliot to approach them at a run while pounding the air with his fists and calling out for attention. Almost. And then he stopped and thought about what someone with a gun might do if surprised by something leaping out of the darkness right now.

Elliot put his hands up and called out to them. He remained where he was as two round lights locked on to his position. He squeezed his eyes shut against the blaze and kept still.

"Identify yourself!" a man shouted, fear making his voice shake.

"Elliot Born."

"Get down on your knees. Put your hands behind your head."

Elliot did as he was told.

A soldier came over, the light at the end of his rifle shining in Elliot's face. "You got your identification card on you, Mr. Born?"

Elliot nodded. "In my pocket."

The man gestured with his gun. "Go on then. Slowly."

Elliot trembled as he pulled out the laminated card. The man swung the light over to it, then back to Elliot's face.

"He's not one of them," someone else said from the darkness. "I know this kid."

It sounded like the geeky guy who analyzed data. "Alex?" Elliot called.

"Hey, Elliot."

Despite Alex's recognition, the soldier still patted Elliot down. He stopped at the military cap peeking from Elliot's pocket. He jerked it out.

"Where the hell'd you get this?"

"An injured soldier," Elliot said. "He's back over there. He's from one of the choppers that crashed."

The soldier rolled back the material of the cap. "It's some kind of metal," the soldier observed. "It's soft as hell."

"Wouldn't touch that if I were you," Elliot said. "I found it. I think it's something left behind when the monsters disappear."

"We need to get that to Dr. Alfredson," Alex said.

The soldier grunted, handing the hat back to Elliot. "First," he said to Elliot. "Show us where the soldier is."

"His name's Castro," Elliot said, shoving the cap in his pocket. "This way."

Shit Runs Downhill

Jennifer

D REW HELD OUT A cup of coffee. Jennifer accepted it with a smile. She placed a hand on his forearm, then slid it up to his elbow. They looked at each other for a long time before Jennifer broke contact, returning her attention to the monitor on the desk.

"Can you spare a minute?" Drew asked.

"Yeah, I need a break. I'm working on a model of the energy patterns we picked up before everything shut down."

They both watched the 3D printer at work.

"It looks like some kind of tunnel, or something."

"Doesn't it? I think it leads directly into the anomaly. But it seems to be missing something. There are places where there aren't enough dimensions to capture what it looks like."

"I'm still trying to get numbers on how many people they've taken through that thing. If that's where they're taking them."

They both fell silent. Jennifer tried imagining what the entities wanted with people. Why hadn't the creatures tried making contact? Why were they acting hostile, or was that merely an interpretation of events? She wanted to believe the people taken were still alive, that there would be a positive outcome to all this.

If those things used this tunnel to move people through the water, then maybe there was hope. The entities may not need oxygen, but she prayed they understood human reliance on it. What about radiation? She wished they had more information.

"What did you want to talk about?" she asked.

Drew pulled something from his pocket. It was a hat, and inside the hat was something metallic. It looked familiar.

"Elliot Born brought this in. He said after the EMP there were dozens of these things scattered around the ground."

"I think I saw them. When Spencer and I were running to get here."

She liked Elliot. She wished his mother and father had made it.

His mother was a strong and brilliant woman. She'd won the New Horizons Prize for Physics for her work on string theory. She'd given the most inspiring speech Jennifer had ever heard. All the women in the audience stood and applauded. The men, too, but the women stood first.

Dr. Born had kept pressing the idea that the anomaly might prove the presence of another reality. Her husband, on the other hand, believed it was the key to another power source.

Both possibilities were fascinating. And dangerous. They could bring the salvation or destruction of the human race.

Right now, it looked more like the latter.

"So what do you think?" Drew asked.

Jennifer dragged her desk lamp over and pulled a magnifying glass out from a drawer. She placed the metal under the light, poking at it with a stylus. The metal reminded her of bismuth.

"You checked for radioactivity?" she asked.

"Of course," he said.

"I have a theory," she said. "These things disappear after they shoot off energy. We saw that. We have video. They aren't entirely solid. Maybe they're like Spencer's Molecule Thief. Maybe they can draw material when they want to be in a solid state. Then once they expend energy, this is what's left behind."

"Bismuth?"

"It looks like bismuth. It isn't. It's too malleable. I don't know what this is."

Jennifer thought about it, and considered that the bulk of this stuff, according to what they knew, had appeared immediately after the EMP. It was like the entities had generated the pulse working together and this is what they left behind. Or what was left of them. She considered the implications of that.

"They have an inherent ability to manipulate energy," she said.

"And why are they taking people prisoner?"

"I don't know."

Jennifer took a sip of her coffee as she glanced around the lab. Too many of the workstations were vacant because of missing personnel.

If the things from the anomaly were from another reality, how were they able to exist in this reality? They made no effort to communicate. Their behavior gave no clues to their psychology, other than to suggest they were all connected somehow.

What if there weren't several entities? What if all the soldiers were a manifestation of a single intelligence?

Jennifer's throat tightened. "Drew, we need to evacuate the compound."

He tugged an earlobe and sighed. "I told you, I put a call in. I'm waiting to hear what they want us to do. It's GERI though. That means it's political, and politics always slow things down."

"Are they sending in more military?" Jennifer asked.

"I've made that request. I'm told there's a naval presence coming up the coastline."

"At the very least, the children should go." Jennifer wanted Spencer out.

"I'm sure they'll get them out. But I don't see them letting the core scientific team go anytime soon."

"We're not prisoners."

"I know," Drew said. "But we need expertise. We need to know what we're facing and figure out what to do about it."

Jennifer shook her head. "I don't know where GERI leaves off and corporate or military interests begin."

"That's always been the struggle," Drew said. "They're being cautious. Everyone is. There's a sense what's going on here is critical. Decisive. Nobody wants to make a mistake or open themselves to criticism."

"Nobody wants to be accountable."

Drew smiled at that. "Maybe they're hoping to make sure that, whatever happens, they share accountability."

She liked him this way, in the quiet moments where the two of them could talk, without their careers and status putting up walls. Jennifer knew it was an illusion. Their careers were ingrained in who they were.

"I don't think anyone is going to be held accountable," she said.

"That's not true. They'll drag me through the mud. Shit runs downhill."

Jennifer took his hand and kissed his palm. With his free hand, he ran his fingers through her hair. She liked that, shutting her eyes to concentrate on the moment.

It never lasted long.

"I have to tell you something," Drew said. "Elliot told me the entities took Maude."

Jennifer's lips trembled. She pressed them together.

"Do you want me to tell Spencer?" he said.

She shook her head. "No." She couldn't swallow. "I'll go do it now."

Maude

Maude was in the dark. And there were others nearby. Dozens of them. Was she awake, or dreaming them?

She reached out, trying to determine where she was, and realized she couldn't feel anything. Not her hand, or arm, or body.

She concentrated on making a fist, but couldn't feel her fingers. She could sense temperature; patches of warmth and cold in different places, but in the darkness, she couldn't tell if the feeling was internal or external.

What if there was nobody to respond?

Freak out time.

Maude screamed, felt her mouth opening, but no sound came out, no feeling of stress at the back of her throat, no physical sensation of expelling air from her lungs.

The dozens of others shifted, sensing the change in her presence. Some reached out while others drew back. All were aware, because all were connected, their presences joined, the sensation both of being split and being many places, shared by many others at once.

Panic rippled through them all, even those who'd reached some level of acceptance. Some didn't fight it; some found merging with the mass comforting. It scared the hell out of Maude.

I'm Maude Faraday. Maude Faraday!

Her name echoed through the shared consciousness.

I'm Christian Klaver. I'm Ibn Batutta. I'm Jarod Wheeler.

Jarod? It was oddly reassuring hearing a familiar name, even if it was Jarod's.

I'm Lucas Wheeler. I'm Emily McGregor. I'm Lisa Sharone. I'm Isamu Yagi. I'm Janine Hamilton. I'm....

The names kept going. Although she didn't know them all personally, they were the names of others from the compound.

Maude let go, drifting for a second. A minute? An hour? It would be easy to drift, to let herself go into the current and join the others becoming something different.

She sensed movement all around; heard it, saw it, tasted it. She could slip off and let the collective melt away all her imperfections.

STOP!

Maude shut out thoughts of surrender, fighting to reclaim the bits of herself that had floated off, concentrating on what felt like *her* and luring it back with focused thought. The effort almost seemed too much. The strain disturbed those who had succumbed.

She tumbled into a moment of clarity. A moment where she was sure of her perceptions.

Inside a dark space, bits of colorful energy surrounded her, ever-changing, beautiful to experience. All these consciousnesses were dandelion seeds on a cosmic wind, and the freedom they offered enticed like nothing else ever had.

There was nothing to fear. Here there was no time, no place, no reason, there was only existence, and the satisfaction of being connected with a whole. That was enough.

Maude sensed a rogue spark nearby. She recognized it. Like herself, it hovered at the fringe of the collective, fighting the allure of surrender.

"Maude?"

"Here." She hadn't said the word or expressed it as a thought. It was simply reality.

A picosecond passed. Or maybe a millennium.

"I'm having trouble keeping it together," he said. It was First Sergeant Martin. She knew his presence without seeing or hearing him.

"Don't give up, First Sergeant," Maude said. Or rather, her awareness reached out in an attempt to ease his doubt.

"Bill," he said. "My name's Bill."

She sensed his fear, following it as it spread through the collective. Others reached for him in reassurance, anger, confusion.

Her desire to connect with him morphed into a golden light traveling through foam-space, faster than thought, an urgent tendril driven by her own fears and needs. He embraced it, and they locked together, away from the collective. An island of calm and purpose.

Bill now drifted inside a swimming pool, arms outstretched, eyes closed. The sun warmed his face and stomach as he floated, half-submerged. Maude bobbed along with him, the water keeping their bodies cool.

"I can't move," he said, sinking as the water closed over his face.

"No," Maude urged.

As he drifted away, she kept track of him through the thickening water, following his thread. But then she found another presence.

Maude?

"Spencer?"

It felt like him, but a kernel of selfishness buried deep inside the presence spoiled the illusion. So close though, she could almost overlook the imperfection. Except the flaw twisted this version of Spencer in an unpleasant way.

Maude struggled, swimming without a body, fighting against the current that continuously pulled her back to the collective.

This was the belly of the whale. Here, the dense space made escape unimaginable, but if she could break through and find the area beyond, maybe she stood a chance. Bits of energy streaked by her in a less organic pattern, as if constructed with intention.

She touched a strand of light. The contact ripped away bits of herself, sending fragments of awareness along the stream into the collective.

Maude, come on!

"Don't yell at me, Spencer!"

She didn't know how Spencer could be here. But he was.

I need you, Maude.

What did he need? It didn't matter. All that mattered was he was here.

"We need to get out," Maude said. "If we stay, it's going to end badly."

Spencer laughed. *It'll end wonderfully.*

It would end both ways. And none of them.

"Come on!" She grabbed onto Spencer and was so immediately repulsed that she almost broke the connection. This wasn't Spencer. Not exactly.

Everything flipped.

"We're on the other side of the mirror," she said.

And became aware.

The Other Side Of The Mirror

Spencer

"COME OUT, COME OUT, wherever you are."

I sit at a desk in front of a mirror in a plastic stand brought in especially for me. Except for my reflection—my unaltered reflection—it's empty.

I've been sitting in front of the mirror for hours, staring unblinkingly. Tears ran down my cheeks until my eyes dried out. Then, I meditated, humming one note in a nasal tone repeatedly, and now I'm talking, hoping in the middle of a conversation with myself I'll hear his voice.

"So what do you say?" I ask. "I need help here. Something."

Nothing.

"Tha? I'm scared."

Still nothing.

"I think we're missing it. I mean, you knew about The Contained, and the only thing you told us was they were coming. Why? What are you holding back? Come on, Tha."

On the far wall behind the desk, a bank of monitors shows pictures from the cameras that were replaced by a tech team that slipped outside after the EMP. When I get bored with the mirror I check them, although I have no idea what I'm looking for. If this were an old detective movie, I'd already have gone through a bottle of whiskey and half a pack of cigarettes on this stakeout.

"What do you think?" I ask myself.

"I think we're missing something big, and I think we're being played," I respond.

"Played?"

"Yeah. If we're not being played, why not come out and say what we're up against? Don't give me this mystery stuff."

"I don't want to spill too much," I answer me.

"Oh?" I say, making my frustration and ridicule clear. "At least tell me what's happening with the people they took. What about Maude? She's okay, right?"

"I can't tell you anything except we all have our part to play."

God, I hate feeling manipulated. Who is he? Who is the man in the mirror? It's not me. I know it's not me.

The door opens, and a soldier slips in. He's the bullfrog from the beach, Cal Johnson. He smiles. I can't help but smile back. He checks the images on the monitors, then sits on the edge of the desk.

"How you doing, Spence?" he asks.

"I'm going crazy."

That makes him laugh. He pulls out another one of those chocolate bars wrapped in green foil that he seems to keep in stock to be used when he's about to say something difficult. He offers it to me.

"No thanks."

He tucks the chocolate away, shifting his weight awkwardly. "Spencer," he says, and then takes a long pause. "I heard from one of my friends that your girlfriend didn't make it. I'm sorry. She seemed like a nice person."

"She is a nice person. And she's not dead."

He leans back, like my words give him a quick push. "No?"

"No. She's something else."

"What?"

"I don't know."

I can't stand the thought of anything happening to Maude. She's not dead, but I'm not convinced she's alive.

Maybe she's Schrödinger's cat. Right now not dead, or alive, but in a state of quantum superposition. The metaphor doesn't ease my mind.

"What about you? You know some of the soldiers they took?"

"Yeah," Cal says.

"Maybe they're alive, too."

Cal studies the mirror, and we make eye contact there. When he speaks, it's as if he's talking to me through the glass. "I'm torn up about it, Spencer. But I know that you have to keep perspective or you're sunk. You have to keep balance."

When he says that it strikes a note. I consider the streaks of energy I've seen in the background when Tha has made an appearance. I imagine touching one and traveling along it, hitchhiking through time and space. What am I missing?

"What are you seeing, Spencer?" Cal asks.

"Just the other side of the mirror."

Cal adopts a thoughtful expression. "I used to imagine what it would be like to step through. But then there would be two of me and I can't imagine that. I don't think the world is ready for two Cal Johnsons at the same time, in the same place."

The door opens and Cal shoots to attention. It's General Dawes. The general gives a dismissive wave and tells him, "At ease."

Cal relaxes, but not a lot. The general checks the monitors and then the mirror. "Corporal Johnson, can you excuse Mr. Newton and myself, please?"

"Yes, General."

Cal offers an encouraging glance and slips out. The general drags a chair over and sits down beside me so our knees almost touch.

His gray eyes probe me. I'm not sure what to say. I wonder if he sent Cal Johnson in here, or if maybe I'm being overly suspicious.

"No progress?" he asks.

"No, General."

He frowns. I'm sorry that I've disappointed him.

"Is there anything we can do to make this easier for you? Anything you need?"

"I don't know," I say.

The general turns his attention to the mirror. Together we watch ourselves and the room beyond.

There's so much pressure on me, so much responsibility, but I have no control over things. I want to do something, but maybe I've given all the help I can. Only I don't believe that.

"People are working outside," I say. We both watch the monitors and the general nods. "Any possibility I can get out there, too? Maybe if I get away from the labs, away from the shielding, I'll have some success."

Dawes shrugs. "I'll arrange it."

"Have we heard from the outside?"

I know I've overstepped my bounds with the question, and the general confirms this with a sour expression. Then his face relaxes.

"Not yet, Spencer. You're talking about a giant bureaucracy in action. There are meetings, phone calls, more meetings, more phone calls, and a bunch of asses running in circles trying not to take responsibility in case anything goes wrong."

I see the general as a young officer, and imagine Cal Johnson years from now. That makes me grin.

The general chuckles and nods at his own words. "Pathetic, eh? Everyone's too caught up trying not to get burned."

"What about you?"

"I'm as bad as any of them."

"I don't think of you that way."

He gets up. The lines of his face are deeper. Maybe the circles under his eyes are darker, too. He looks tired. Older. He's worried, which makes me feel both reassured and unsettled.

"How long do you think, before I go outside?"

"I want to go with you. And I have a few things to do before that. What do you say you try to get some sleep? Come back here at oh-six-hundred."

I nod.

The general and I are going outside. I want to feel safe, but he can't protect me. Not out there. Not against *them*.

Blockade

Spencer

S LEEP VISITED ME IN fits and starts and so, an hour ahead of the appointed time, I'm lying on my back, staring at the base of the top bunk, listening to someone breathe. There are three hundred and twelve springs on the bottom of the mattress.

I shift from my back into a fetal position on my side, then roll onto my back again. I'm determined not to let the restlessness drive me out of bed. God, why can't I be normal and sleep until my alarm goes off? But no, I have a goddamn internal alarm set by anxiety that goes off prematurely.

Don't be late, it blares. *Are you sure you're not late? Look at the clock. Look at it!*

As the seconds turn to minutes, tightness builds in my throat that I can't swallow down. Something is going to happen that will prevent me from going outside. I can feel it. Stupid. Paranoid.

Maude. She's all I can think about. The contours of her face. That sideways smile she gives whenever she makes a smart comment.

I haven't known her for long, but that's no reason to let her go. I'll find her.

I can't stand it any longer. I bounce out of bed about twenty minutes early. I grab clean clothes and shuck them on while in motion, staying vigilant about not disturbing anyone still sleeping. That's most of them.

When I get to the command center, my mother and the general sit close together, her hand on his. She leans in, and he tells her something that makes her laugh.

I walk up. "Morning."

"You're early," Dawes says.

Something on Mom's computer grabs my attention. It's a copy of an assignment I did for Alfredson; a mind game to create a model for a five-dimensional universe.

"What's this?" I ask. "Where did you get this?"

Mom sees what I'm referring to. For a moment, it looks as if she's been caught doing something embarrassing.

"I did some modeling based on what we know about the anomaly. Dr. Alfredson saw similarities between some work you completed for him and the information I kept coming up with."

My model showed time as a fourth dimension, and velocity as the fifth, working at the quantum level, creating a defined superposition, like the ability of something to be in two places at the same time until an observer determines whether it's at one spot or the other.

That's where the Molecule Thief is. That's where Maude is, too. I know it in my heart.

If the model of the anomaly were real, I'd contend with length, width, depth, and time, where time existed in its entirety; past, present, and future. Moving through time would be as easy as walking from one room to another.

I again think of Maude, and then the Molecule Thief. She's not dead. I know it somehow. It's not merely a hope, it's real.

With what I've seen when the Molecule Thief visits, and all the math I've done related to the anomaly, I'm certain. And I'm sure there are others survivors out there, too.

Something nagging at me edges closer. An image of Tha pops into my head, driving a wedge between Maude and me.

"Spencer? Come back."

I've zoned out. The general watches me with a slight jiggle of his foot that I interpret as concern and anticipation. He's nothing like my father, not in appearance, not in temperament.

Dad understood my flights of attention. He had them, too, I think.

The model beckons me; numbers rushing along, following a predictable pattern. I know the computer can't model what I suddenly have in mind, but I reach over and create a second version of the model, anyway. Now the computer has two versions.

"What are you doing?" Mom asks.

"How does something from one reality affect the other?" I ask.

"Do we know?" Dawes asks.

I shake my head. "But what if there is an effect? What if that's why The Contained are taking people?"

"What effect?" Dawes asks.

"It would be some sort of disruption," Mom says. "But Spencer, if you're right, then what about when the entities leave the anomaly to come here?"

"I think they have an effect," I say. "But, maybe having us enter the anomaly is more dramatic, maybe the effect is localized because the anomaly is limited, or whatever is on the other side of the anomaly is limited. Maybe that's why Tha keeps calling them The Contained."

I watch the two models. I touch the screen, dragging one closer to the other.

"Energy is the capacity of a physical system to do work, right? But what if that physical system is overloaded? The matter and energy within one system can't be created or destroyed. But what if matter or energy from another system is introduced?"

The two models touch. Both take different forms. But the models can't accommodate what would really happen.

And then I'm hyperventilating, almost on the verge of passing out. Shit. I haven't done this in years. Let it sneak up on me this way. I fight to regulate my breathing and calm myself. Focus.

"You okay, Spencer?" Dawes asks.

My mouth is dry. I lick my lips.

My mom puts her hands on my shoulders and looks me in the eye, though I'm not sure what she's hoping she'll find. I relax my body, but my brain is still revved.

"I'm okay," I say.

Dawes furrows his brow. I'm sure he's trying to sort all this out by the way he looks at me and then at the computer models. "So, The Contained are trying to upset the system. Why?"

"I don't know. Maybe to close off the anomaly? Maybe to create another portal somewhere else? When they're in the anomaly, The Contained are in a different state. They exist, and they don't exist. Not in a fixed state, anyway."

"It's almost like you're describing their situation as a prison," Mom says.

The general stands for a moment, then sits again. This time his back isn't as straight, and his shoulders drop a bit. Dawes gestures for one of his men, and Cal approaches.

Cal gives him a crisp, "Yes, sir?"

"Are we ready outside?" he asks.

"Yes, sir."

"You ready to go, Spencer?"

I almost forgot why I'm up so early. I nod.

My mom doesn't look as calm. "How do you want to do this when we get out there?" she asks.

I hadn't thought about it. Apparently the general has. He gestures and Jeff and Rod pick up a full-length mirror. He gives a command and they carry it between them down the hall, heading toward the lab's exit.

"I had some questions prepared, if it's okay, Spencer?" Dawes reaches in his jacket and pulls out a sheet of paper. "If you contact him, I'd like you to ask these. They're printed out in order of importance."

They don't know him. Good luck with this. The Molecule Thief is as scattered as I am. I scan the list and shake my head at the first question: 1) Are you a time traveler? If so, are the entities from the anomaly also time travelers?

I'll ask, but I know what the Molecule Thief is going to say, or at least I know his tone. "I can't tell you that, Spencer. I can tell you we're all time travelers." And my follow up would be, "Are you me?" And he'll say, "Yes." And it will mean nothing, because he speaks in abstracts.

As I finish my review of the list, the general gives a signal. We move down the hall, through the entrance area, and out the front doors of the labs.

It's cool outside, with a gentle breeze stirring the nearby trees. About fifty yards away from the building, they've set the mirror into a frame. They've positioned two cameras to record the entire production.

"Are you up for this?" the general asks.

I shrug. I'm sure that doesn't inspire confidence.

When you're a little kid, you believe there are monsters in the closet. You've seen them. You've heard them move through the dark and bump against the door. Yet, when your father comes in and turns on the light, and opens the door, there's nothing there. Just your clothes. But you know, as soon as he turns the lights off and shuts the door, the creature will be back.

That's the feeling I have now. My dad is here opening the door and the Molecule Thief is nowhere to be seen. But wait until I'm alone and it's unexpected. He'll show up.

I approach the mirror and see myself. I have a ridiculous urge to giggle. I don't, because I don't want them to shoot me.

I try to relax. I need to clear my mind and open myself as much as possible.

Where is Tha? I empty my head and stare. Forget that people are watching and cameras are recording; forget all that. Make contact.

Pretend he's there. Pretend you can see him, then listen. I lean closer to the mirror and let my vision blur. Come on. Where are you?

I know our connection isn't broken. He's somewhere out there. I can feel him.

I imagine him drawing close. He's not solid, just a network of impulses, and those impulses form an intelligence, and that intelligence draws in matter from the surrounding reality; molecules coming together, helping that sentience gain a foothold in reality.

I wait as I focus on this image, but something is missing. No, something is different. The energy patterns have altered, but I don't know how, and I can't be certain it's not just my imagination.

I sense him, but I can't call him. I'm relieved, because for the first time in a long time, I'm uneasy about him. More than that; I'm afraid.

I roll that around inside my head.

"General, that call's come in," Cal says.

I'm careful to keep my eyes on the mirror, but the words hook my attention.

In my peripheral vision, I watch the general accept the satellite phone and press it to his ear. He puts a finger in the other ear and steps back for privacy, lowering his head, as if that provides an extra dimension of secrecy. His expression hardens.

"What about New York?" he asks.

When he lowers the phone, his brow is flat, his mouth sour. He rubs the side of his chin, then he picks up the phone again and dials. His eyes narrow, the muscles along his jaw tighten, and the tension in his face is contagious.

Cal, Rod, and Jeff stand guard close by. They attend to the general's conversation with worry in their eyes.

"Anything?" Mom asks me.

Her reflection in the mirror startles me. "Not yet."

"It's okay if this doesn't work. We can try later."

"I know."

I try again, attempting to shut out all distractions. I take a deep breath, then release it. Nothing.

"Maude?" I say her name into the mirror. I can almost feel her waiting on the other side. Stuck in another reality. Or maybe I'm fooling myself with wishful thinking.

"What is it?" My mother's touch brings me back.

"I'm picking up something."

I don't know why I lie to her. It's been so nice not having to hide things from her, not having to omit anything about what I see in the mirrors. And now I'm making up stuff that isn't there. Nothing tangible, anyway. It's more like a tickle in my subconscious.

"I think I'm sensing the people who went with the entities."

"They're alive?"

Maybe. It could be true. I nod. "But I don't think they have much time."

Mom searches my face. I'm careful to keep my expression neutral.

"We need to go after them," I say.

"I don't see that happening."

"We need to. The energy patterns in the mirror are different." At least that part's not a lie.

"In what way?"

"I don't know." My mom gives me time to develop an explanation. "It's like what we were talking about with the models. The entities expend energy here. And our people expend energy there, stressing the system. If we wait too long, we'll lose them."

My mom chews her lip, then inclines her head a fraction. "It makes sense."

"Can you talk to the general? Can you convince him to let a team go into the anomaly?"

Mom shakes her head. She glances at the mirror as if she can see what I'm doing. Maybe she can. Maybe everyone can see it but they refuse to acknowledge it.

"No way," she says. "It's too dangerous. We can't send people in there."

"I'd go."

"Like Hell. Spencer, we don't know enough."

"What about the people already there?"

"The anomaly is unstable, the readings change. What happens if we send people in there, and it disappears? And what kind of environment is it? It's too dangerous. We don't have enough data."

The general's still talking into the satellite phone. "Quit jerking me around." His voice is hard to hear. I'm sure that's the idea. "I called GERI, and now I'm calling you... A blockade? Who authorized that...? Don't give me that shit. Call Kilgore. Call Ponepinto. I don't have time. Do this for me."

I wish I could hear the other side of the conversation.

"That's a goddamn arbitrary deadline. What am I supposed to do? There are civilians here goddammit."

The general puts the phone down and gestures for his men to follow him. With the soldiers close by, he returns to the lab without a word. That can't be good, right?

The Net

Maude

M^{AUDE?}

M AUDE?

The voice came from inside a fog of thought. She struggled through the haze to find it. It took so much effort, more than seemed worthwhile, but something in the back of her mind warned that she needed to resist.

Maude shoved through a gelatinous bubble, only to fall back exhausted. What was this? Where was she?

Her memories drifted away, but she jabbed through the denseness so she could hold on to them. If she let them go, it would be over.

She thought of her parents. The anger and pain helped her keep from letting go.

Don't quit on me.

The voice again. She almost recognized it. It wasn't real, was it?

"I want to go home," she said. "Help me."

I'm trying.

"What's happening? Where am I?"

The Contained are draining you. Then they'll take you apart molecule by molecule. You'll be nothing more than a mound of residue. Not even that. You'll be nothing.

An internal shudder passed through Maude, and she fought to keep calm. It felt like treading water now; the whole time her body worked to stay afloat, another part of her offered soothing suggestions that surrender was inevitable and how good it would be.

Come on, Maude. Stop feeling sorry for yourself.

"Spencer?"

A wave of amusement lapped at her consciousness. It had an edge of schadenfreude Spencer didn't possess. Her consciousness shuddered in a way similar to a shiver.

You're on the edge of disappearing.

"Help me."

Help yourself.

What was she supposed to do? It was hard staying awake, harder keeping clear thoughts.

Tha.

The word came from within the darkness, an awareness within a collective. It referred to the voice, to the identity of the sentience that darted through her skull. It offended. The Contained hated it.

What was The Contained?

Ideas came from the web that sought to devour her. The disorientation hurt. Information sliced through her awareness like shards of glass.

The Contained, the things that came from the anomaly into the compound, the things that formed this collective. They couldn't exist long in her world, and she couldn't exist long in theirs.

That's what they were hoping for, wasn't it? That's what The Order wanted to stop. The humans created an imbalance, and the universe always sought correction, right?

You're drifting, Maude.

A rumble moved through the net. The Contained hated Tha, The Abomination. Tha went against everything that should be.

Maude, listen. Listen for where it sounds less dense.

"You're not Spencer," she said.

No. I'm better.

The contempt of the response angered her. Why was it deriding him? What was the connection between Spencer and this thing? "He called you Molecule Thief," she said. "At the beach."

Spencer needs you.

Through Tha she saw him. Spencer. Large ears, blue eyes, high forehead, unruly honey-colored hair, a broad smile that could at once be mischievous and shy.

Listen!

His command startled her out of her reverie. If he hadn't rattled her, she could have kept drifting and not come back.

Maude drew in what willpower remained and listened. She heard a low buzzing, and then a constant crackling beyond that. She could hear the patterns of energy weaving into some sort of netting or field, and she sensed it getting stronger as it absorbed the people within the netting.

One spot didn't seem as dense. That's where she heard Tha. She wasn't sure if the dead spot was his doing, or if he was taking advantage of a flaw.

Go that way. Spencer already knows you're here. He'll be able to find you once you're out.

His voice irritated her. It rang false, and she knew Tha held back. What did he want, and why did she feel manipulated?

Go. And listen for Spencer. Listen for him.

She resisted being dipped into the churning pool pulling her apart and screamed with the effort. Her presence rippled through the netting. She tried again, aiming her will at the thin spot, and collapsed back after expending herself.

She wanted to give up. She might have, except for a familiar presence.

"Keep going," it said, and she heard Bill inside her head.

He was afraid, but his determination was iron. As terrified as she was, he still sensed her, and fought for her through the others, battling the avalanche of raw feelings stripping him of his identity, hurling him into madness.

Bill.

Maude reached for him, and their energies connected. He ripped through the confining energies with abandon, joining her, helping Maude battle through the webbing imprisoning them.

He pushed to free her, but it wasn't enough, and he was spent. He sank back into the white nothingness, fading fast.

"Bill, don't stop," she cried, stretching back for him. She wrapped a hand around what might have been a wrist and pulled, even as he struggled against her.

He didn't answer as he slipped further away.

"Fight. Come on, fight."

He rallied, and she kept at him.

A vibration traveled through the web and penetrated the consciousness of the others. Their inner voices shrieked with the loss of themselves, reaching for Maude until she couldn't bear it.

They're beyond you. Leave them.

"No," Bill said. He heard Tha, too?

They aren't in pain; they feel nothing. Soon they won't even be a memory, just a flash of energy.

"I can't," Bill cried.

Maude felt his panic and frustration over losing, letting the others tumble into the maw of nothingness. She almost gave up on him. Maybe it would be better for both of them.

No, not when they were so close. One last chance. They would try once more, expend everything, and this time if they didn't make it, they would both tumble back into the collective with nothing left to try again. It was a reckless move, but Maude didn't have any other choice.

She reached through the whiteness and pulled, perhaps igniting some spark of self-preservation within him. He didn't want to die like this, not sinking into nothingness, without meaning.

Time screamed, stretched, snapped back. A hundred thousand versions of themselves shot by.

And then, with a last push, they were free, whatever that meant, and wherever they were.

Inventory

Elliot

E LLIOT SAT AT THE end of a corridor inside the labs, his mind racing. The images from the day before bombarded him, screwing with his emotions.

He needed a clear head. He had options to weigh and plans to make. Maybe he didn't have Newt's giant brain, but what he didn't have in smarts he made up for in grit.

Newt lumbered down the hall and sat beside him like they were two old friends enjoying a moment of quiet and nothing had happened. He looked at Newt's profile, then turned away, clenching his jaw.

"You were with Maude," Newt said.

Elliot's lip curled. "I was with her."

"When I was outside, I felt her. Or maybe I heard her. I don't know which. I know she's alive."

Newt's proclamation made him ball his hands into fists. He wanted to change the subject, but nothing came to mind.

"She's there. And someone else," Newt said, bird-bobbing his head. "Anyway, she's alive."

Newt shifted and faced Elliot, making direct eye contact. Elliot noted something different in him, a subtle change. He didn't like it. Newt wasn't one for eye contact, and he definitely wasn't someone who took things head on.

"You know what your problem is?" Elliot said. "All that shit bouncing around inside your mind makes you too weird for your own good."

Newt stared at him with round eyes, fueling Elliot's anger.

"If something from the anomaly is contacting you, you should be creeped out. Not talking to it like an old friend."

"She's alive," Newt said again.

"Whatever." What did he want him to say? Did Newt blame him? The image of Maude collapsing as a rain of white sparks showered her body roiled through him.

It wasn't his fault. There was nothing he could've done.

"She's not alone," Newt insisted. "There are others with her, but I don't think they'll survive long. I need you to help me convince people. We can't give up on them."

"Me?" Elliot's gut contracted. He put his head down, fighting back the shame he felt, not wanting Newt to see it.

"Elliot?"

"Enough. I don't want to talk anymore, Spencer. Leave me alone."

Spencer held up his hands like Elliot was a cop with a gun. "But she's our friend."

"Stay away from me."

Elliot stood and stumped down the corridor. He ignored the roaring in his ears and the fire burning his cheeks. Tears stung his eyes. He wiped them away before anyone passing could see.

Jennifer

Jennifer entered Drew's office, closing the door behind her. He sat at a desk, leaning on both elbows, his head down, as if asleep.

He looked up as the door clicked shut, and she wondered how much sleep he'd gotten in the last twenty-four hours. Probably none. His lips were dry. A shadow of stubble dotted his chin.

"What's going on?" she asked.

He pursed his lips and gave her a sardonic expression. "I don't know."

"What about evacuation?"

"They won't. None of us."

"What happens next?" Jennifer asked.

"I'm still trying to get through; I'm calling in favors, using whatever influence I've built up. But I'm running into walls. A lot of important people have their futures and fortunes tied into GERI. If there's a crisis, they stand to lose a lot. Not just individuals, but governments."

"Only if they're responsible for the crisis."

Drew nodded.

Jennifer paced across the room, her mind spinning in different directions. She had to stay disciplined. For herself, and for Spencer.

"They've got us quarantined. There's a naval presence off the shore that will stop any craft from getting across to the mainland. They've blocked all communications. And I have my orders."

"To keep us here."

He didn't answer.

Jennifer moved behind Drew, slipping her arms around him. She leaned forward, resting her cheek on the top of his head.

He reached back and pulled her around until their lips met. The exchange of intimacy was reassurance. The kiss said they were there for one another, and they would get through this.

Jennifer took his hand and squeezed it. She left without saying more, without arguing with him. Drew didn't need any more stress.

She didn't like how far GERI had strayed since its inception, when its purpose was to find alternative means of energy and to help deal with the increasing climate change.

Out in the corridor, she thought about the anomaly, and about the people trapped there. Someone needed to do something. If the people within couldn't be saved, then the singularity had to be collapsed so more people couldn't be taken.

Elliot walked toward her, striding as if in a hurry. She watched him as he passed by without offering a greeting, anger clouding his expression. Given what he'd been through, she wasn't surprised.

She wanted to stop him, but thought better of it. He needed space and a chance to process what had happened to him. She'd keep an eye on him, though.

Around the corner, sitting with his head up and mouth agape, she found Spencer. Had the two of them been in a fight?

"How are you holding up, kiddo?"

He gave a perfunctory response. She put a hand on his shoulder.

"You and Elliot not seeing eye to eye?"

He shrugged.

She took Spencer's hand in her own and squeezed.

"I have a favor to ask of you. It will give you something to do other than worry."

Spencer shook his head, but she pressed on.

"I need equipment inventoried and checked out," she said.

"What equipment?" Spencer asked.

She took a moment before answering, afraid he'd discover her real motive.

"AMOPP suits. Breathers. Medical stuff. Sensory equipment."

"AMOPP suits?" Spencer asked. "You mean, like Hazmat suits?"

"These are a bit more sophisticated," she said. "Advanced Mission Oriented Protective Posture suits."

"What are they for?"

As Spencer asked the question, she could see his mind racing.

"We need to be prepared."

"For what?"

Too perceptive. He'd pressed her into a corner about her reasoning.

"Mom?"

"In case we have to travel into the anomaly."

Having said it, she wanted to take it back.

"Wouldn't that be something the military would do, and not us?" Spencer asked.

"We have expertise they lack. I don't know. Maybe I'm wrong, but I think it helps to be prepared. I think doing something like an inventory will take your mind off everything. I think Elliot needs it, too."

"Elliot and I..."

She squeezed his hand. "Give him about a half hour. Then go make things right."

"But I didn't..."

"He needs a friend right now, Spencer."

"Maude needs a friend, too. What about her?"

"I'm not giving up on Maude." She didn't want to give voice to her belief that Maude was gone.

"I'll print off a list of supplies for you to go over," she said.

Spencer shook his head. "I should go over the computer models, look at the energy patterns. I should try to contact Tha. I should go down to the beach, maybe we need to get closer to make contact."

Spencer spoke so fast it was difficult to understand his words. He was revving.

"Spencer, all of that is important," she said. "You're right. But I've asked you to do something important. I need you and Elliot to go through the inventory."

His woeful eyes broke her heart.

Scrub The Area

Elliot

ELLIOT AND **S**PENCER WALKED down the narrow corridor that ended at the heavy door to the supply area. A soldier waited there, a younger man with a nervous but mischievous expression on his face. Elliot liked him immediately.

"Specialist Haas?" Elliot asked.

"Mr. Born? Mr. Newton?"

He opened the door and followed them into an area with wire cages where they'd stored away tons of equipment. They should've checked all of it when they carried it down here, and they'd also done regularly scheduled inventories. Elliot wondered if this was a bullshit task.

Newt showed Haas the list. He scanned it and handed it back.

"Do they want all this stuff taken out and tested?"

Newt nodded. "I think they also want it put aside for access."

"For what?" After Haas asked, his mouth clamped shut and worry lines wrinkled his nose. He turned and led them to a large area, using a key chain attached to his belt to open a sliding door.

"If you need anything, I'll be outside," Haas said, then he left.

Elliot started dragging equipment from the shelves and sorting it into piles. He gave Newt instructions and noted with satisfaction that he followed direction without hesitation.

When Newt sought him out earlier, he'd been in a bad place. Hell, he still lived there. But Newt's seriousness about the task cut through his defenses.

And Elliot didn't mind the work. It cleared his thoughts.

Elliot examined a piece of equipment, not sure what he held in his hands. Newt watched him.

"That's a breather," Spencer said. "It's kinda different, isn't it?"

"Yeah."

Elliot held the soft plastic piece to his face and inhaled, trying to figure it out. He lifted a section of tubing that seemed to fit over a nozzle running from a gallon-sized clear canister of blue liquid.

"It takes oxygen out of the water," Newt explained. "You know, water is just hydrogen and oxygen molecules."

"Duh," Elliot said. Newt wasn't trying to act superior, but his knowledge pissed off Elliot, anyway. "What if you're in an environment with no water? What're you supposed to do without oxygen tanks?"

"That's what that blue fluid is for. It's oxygenated concentrate."

Of course it was. Elliot put the breather down, counted out how many they had on the shelves, then gave the information to Newt, who jotted it down on a tablet.

"We've got to check the suits, too," Newt said. "We have to look for tears, obvious defects, missing pieces."

"That'll take forever."

"Maybe that's the point."

Elliot surprised himself by chuckling.

He finished checking one suit and paused, tossing it casually aside when he noted that Newt meticulously folded the one he'd finished examining, then set it down with care.

"I never figured you for a neat freak," Elliot grumbled. "I don't think you even own a comb."

Newt grinned.

Elliot held up another breather, again slipping it over his face. The units were light; the suits looked almost flimsy. He lifted the material, pulling it back and forth. Strong. He suspected puncture resistant, too.

An idea poked him.

How far could someone swim wearing this suit? How long would the breathers last?

He heard military ships watched the area, making sure no one tried boating to the mainland. What about under the blockade? One person in a suit like this could swim. It would be a long way, but he could try.

He tossed out the idea. The mainland was way too far for him to swim. And there were way too many impossible currents to navigate.

But then, maybe he wouldn't have to swim. The equipment sheds down by the beach had traditional underwater gear, and some machines for traveling below the surface.

Newt had stopped working. He squatted by the lower shelves, one hand on a piece of equipment that wasn't familiar to Elliot. It looked like something that went around the wrist.

Newt's mouth fell open, and his eyes adopted a vacant gaze.

"Hey," he said. "Newt."

"We could stow a couple of suits," Spencer said. "We're the ones doing the inventory, it would be easy."

"For what?"

Was Spencer coming around to his point of view about getting the hell away from here?

"These suits could get us into the anomaly."

"Are you serious?"

"Why do you think we're inventorying these? They're planning a search and rescue. They have to."

"No one is going into that anomaly. Let it go."

"Maude..."

"Oh my God. You know I lost my mom and dad, right? You know I held my mom in my arms and felt her die. I saw people we knew slaughtered."

Newt shut up.

"If I took one of these suits, the only place I'd head is off this island and not into a deathtrap."

"It's not a death trap. We need to get Maude,"

"Maude's gone!"

Newt shoved him. Elliot acted instinctively, ramming Newt against the wall beside the wire cages.

He hadn't meant to hit him that hard. Newt bounced right back and charged at him, yelling his name like a battle cry.

They both went down, but it only took a second for Elliot to flip him over and pin him down, fists ready to fly.

"Stop it!" Specialist Haas came into the room, using the bottom of his boot to knock Elliot over, letting Newt scramble back.

"Are you guys kidding me?" he asked. "Really? You're going at each other?"

Elliot scrambled to his feet.

"If I have to come back in here, you'll both be sorry," Haas warned, and then left again.

Elliot picked up a pile of suits and set them aside for further inspection. When he looked up, Newt was staring at him.

"I'm sorry, Elliot," he said. "I'm sorry for everything."

Elliot didn't know how to respond. "Don't worry about it. Let's just get this done."

He didn't want to talk any more, but he had so many questions. Elliot glanced at the metallic wall behind Newt.

He saw a distorted image of himself and wondered what he would do if his reflection spoke to him. The thought creeped him out.

Worse, he thought about his parents. If there was another version of you, then what happened to it when you died?

Elliot wanted to smash every mirror.

"I'm getting the fuck off this island," he mumbled to himself.

Jennifer

They went outside again, as they'd done early this morning. Spencer walked between two large guards, looking more like a prisoner than someone being kept safe.

Jennifer smiled, as she often did when she watched him, especially when he reminded her of his father. Spencer hadn't had it easy, and she didn't think adulthood would hold any breaks for him, either.

They headed for a bluff overlooking the beach. They'd considered going down to the water, but after all that had happened, Jennifer wasn't about to let Spencer get that close without a fight.

She liked being outside. The soldiers seemed to liven up with the change in environment, too. Maybe providing protection gave them a sense of control.

At the bluff, they'd set up some equipment and cables ran along the ground back to the center of the compound. Jennifer gazed up at the clouds crawling across the horizon. The shades of yellow and red looked as if an artist had lazily splashed color across the sky.

She put an arm around Spencer and pulled him close. "The sky reminds me of your grandparents. When I was little, they'd take me on these long road trips," she said. "Sometimes they would stop by the side of the road, and we'd spend the longest time just looking. Your grandfather called it memory shopping."

"Dad used to say things like that," Spencer said.

"He was a poet."

"I can still hear his voice," Spencer said.

Jennifer nodded. She could still smell him sometimes. He always wore that awful cologne with witch hazel in it. How funny she could remember things like that. Memories were like kindling, ignited and then gone.

"You ever think some memories aren't real?" Spencer asked.

"What do you mean?"

"Maybe some of them aren't actual memories, but things that might have been."

"False memories?" Jennifer asked. It was a strange question, so she knew her son had something on his mind.

"No, events that could have happened but didn't."

"How would we know which memories to trust?" she asked.

"Maybe that's the point."

When Drew came walking up to the bluff, he looked exhausted. He'd shaved and changed uniforms, but he didn't look refreshed.

He walked over to them, giving Spencer a pat on the back. "You ready to attempt contact again?"

The comment snapped her back to the present, and she felt silly for letting her guard down.

Spencer nodded and went over to the mirror they'd brought along. Someone had set a metal chair before it. Spencer settled into it and leaned forward, elbows on his knees.

Jennifer watched, trying to read his features, attempting unsuccessfully to put herself in her son's place.

Drew stood beside her, staring out at the ocean.

"What aren't you telling me?" She kept her voice down so only he could hear.

Drew didn't respond for a long time.

Her heart tightened. Now she didn't want to hear the answer.

"I tried calling GERI," he said. "I can't get hold of anyone. They're blocking all contact. Before they were giving me the stall, now they aren't even trying."

"And that surprises you?"

"I think they've made up their minds, and they don't want me talking to anyone and fouling things up." He reached down and picked up a stone. With a grunt, he hurled it at the ocean, where it made a satisfying splash. "I think they're getting ready to scrub the area. Maybe I'm being ridiculous, but I think that's what they're up to."

What a horrid metaphor. Scrub the area.

"How?" she asked.

"I'm not sure."

"You think they'll use a bomb," Jennifer said.

It made sense. A bomb would create an electromagnetic field and maybe close the anomaly. Maybe.

"I've tried other means of communication, but the communications satellite is being blocked."

"They're covering their tracks," Jennifer said.

"That's my guess."

"GERI hired us to do the investigation so they could contain the results of our research. If they blow up the area and disrupt the anomaly, won't they have to account for the explosion?"

Drew hurled another stone and watched it land short of the surf. "Maybe they'll say the blast was part of an effort to head off further seismic happenings. It seems more likely they'd say it was a successful detonation, as opposed to something gone wrong."

"That's what you'd do?" she asked.

"That's what I'd do."

"Benjamin Franklin said, 'Three can keep a secret if two are dead.' But it will get out eventually."

Drew glanced at Spencer, who was still staring at himself in the mirror, then looked back at Jennifer.

"We need to get off the island," Jennifer said.

Drew didn't answer.

"We can take a few boats. We can leave immediately."

"And the blockade?

"Well, what then? We wait for a plane to fly overhead and drop a payload?"

"Shit," he said. Then louder, "Shit!"

Jennifer looked out at the water, focusing on the area near where she imagined the anomaly to be.

Drew studied her, then followed her gaze to the water.

Escape Plan

Elliot

E LLIOT COULDN'T STOP STARING at the rec room photograph of Mt. Baker. He wanted to be there now, jogging down the trail near the bottom, tearing through the trees, filling his lungs with forest air as he kicked up black dirt.

He leaned back against the couch, his eyes half-closing, letting himself drift off, as if imagining hard enough could transport him there. He could make it out of here.

He remembered the mini-subs the twins always bragged about nabbing, and smirked. Assholes. God, they were assholes. And now they were probably dead assholes.

The grin slipped from his face, but he didn't dwell in mournful reminiscing. He had the living to worry about. Namely, himself.

He could snatch one of the underwater scooters. They weren't like the ones at the marine stores. These had been modified with extra power and could travel much longer than two hours underwater. He could get past the blockade, maybe, and follow the coastline, or land and make his way to Washington, somehow.

Was he daydreaming, or could he pull it off? Elliot shifted in his seat, the picture inciting courage.

They kept the scooters in a shed by the docks. While he wasn't happy about going anywhere near the anomaly, he wouldn't have a choice. The scooters were small. They should avoid detection.

Someone monitoring sonar, or whatever they used, might write him off as a dolphin or a small whale. Or maybe they'd drop a charge and blow him apart.

What if the blockade was being coordinated by satellite? Why waste personnel and ships when it was easier to program surveillance from space?

No, he couldn't imagine it being that tightly patrolled.

Maybe the blockade was a lie to scare people and keep them there. But why not evacuate them as soon as possible? At least all unnecessary personnel? Hell, he was as unnecessary as they came.

People wandered in and out of the rec room, checking the vending machines, sitting at tables talking, hanging out on the couches, and pretty much ignoring him. Which was a good thing. He wasn't in the mood to have people pretend concern for his emotional well-being.

Specialist Haas strolled in and slouched onto a couch, leaning over and saying something to some tall guy he called Jeff. Haas's eyes brightened, and he grinned. Then he laughed, slapping Jeff on the leg, before he sat back, apparently pleased by his own wit.

If people knew he planned on leaving the compound, would they try to stop him? Why would they give a damn? Most people were too focused on the crisis to worry about him.

Elliot again shifted in his seat, unable to get comfortable. He hugged his knees and thought about his options.

He could slip down to the beach easy enough, and make his way to the docking area, but the shed might be a problem. Bolt cutters should do the trick. The shed was just a shed, after all.

They didn't keep important equipment there. Much of the stuff was used for recreation and simple work activity.

Although he'd find wet suits and other underwater equipment in the shed, he wouldn't have access to one of those breathers they'd inventoried, or one of those environmental suits, and both would be worth having, especially the breather. He didn't know how long he'd have to stay underwater.

But confiscating a breather from the supply area might be tough. But then again, Specialist Haas knew him, and knew they'd tasked him and Newt with checking out the equipment. Would it be such a stretch for Haas to imagine they needed to take one suit out?

Even if he couldn't get away with it, Elliot figured it was worth a try. And he could fall back on oxygen tanks and a wet suit, if necessary.

"Hey pardner," someone said.

The last person he expected to see hobbled in on crutches and struggled to sit next to him. Castro lowered himself onto the cushion next to him with a grimace.

"Two broken ribs, a collapsed lung, and a nasty broken leg," Castro said, as if it was an accomplishment. He grinned and added, "Oh, and there was some internal bleeding, too. Maybe a concussion."

"How's it they let you out of bed?" Elliot asked.

He laughed. "Who says they let me out?"

The soldier settled back on the couch and surveyed the room. He waved to a few of the other officers, then looked back at Elliot.

"You know, I didn't think anyone would come back for me. I thought when you left that was it."

"That's what you thought?"

"I thought you were a little puta. But you're okay."

Castro sounded fine, but his eyes showed his pain. Elliot didn't think Castro's being out of bed was a smart idea, but he wasn't sure if he should say something.

"I'm sorry about the girl not making it," Castro said. "She was something else. What an ass kicker, eh? That girl was something. Yeah, I'm sorry about her. I'm sorry about my buds not making it, too. I'm sorry about life."

Elliot agreed.

Castro rubbed his rough hands together and shut his eyes. "I'm on good medicine," he said. "Too bad they won't give me sample packs so I can enjoy them after I heal."

Haas and Jeff had apparently been listening in because both laughed at that.

"Don't believe him, kid. Castro is an oil can man."

"What's that?" Elliot asked.

"It means he bleeds beer."

Elliot laughed.

"You're a sharp guy," Castro said to him. "Why did you let yourself get talked into coming to this island in the first place?"

Elliot didn't want to talk about that. It was too hard to keep the anger and the guilt under control. He changed the subject. "Why did you come?"

Castro didn't answer either. He turned his attention to the picture that Elliot had been staring at earlier.

"I understand that mountain's a little shorter since the earthquakes," he said. "But what the hell? People shouldn't expect things to stay the same. People don't. Why should the Earth? Spencer Newton is one of your friends, eh?"

"Yeah," Elliot said.

"They say he sees things. What do you think?"

"Hell, I don't know."

Castro held his side and appeared to ride out a wave of pain, confirming Elliot's first impression that he shouldn't be up and walking around.

"I don't know nothing, either," Castro said. "Nobody here knows nothing. That's fine by me. Not knowing is why we try to find out something in the first place, isn't it?" He let the comment float there, then put a hand to his chest. "There I go getting religious again."

"You heard what's going on with the anomaly?" Elliot asked.

Castro shook his head. "You know more than I do, kid. Usually there's talk, but I'm hearing nada."

The soldier shut his eyes again. Elliot thought maybe he'd fallen asleep this time. Then he opened them.

"I'm going back to bed. I'm hurting worse. Would you mind giving me a hand?"

Elliot helped him up and settled him on his crutches. They shuffled through the door into the hall. Castro's face looked pale.

"You going to be okay?"

"I'm fine," Castro said.

It wasn't far to the soldier's room. The place smelled of antiseptic. A small TV was on. An old horror movie played on the screen; zombies stumbling through a farmhouse. Castro eased himself onto the side of his bed. He grunted and thanked Elliot.

"Nobody likes being helpless," he added. "That's too much of a reminder that we don't have control over things. I hope people get the hell out of here, any way they can. I mean it."

Castro settled back in bed and closed his eyes. He sighed with relief. "But people do what they can to survive, don't they?" he said. "Even if they have to climb over bodies to get out."

Elliot backed out of the room, thinking about Castro's words. He headed along the corridor, passing through the main labs on his way to the supply rooms.

Newt and Dawes came in the main entrance from outside, talking, the two of them looking like equals. How was that even possible? Spencer Newton, who didn't notice when he rubbed bird shit all over his jeans, who moved with the jerkiness of a chicken in meth withdrawal.

Holy shit.

Spencer Newton.

He was at the center of it all, wasn't he? Newt was going to get them all killed. Elliot included, if he let him.

Blast Radius

Spencer

I TELL THE GENERAL I want to head outside again to try contacting Tha, but what I really want is to contact Maude. I keep feeling her.

It's driving me crazy, because I don't know if I can trust my gut. I don't know if I really sense her, or if I think I do because I want to. Or need to.

"I'm sorry, Spencer," he answers. "Show me again how this thing works, I can't wrap my head around it."

We're looking at the computer model I created. He's struggling to think of time as something other than what's on the face of a clock. He can't accept it as a dimension, as something that can exist all at once instead of our linear point-to-point experience of it.

"So, if what you're saying holds true, what would we perceive in the anomaly?" he asks.

He sounds as if he's looking for hope. I don't know how to answer him because it's all abstract. What would we see in the anomaly? I've asked myself that a thousand times.

Dr. Alfredson drifts over, listening for my response.

"That's hard to say," I answer. "I mean, our brains are programmed to perceive things in our world. Maybe we would interpret the experience so we could understand it? Maybe we wouldn't. Maybe it would look like our world, because that's what we're limited to, or maybe we wouldn't see anything at all."

"We sent out an underwater drone," Alfredson says.

"And?" Dawes asks.

"Nothing. It went to the edge of the anomaly and then stopped transmitting."

"Maude's alive," I say.

I wish I'd stayed silent, because I can see from their expressions that they don't share my conviction, and that maybe my words remind them of everyone they've lost.

Alfredson changes the subject. "Have we heard anything from GERI?"

"I don't have access," Dawes says. I hear the frustration in his voice. "They're blocking us. We can't get a call out."

Dr. Alfredson's not happy. He keeps licking his lips. The action distracts me. I want to tell him to stop. "I'm not an expert, but isn't there a way to get around that?"

"It's got quantum encryption. I'm sure there are people who could pull off breaking through, but none of them are on this island."

"What about those ships allegedly cordoning us off from the mainland?" Alfredson suggests. "Couldn't we send someone out and make a case to one of the skippers? Maybe they would place a call to command."

"They're just following orders."

Mom comes by. She runs a hand along my back, and I notice her touch the general's arm. He gives her a quick nod.

"Nothing?" Mom asks.

Dawes shakes his head.

"I've been thinking this through," Mom says. "GERI isn't blocking us because of the anomaly. They might order a communications blackout, but they wouldn't isolate us. If anything, they would be in constant contact."

"So why?" Alfredson asks.

"I've been banging my head against the wall, asking the same question. I think it has to do with the earthquakes."

Alfredson stares at her, then at Dawes. I'm confused, too.

"We helped stop the quakes," Alfredson says.

"When I started researching the data from the quakes, GERI kept sending me summaries, not raw data. They blocked me. And then they instructed the military to set up a separate station at the beach. I think they were getting ready to shut us down."

"Why?"

"Because I was seeking a link between what we did to the quakes and the appearance of the anomaly. Maybe we were on our way to finding another link. GERI had other experiments manipulating electromagnetic fields that might have affected the plates in the first place."

I hold my breath, not wanting to hear more. My heart beats faster and my last meal churns in my stomach.

"You're saying GERI caused the earthquakes in the first place?" Alfredson asks.

"I'm not saying anything," Mom says.

He turns to the general. Dawes shrugs.

They all fall silent, and I keep my head down, my fingertips poised on the computer keyboard. If GERI did this, if they caused the quakes that wrecked much of the northwest, they were responsible for the deaths of over fifteen thousand people, including my father.

Wrestler Rod enters the main lab, and he's in a hurry. His face is pale. I notice his cheeks are damp. He snaps a salute to General Dawes.

"Sir, forgive me for interrupting, but we have a situation developing."

"What kind of situation?"

"We weren't able to make contact, but we've been able to pick up some protocols from the satellite."

"What protocols?"

"They were red protocols. Now they're brown."

This means nothing to me, but I notice the general stiffen. It's almost imperceptible, but it's there.

Whatever the implication, it's like someone punched him in the stomach. He's making a tremendous effort to remain cool.

"Let's head over to the communications station," he says.

With no explanation, they leave the room.

"Brown protocol?" I ask.

"I don't know," Dr. Alfredson says, and seems to tell the truth.

"Whatever it means, it's not good," Mom says.

She sits down beside me and glances over at the model I was using to discuss the anomaly with the general. She shakes her head.

"Spencer, sometimes I worry you don't realize how smart you are," she says.

"I know I'm smart."

"And funny, and kind," she adds.

My mother has always been affectionate. She's always supported me, going out of her way to make me feel special while making things happen in her own life. Only now I hear sadness in her voice, and it makes me sad, too.

The rec room is quiet, although a couple of techs are playing a video game and sucking at it. I suck worse, so I'm basically watching them for pointers. So far, the only pointer I've picked up is "don't suck." I know.

I looked for Elliot earlier. He might be outside somewhere. I hope not, because unless he's gotten permission, he'll get in trouble.

I get up and wander over to a picture on the wall. It's of Mt. Baker, in early spring, with snow still thick on the slopes. There's a large bird there, but I can't see it. I know it's a kestrel falcon, investigating the area before dropping on a large carcass left by a pack of grey wolves.

When dad was alive, Mom took nature pictures. I remember her pictures throughout the house, but I can't remember what happened to them.

She took magnificent pictures, spending hours waiting for the right shot, trying to stay unobtrusive. I never understood that. Just by being in an area, you're affecting it, regardless of your intent.

I turn as three people enter the room, techies. They have solemn faces. There's something fatalistic about them.

They stand by one wall and whisper among themselves. Soon two more people enter, officers. They stand by the door.

What on Earth?

Five other people come in, and there's more in the hall behind them. Everyone has expectant, nervous looks on their faces. I tally up the new arrivals. It isn't long before we have everybody from the compound who made it through the initial attacks from The Contained.

Elliot leans against a snack machine. He somehow slipped in without me noticing.

He's fidgety, and it's contagious. Soon, I'm tapping my hip with my fist, and shifting weight from one foot to the other.

"What's going on?" I ask him.

"Didn't you hear the announcement?"

"I didn't hear."

"Meeting."

My mother and Dr. Alfredson appear. Behind them, General Dawes and a handful of military men march in. Seeing them, the quiet in the room deepens.

Dawes stops, standing with his hands clasped behind his back and his feet spread apart. His expression isn't encouraging. He lets his gaze travel around the room. It falls on me, then continues.

"I don't think we're missing anyone," he says. He thrusts his hands into his pockets. A grim smile flashes across his face, and then it's gone.

"We have another situation," he says. "A few minutes ago, we picked up an encryption in the satellite feed they would only enact with imminent threat and response."

No one moves.

"I don't have confirmation, and we aren't likely to get confirmation, but I believe a countdown has begun for delivery and detonation of a small tactical nuclear device. I don't know when they'll deliver the device, but I believe it will be sooner rather than later. We might have hours. Probably less."

Silence in the room.

"This can't be real," a man says, he's one of the people responsible for the grounds. He watches the room, as if hoping someone else will echo his disbelief. "It can't be real, right?" he says again.

"I'm sorry," Dawes says.

"Why? Why would they do this?"

Several people in the room murmur things, making it difficult to understand any single person.

"I can only provide speculation," Alfredson offers.

He looks like he's about to cry. I don't think he's frightened, but feels responsible for what is happening. Alfredson has always been a dick, but that's not who he is when you get to know him.

"Speculate," Mitch, one of my mother's co-workers, says.

"We believe we can draw a connection between the anomaly and the earthquakes along the west coast. There's further speculation that those same earthquakes resulted from massless particle experiments GERI conducted, and some unexpected happenings at the quantum level."

People grow quiet once more.

"Options?" Cal Johnson asks.

Dawes shrugs. "We have enough AMOPP suits for everyone. We head into the anomaly and hope it gives us protection from the blast."

It's like someone has tossed water on a grease fire. Voices rise as people panic. My temples throb. It's like all the tension in the room is vibrating through me.

"The data suggests it should provide us protection," Alfredson adds.

"The data suggests," Mitch echoes in a mocking tone.

"The island will be in the blast radius," Dawes says, "including this compound."

It's a few more minutes of chaos. Dawes isn't used to having his authority challenged, but half of these people aren't soldiers.

My mother raises her hand and waits. It takes a moment, but the room settles down and all eyes turn her way.

"They want to close the anomaly," Mom says. "They want to bury the evidence. A sizable blast should do it and remove us as witnesses. We don't know when this will happen, but this is not the time for discussion or argument. I think everyone here needs to know what's happening and choose their own response. Some of you might decide to make a run for it by boat. Others might decide to wait it out here and hope for the best. If you're considering the sea, you should know that, even if you make it past the currents, there's a naval presence out there waiting to intercept those who try."

"Wait, if they detonate a bomb that will close the rift, we'll be stuck in the anomaly," Alex, one of the techs, says.

"That's if we survive entering the anomaly in the first place," my math teacher, Mr. Labon says.

"That's if we get there before they drop the nuke," Alfredson adds.

Hearing this, I'm thinking I should be scared as hell, but it's as if someone else is trying to process the information. Entering the anomaly; I know what I'll see there, don't I? I've seen it before in the mirror—the flat expanses, the lines of energy, the blurry forms drifting deliberately into view.

THA.

So Long, Elliot

Spencer

IT'S A PERSONAL CHOICE you all face," Dawes says. "I'm leading whoever wants to follow me into the ocean and into the anomaly. Do some soul searching.

"Whatever you decide, no one will fault you. I know there are some who will elect to remain behind, and I respect that. When the strike hits, you won't feel a thing. Maybe that's the smart choice. I don't know.

"Unfortunately, we don't have time to mull things over. As I said earlier, we don't know what the countdown is. It could be hours, days. I honestly don't think we have long.

"Gear is being set outside. Those that are following me, if there's something personal you want to take with you, you have precious few moments to grab it. Don't waste time. We leave in twenty minutes."

With that, the general glances at me, then strides from the room.

Some people are staying. You can see it on their faces. I don't blame them one bit. Dr. Alfredson looks stoic. One woman, a military communications specialist, bites her lip and watches those around her as tears well in her eyes.

Maybe they're all waiting for someone else to stand and make a statement. What else is there to say?

A few people keep staring in my direction. I want to vanish. You're at the center of it all, Spencer, they seem to say.

The group files out of the rec room. Conversation is almost non-existent, and those who are talking do it in whispers.

Before we went outside earlier, Alfredson and the others peppered me with questions. I know my answers must have been part of the discussion they had about whether to head into the anomaly.

"You keep describing lines of energy. What else?"

"You say there are entities after Tha. Why?"

"You and he are connected. How?"

"Do you see an actual horizon in the mirror? Are there any visible features?"

"What about life forms? Describe whatever comes to mind."

I go over to Elliot. He's frowning, and studying the floor, maybe looking for answers there.

"You're not going into the anomaly," I say.

He shrugs. "Nope."

"Then what?" I want him to come. Suddenly it's important. He's been my closest friend. Sure, we've had our differences, but I can't lose him.

"Not hanging out here's what," he says. "I'm going for a swim."

I can't help laughing, and then so does he. For a second we relax, but the moment passes as if it never existed.

"Keep it to yourself, Newt, all right?" His request has a hint of intimidation behind it.

"What are you going to do?"

"Take a sea scooter to Washington."

What? The absurdity of that plan makes me shake my head. But is it any crazier than heading into the ocean and disappearing into some tear in space?

"That's sixty miles," I say. "It'll take you at least ten hours. And there are nasty currents. You'll never make it."

He doesn't look at me. I know I'm pissing him off. The last thing he needs is me telling him he's screwing up.

"Maybe I won't," he says.

I'd never have his courage. Sixty miles, even with the help of a scooter, is overwhelming. Well, at least he's got a plan, and he's following it through.

He's not feeling sorry for himself or complaining. He's accepting the situation and moving on. His survival instinct is in hyper-drive.

"You're all going to die, you know," he says. "There's nothing in that anomaly."

I almost expect him to invite me along with him, but he doesn't.

"There's something out there," I say. "I've seen it."

"Seen what? You can't even describe it, Newt! All you say is there are these lines and things. Oh, and some blurry shapes. Shit. That's where those monsters came from."

"We can survive there."

"How do you know?"

How can I explain that I just do; that I know with certainty inside the rift is a contained environment, and that somehow we can survive? And Maude's there. And Tha. Waiting, but silent.

Elliot picks up a duffle bag and heads down the hall. I'm not sure why, but I go after him, and we walk together as I match his steps.

We pass the sleeping quarters and then make a right, going down a few steps to the supply rooms. No soldier is on duty. Elliot tugs the door latch and finds it locked.

"Shit!"

"Now what?" I ask.

He checks the hallway, then puts his head down in thought. I watch and wait. Simultaneously, I want to suggest something, but also not help him.

He pushes away from the wall and is on the move again. I stay with him.

"Now what?" I ask again.

"I don't know."

We swing by the rec room, and he pops his head in. A few people sit at a table where they work on laptops and tablets, ignoring one another.

"Hey, I gotta get into the supply room. Anyone have access?" he calls out.

A couple people shake their heads. The rest ignore him.

That's his plan? Walk around asking people until someone hands over a security card or gives him a code? Really?

In the hall again, he walks right up to Jeff. "Hey, I gotta get in the supply room, and I don't have a card."

"What do you need in the supply room?" Jeff asks. "We dragged everything outside."

"We were doing inventory, and I left the tablet there with the counts. I just need to get in for a sec to grab it."

That's the best he can come up with? Jeff studies him. Elliot offers a huge, ingratiating smile.

"You'd really be saving our neck," Elliot says.

So naturally Jeff shrugs. We all head back to the supply room where he swipes a card and lets us in with a warning not to screw around. How is this possible?

Is that Elliot's super power? I see things in the mirror, and Elliot gets people to do things for him with a smile. When Jeff leaves, Elliot takes a dry suit down and tugs it on.

"Don't do this," I say. "Elliot, it's sixty miles."

"I'm not swimming."

He stops and stares at me. "Who stands a better chance? Me or you? You're going into the anomaly."

I can't argue.

He puts his pants on over the dry suit. Then he slips on a heavy sweater to hide the top portion.

He's in a rush. Maybe because he expects Jeff to come back and check on us if we take too long. Or maybe because he doesn't want me to talk him out of his plan. Or like the general, maybe he's afraid any minute there will be a flash of bright light and then nothing.

"What are you going to do if you make it to shore?" I ask.

"Stay off the road, and head into the woods. I'll keep a low profile, and if I see anyone, I'll hide. Or if I can get a gun, they'll hide."

"Then what?"

"Then I'll be alive. What else is there?"

If anyone can get out, it's Elliot, but I don't think he'll make it. I'm sure of it. But I don't say anything because I don't want to provoke his anger.

He grabs a mask and slips it over his head. He takes it off and studies the device.

"What do I have to do to make this work?" he asks.

"Make sure the switch is green before going under water. Then just breathe normally. If you feel a vibration while you're swimming, then it means the unit is failing."

"You've used one before?"

"I read the manual," I say. I read manuals because of course I do.

"How deep can this go?"

"It can handle pressure, but you don't want to go too deep because you'll have difficulty. Every foot you go down the amount of pressure increases. Keep close to the surface and you'll be okay. The AMOPP suits offer some protection, but they aren't pressurized. That dry suit offers no protection."

"I knew that."

He shoves the mask in his duffle bag. As I watch him, I wonder how he plans to walk out of here. Somebody will stop him.

Maybe he hasn't given it much thought, or maybe that's what he wants. I suspect he hasn't thought it out. Elliot isn't the sort of person to mull things over for too long.

Elliot slings the duffle over a shoulder and turns for the door. He stops, and I'm glad he hesitates. I hoped he wouldn't just leave and not say anything.

I'm ready, either to say goodbye, or to engage him in further argument against his departure. He pats his back pocket, then his side pockets.

"Newt, I want to say something, but I don't know what to say."

His voice comes out in a rush of emotion that's mostly fear. He stares at me, and I think maybe he's going to hold out his hand, or hug me, but he doesn't do either. He turns and heads outside.

Going Under

Jennifer

J ENNIFER STOPPED AND FORCED herself to swallow.

She stared out at the water and didn't have the courage to progress further. Her heart was beating in her temples. She forced herself to calm down.

A small group of soldiers stood several feet behind her, led by Cal Johnson, who seemed to have developed some sort of friendship with Spencer.

She turned to face the sky. How long did they have? Where was the plane with the bomb?

What if they entered the ocean and found the anomaly gone? Return to shore and wait to be vaporized? She almost laughed at that.

Jennifer checked her bolometer, measuring changes in radiation, and pointed out the direction. She watched the hypnotic motion of the gray swells and white crests.

"You ready?" Drew asked. He moved in beside her and took her hand.

No. What the hell am I doing? Out loud she said, "I guess so."

"Would it help if I said, I'm terrified, too?"

"Still silence from GERI?" she asked.

"Still blocked."

"Anything different on the satellite?"

"Nothing."

"You know I'm stalling, right?"

Drew gave her hand a squeeze and slid his faceplate down. Jennifer squeezed back before she left him and went over to Spencer. Her son's face was slack as he stared out at the waves.

"Spencer?"

He responded with a slow nod. He had the sort of face that would always stay youthful. Sure, telltale lines would eventually score his forehead, but those would come slowly.

"Are you okay?"

"I don't want to die," he said.

The comment stabbed her. She resisted wrapping her arms around him. She pressed her lips together, trying not to say things were going to be okay.

"I don't either."

Alfredson moved closer and said in a wary tone, "I just got information from the connection we re-established with the sensor grid. The anomaly is changing."

"Changing how?"

Spencer nodded. "The anomaly is in constant flux. I think that's why the Contained took the others. They're trying to implement and control changes."

Alfredson spoke as though thinking out loud: "The human body is mostly water, but who we are is mostly energy. They're using that energy to implement change."

"We're fuel," Jennifer said.

"So maybe they're using us because we don't belong," Alfredson said. "We're like a foreign object in the skin that makes the body produce white blood cells."

"But why?" Jennifer asked. "What are they hoping to provoke? What's the end result?"

Her mouth felt so dry.

Perhaps Spencer was right, that the people taken into the void still lived. But for how long?

She looked back at the others, counting those who chose the anomaly over waiting for the bomb. Fourteen. Andrew, Cal Johnson, the pair Spencer had nicknamed Wrestler Rod and Giraffe Jeff, Castro on crutches, Specialist Haas, and two young soldiers she didn't know made up the eight military. Spencer, Alfredson, Mitchell

Plummer, Alex Schwedt, Phillip Labon, and herself were the six civilians. Not a very mighty party to charge into unknown and likely hostile territory.

More people chose to stay than she expected. Some were determined to find a way off even if it meant running the risk of getting shot by the blockade. Some were in denial and didn't believe the bomb would drop.

No one would get off the island. And the bomb would drop.

She tried to take solace in what would happen to them. No pain. Only a second of light. Then nothing. Maybe they were the smart ones.

Drew gave the signal.

Jennifer dug at the sand with the toe of her boot, longing to stay there rather than enter the uncertainty of the anomaly. As if reading her doubt, Spencer put a hand on her shoulder and adjusted his mask. His long fingers fiddled with the radio controls.

She looked over his shoulder at the others, all making the final adjustments. She noticed Castro put a lot of weight on his crutches. He must be in extraordinary pain. Inside the water, he wouldn't need the crutches, but who knew what the anomaly would bring?

Rod and Jeff stepped to each side of Spencer. Both carried a monstrous gun they wouldn't talk about. Energy weapons, she guessed. Maybe plasma rifles.

Cal Johnson and Robert Haas carried assault rifles, which they assured her would fire under water.

"You okay?" Jeff asked Spencer.

Her son smiled and gave a thumbs up. Spencer had a mirror sewn onto the forearm of his AMOPP suit, and he looked at it now, as if expecting to see something there. He might once they were in the anomaly. That was the hope.

"Okay," Drew's voice came through the radio. "This is it. If anyone wants to turn around, this is the time. I won't hold it against you. Otherwise, let's all take a moment, and then get on with our plan."

A few seconds of silence followed, then Drew gave the signal. Rod and Jeff took the lead, then Alfredson, Jennifer, and Spencer, with the two younger soldiers on the outside.

Jennifer stepped onto the rocks, trying not to fall. A small wave splashed her, but she leaned hard against it and kept moving.

Another swell knocked down someone in the rear, she assumed Castro with the crutches, but she heard Drew checking with him and buoying him up.

Cal Johnson took her elbow to steady her. She was grateful for it.

Sunlight danced in fractals across the tiny crests and troughs of the surface. Jennifer controlled her breathing, noting how sweaty her hands felt.

She wanted to rip off the suit and run back onto land. She didn't want to go underwater. It was like seeing a trap closing ahead and dashing into it anyway.

She checked on Spencer. He moved with hesitation. Beside the powerfully built soldiers, her son looked small.

The water splashed their waists now. Jennifer's foot slipped, and she went down, the sunlight replaced by gray and green as she went under the water.

When she surfaced, her string of curses elicited laughter, breaking some of the tension within the group.

"Pretty creative use of profanity, Dr. Newton," Alfredson commented.

The laughter intensified. They pressed on, following a slope under water, and as the ocean swallowed them, Jennifer experienced vertigo, the world spinning around her. She didn't know what direction to follow until Jeff and Rod turned on the lights mounted on their plasma weapons.

Intense beams illuminated the area ahead of them. A school of fish darted off, a mass of silver blades wriggling in the light. Jennifer tracked their synchronized movement as they cut through the water with hypnotic grace, and felt her shoulders relax a fraction.

"Everyone okay? Spencer?" Drew's voice came through the headsets on the radio system.

Jennifer checked on her son, who'd stopped and was leaning forward in the water. Jeff hurried over to him.

"Affirmative," Spencer muttered. "I'm okay."

"Keep it moving."

"Yes, sir," Spencer said.

Jennifer noted with amusement the bit of sarcasm she heard in his voice.

"About fifty meters," Alfredson said.

"I don't see anything," Haas said.

"We didn't see anything from the drone when it went through," the general reminded him.

"That's comforting," Cal replied.

After a few more meters, the water got lighter, and the world took on a metallic tint.

"The anomaly is close," Alfredson announced. "Readings seem less stable. I don't like the fluctuations."

They kept going toward the brighter water. The silence on the radio system became unbearable. Jennifer swore she heard their heartbeats and individual breaths. She shut it out of her mind, but the more she tried, the more she focused on it.

They were brave. Each of them. They were explorers pushing into a dangerous unknown.

Spencer held up a hand for everyone to stop and took a step forward. Jennifer listened, glancing at her son before peering into the water ahead of him.

"Do you see them?" Spencer asked. "The lights?"

Jennifer saw the opening, a bright circular spot surrounded by darker ocean. But no lights. She envied her son's perception, but not the grief it caused him.

Cal stepped in front of Spencer, blocking his path.

"Do you think it's some kind of biosphere?" Alfredson asked.

Mitchell, who had a background in biology, answered, "We have to stop thinking of those things as carbon-based life forms. They're something else."

"They could live outside their environment," Alfredson said. "So, shouldn't we be able to live inside theirs? Maybe?"

"I don't know," Mitchell said. "You know, that illumination looks almost..."

"Chemical," Alfredson finished for him.

"More like magnetospheric plasma," Spencer said.

"What?" Dawes asked.

"You know, cosmic radiation. Like what produces the aurora, the northern lights."

"Do you think it's dangerous?"

Jennifer stretched out her hand and reached around Cal Johnson, fingertips grazing the brighter area. "Even if it is particles decaying and emitting radiation, it shouldn't be able to touch us through these suits. Right?"

"Right," Alfredson confirmed.

Phillip Labon spoke up, "I don't think they require oxygen."

Jennifer knew the conversation was a stall. They were all going to die.

No immediate threat was in sight, but her mind screamed there was no way this could end well. How did any rational person believe they could get away with this?

Dawes asserted himself. "Johnson, Haas."

The two soldiers stepped forward and disappeared.

Although she'd expected something like this to happen, the sudden reality of it still shocked her.

"Gentleman, report," Dawes instructed.

Nothing. Not that they'd expected any communication from inside. They knew there was a possibility that perception of time within the anomaly might be different, and therefore they'd agreed during planning that the next group would pass through within two minutes if nothing occurred, and if the first through didn't return.

Haas stepped backward out of the opening, and Mitchell muttered his thanks.

"No immediate threat," Haas reported, and stepped back through.

Alfredson moved, and Spencer and Jennifer had to move, too, or get left behind.

And then they were across the demarcation line. Warmth spread through her body, and she struggled to stay in the present. It was like she was stretched, and images from her life dropped into expanding holes as she elongated.

In this confusion, reality twisted, and doubt expanded. Her stomach dropped. Her muscles felt slack. It would be easy to surrender, let go, follow different paths until a million different parts spread out, each in search of their own niche.

But that wasn't something she'd let happen. She kept moving.

Jennifer willed herself forward and plunged over the edge of a precipice, floating down through an aether of azure coruscations, until she touched spongy bottom. Water droplets ran down the outside of her faceplate. She knew they were no longer underwater.

"I don't see anything," Jennifer said. "It's like there's a film over my eyes that's brighter in some spots."

"And it's cold," Haas said.

Even through her suit, Jennifer noticed the drop in temperature, and the quiet that enclosed them. Chatter began over the com as more people came through, but even that couldn't mask the hush of the place, the lonely silence.

"It's like walking through a fog," Alex said.

"Everyone stay close."

"Look!" Haas said.

Down in front of them, about twenty meters away, the underwater drone sled lay on its side.

Jennifer approached the piece of equipment cautiously. Then she checked her monitoring device. The energy levels were different here, the fluctuations more dramatic, especially ahead of them.

"What sort of light is this?" Mitchell asked. "What's its source?"

"I see a grid," Spencer said.

The voices quieted.

"It's above us, below us, and stretching out on both sides of us. It goes on a long way."

"What else?" Alfredson asked. "Can we breathe? Is there oxygen here? What about radiation levels?"

"What do you mean by a grid?" Dawes asked.

"Energy lines running all around us," Spencer said. "The lines are blue, like we're inside a basket woven from vibrant light. And..." The last word rang with fear, before Spencer's voice trailed off.

Jennifer turned to him. "And what, Spencer?"

"It's them."

All she saw was a white landscape, featureless and disorienting.

"There," Spencer said. "The Contained."

Venus Flytrap

Spencer

T HE GRID DISTURBS ME. This can't be all there is; a sphere knitted out of energy, hanging unsupported in space. Outside the grid, what's holding it all together?

It's hard to see through the brightness, but beyond the lines, it looks like there's a landscape, maybe even buildings. Below my feet, the weave is tight enough that it's like walking on a spongy grate.

But, right now, the entities are even more concerning than the grid. I see at least a dozen of The Contained heading in our direction.

They have a dense, cobalt blue core, but it's constantly changing shape, as if it's gaseous. Around this nebulous center, a small satellite of matter orbits.

Their core tints the surrounding space, and I can't be sure if the core floats above the grid on its own, or if it is suspended within a gaseous shell. Sparks of energy dance through each entity; white and violet spider-webs erupting without pattern and fading as fast as they appear. Living Van de Graff balls.

"They're getting closer, I think," I say. "It's hard to tell because they're both far away and close, moving and standing still. It's crazy. It's like they're many places at once. But when I fix my gaze on them, when I stare at one entity, it's in a single spot. It's like by looking at it, I force it to condense, to commit to one area."

But I can't fix on one for more than a second, and when I let my concentration wander, the nebula expands again, moving to new points.

"It's like watching a time-lapse video of the northern lights."

I'm sure my explanation is confusing people. Maybe that's best. Maybe that gives them a true sense of the confusion I'm experiencing at what I see, too.

I check the mirror on my arm, hoping it helps clarify what I'm seeing with my unaided eye. It doesn't. Maybe if I look hard enough though, I'll see my old room, or myself looking back at me from the other side.

Several of the entities are simultaneously yards away and feet away from where we stand, and then they're within arm's reach. Which makes sense from a quantum physics perspective, but seeing it in real life, at this scale, makes me shuffle back a step.

"Are you sure about what you're describing?" Dawes asks.

"There's one right in front of me."

"I can't see anything."

The soldiers ready their weapons, but I don't think firing will make any difference. Maybe a bullseye shot to that blue core. But how would they aim? They can't see them, and if they could, would they be aiming at the center of the entity where it is now, or where it was, or where it will be?

One flickers, and then it's inches from my face. The sudden movement startles me and I cry out, stumbling backward, trying not to fall.

A burst of plasma erupts from Rod's rifle. The plasma's trajectory should follow a straight path, but it disperses, and breaks into hundreds of pulses that are attracted to the energy lines making up the grid, as well as the other streams of energy flowing all around us. I run through all the laws of physics filed away in my mental store, and none of them explains what I see.

"Weapons down." Dawes doesn't sound angry, and that's more frightening than if he yelled. The soldiers lower their weapons.

"Spencer, did they react?" my mom asks.

The one closest seems like it's fighting to remain here, in the present. Or in one spot. It's hard to wrap my mind around it.

The point is, they have more than one speed. It's a state of being. It's like seeing time.

A silver thread of energy shoots from one entity to the next, and then to another, and where there were several of the entities seconds ago, they are joined together, but still maintaining the individuality of the different parts.

The space around us is changing, crackling with energy.

"We've got to move," I say.

My legs are tired, and walking takes effort. I lean forward, as if struggling against a heavy wind, and trudge on.

"They're doing this," I say. "They're trying to trap us here."

I force myself to move forward, but it's a slog through waist high mud while walking on unstable ground. My muscles protest, but if we stop, we're dead. We can't see it, but there's some kind of entanglement in process, and we're being drained.

"This is what happened to the others," I say. "They were netted, and then the things started converting them."

"What the hell does he mean?" The fear in Mr. Labon's voice spreads and creeps inside of me.

"You mean it's trying to convert us to energy?" Mom asks.

Her statement petrifies me. Yeah, we're being converted into a different form of energy, changing, dissolving into something else.

"How much time do we have?" Dawes asks.

"There's no time here," I say. "It's like in the exercises Dr. Alfredson had me do."

"No time?"

"Not as we understand it," Alfredson speaks up.

I want to add that it doesn't exist, but that makes no sense. That we're aware and acting is proof time is real. Only maybe we no longer experience time in terms of one single moment following another single moment, maybe here time exists in its entirety.

Right. Good luck explaining that, Spencer.

"Get up," Rod cries.

I look over my shoulder and see Mitchell on his hands and knees, head hanging, surrendering.

"If plasma rifles don't work, then what about assault rifles?" Dawes asks.

"I don't know."

"Fire at will," he commands.

Weapons point in the wrong direction, but it doesn't matter. The discharged slugs slow down and then descend to the unstable ground. I moan at the sight, and there are similar noises from the others; gasps and sharp intakes of breath.

"Kinetic energy," my mother says. "We can't use guns, because the kinetic energy is converted almost immediately. We're giving them more energy to use against us."

"Are you fucking kidding me?" Rod blurts out.

"Can we go back?" Mitchell says quietly.

"What happens when the bomb goes off?" Alfredson says. "What about that energy?"

"Seriously, can we go back?" Mitchell sounds on the verge of tears as Rod hauls him to his feet.

Cal responds, "Calm down."

Several entities close on us, constantly shifting shape and position. A tendril shoots out and lashes around Jeff's arm. He may not see the thing, but he feels the tug. He shouts and jerks back, but the tendril tightens.

"What's happening?" he screams.

The entities feed off the AMOPP suit, where they touch it, converting the material to blue energy. How long will that take? Seconds, minutes, years? It's already happened, it's going to happen, it will never happen.

I can't think, my mind isn't built for this. But it seems mine is meant for this more than anyone else's. Damn it. I need to figure this out, to use those overactive, detached circuits in my brain.

"The suits won't protect us," I say. "We're not dealing only with radiation, or gasses. They'll breach the suits and break them down molecule by molecule. And then start on us."

"Molecule by molecule." The general's tone is incredulous.

"So we're going back, right?" Mitchell whispers.

Jeff cries out, his feet inches above the ground. As the silvery tendrils reel him in, he's lifted and appears to snag on something, then continues to rise as if on an unseen wind.

Again, there's a snag. And again, he lifts. He ascends in this stop-and-go motion, and he's shouting and struggling; an insect caught in a Venus Flytrap.

"Help me!"

Jeff drops his plasma rifle, and I struggle for it, my fingers flexing in anticipation. My hand closes around the grip, and my lips pull back as I roar.

I'm not thinking, I'm acting. I hurl the gun at the core of the creature that has Jeff in its grip. The gun spins for an eternity, end over end, before striking the dense blue hardness of the core.

The entity drops its prize and Jeff tumbles down. Easy prey if it attempts recapture.

The Contained hesitate, watching me without eyes, my presence startling them.

"How did you do that?" Dr. Alfredson's voice crackles.

Good question. I relive the moment, and it hits me. I didn't aim at *where*; I aimed at *when*.

I turn back to the group, ready to say something, fumbling for the words to explain what I intuitively know, but they're transfixed by something over my shoulder.

The entities are attacking, wrapping wispy threads around Mitchell Plummer and Specialist Haas. One has Cal Johnson, bright tendrils slashing him about his body, plunging into him.

Screams rip through the radio system.

Cal's suit breaks along the edge, bits and pieces crumbling away. He swings a fist, plunging it into one of the gaseous shapes descending on him. His hand disappears, then his forearm.

I want to turn away, run, do anything, but I'm frozen with shock, watching. His fight is useless, but he keeps struggling as his flesh shears into blue particles.

And then he deconstructs, his molecules coming apart. His writhing form dissolves into a blur, a concentration of specks where there was once a body. His energy seeps into the grid lines, seeking areas of greater concentration.

Cal is gone. The realization punches me in the stomach. My knees weaken.

Behind him Haas and Mitchell are repeating the struggle, but it's over quick. Nothing left but blue particles that merge with the energy grid.

People backtrack, desperate for a retreat through the opening, but no one can find it. The whiteness behind them gives no evidence of a break. Castro mutters a prayer. Mr. Labon utters something nonsensical.

I step into the area where Cal Johnson discorporated. I still sense him. Maybe it's like when someone loses a hand and still imagines it at the end of their arm. A phantom limb.

He's gone though. And it's my fault.

I feel like I'm about to break down sobbing when my mother shouts and I move, propelling myself in her direction. I'm ten feet away from her. I'm right next to her.

An entity strips away some of the suit's material from her arm. She's falling back, trying to escape, but her body's in slow motion, and the entity has anticipated her.

I grip the tendril, and my hands go numb. Clarity.

I'm in a nanosecond, a pocket of peace within the chaos. I move through time, seeing us minutes ago, seeing us as we'll be in the next few minutes, both of us reduced to millions of particles blown along an energy stream.

We're here now. And right now is as brief as an eternity, and as never-ending as a Planck length.

Time moves. A stutter. My mother and I are close, her mouth frozen open in a scream. Another stutter, and the entity pulls away from me.

It's terrified as it retreats, reaching out, latching onto a stream of energy, and riding it into the distance. Another of the creatures stretches into a stream and is gone.

"I think they're going," I say.

The closer we are to one of the energy streams, the more interference we encounter. It's harder sensing things, but The Contained are definitely fleeing, sending out anxiety like inky octopus clouds.

My mother checks me for injury. I don't show her my hands; I don't want to see them myself. My fingers are still numb, and I'm horrified that, if I look down, I'll find them gone. A white line around my mother's waist leaves evidence that the entity grabbed her.

When I find the courage I look, and let out a breath when I find all my fingers intact.

"Jenn, are you okay?" the general asks.

He's at her side, gripping her shoulders, staring at her through her faceplate. When she nods, his body relaxes. He holds her a moment longer, then turns to me.

"Where are they?" he asks.

"I don't know. I think something scared them." It's a stupid statement.

"Did you do something?" my mom asks. She sounds amazed.

I don't need to see her expression to sense that she's grasping for any sign that would ignite hope. I wish I could say I had, that I'd saved her. Maybe I did, but I don't think so.

My mother's eyes widen, but she doesn't say anything. Neither does anyone else. Something is wrong, and we all feel it.

The space around me thickens, like quantum foam condensing, or slowing down. Movement is difficult, then impossible. We're insects caught in sap.

Again, I'm fighting myself, struggling to find calm. It's horrible being unable to move, or even talk. And now thinking becomes difficult, and I imagine the electrical impulses taking a lifetime to move along the synapses between the nerve cells in my brain.

Something's inside me, and I'm spinning through the dark, trying to escape, but it pulls me back.

—*This one?*

The communication is one thought, but many voices.

—*This one is different.*

—*Different, but the same.*

The voice converses with itself. There's something like emotion in the communication. Anxiety. Repulsion. But neither of those are right. The emotions are alien, but I sense that they're not positive. And that the voice is referencing me.

—*There are traces through it.*

—*Yes.*

—*Tha is near. They're linked.*

—*How can they be here together?*

—*Bring them. All of them. Their presence creates instability. They weaken the enclosure. They're making it fragile. We need to know more. Keep them safe against the abominations, keep The Contained from using them.*

And we're moving, flowing along one of the lines as the entities guide us across the grid, or as they refer to it: the enclosure.

The others in the group can't talk, but I sense the terror they feel, the crippling helplessness. Too much stuff to take in at one time. An avalanche of information and emotion.

And we're through the grid.

Underwater Scooter

Elliot

E LLIOT PLANNED TO STAY underwater as long as possible, but it had probably already been an hour and he felt on edge. He rotated his shoulders, gripping and regripping the handlebars, shifting on the seat. He tried distracting himself by thinking about great basketball games and good times with friends he'd left behind, but nothing worked long.

The dark ocean slid past the scooter's headlight. Not much to see, except grey and brown fish camouflaged against grey and brown rocks, with the occasional pink shrimp and darker pink starfish.

He kept his eyes open wide, studying the path ahead, more concerned about what he couldn't see. His imagination ran away with what might lurk outside his stab of light.

He imagined predatory eyes following him, anticipating his path. He couldn't scan in all directions, and there was no telling where a threat might emerge.

He slowed his breathing and focused on the GPS. It would be pretty stupid to lose track of his heading.

Elliot had difficulty judging the water's temperature, but the wet suit, or whatever it was, kept him comfortable. Supposedly, the water was warmer than it used to be, allegedly because of the quakes. The images of the massive tsunamis that devastated the coast after the quakes ran through his mind, and his jumpiness escalated.

He checked the GPS again and decided to surface in another thirty minutes. He didn't think any ships were actually nearby, not if someone was planning to drop a bomb on the island. Maybe a ship would come in if ordered, but he bet they'd send a helicopter instead. Those suckers traveled fast and were good at getting in and out.

The scooter worked better than he'd hoped. He traveled at 6 knots, and so far the thick plastic shielding had protected him from floating debris and fish. Sure, he could travel at higher speeds on the surface, but he didn't want to risk it yet. The scooters were good for sixty or seventy miles, and then there was the additional fuel tank he'd tied to the side.

The slow pace felt like drifting. More like he was a giant sea horse than flying at high speed like they show in spy movies.

A strange sensation made Elliot cut the engine, and the scooter immediately descended. He couldn't spend more than a couple seconds doing this. The last thing he needed was decompression sickness, but he knew he felt something.

A moan traveled through the water. It was an eerie sound, lonely, inhuman. Several guttural calls followed, and then squeaks. A whale, for sure. Maybe a humpback.

Too bad he didn't know more about sea life; he'd seen a couple of shows. Most of the stuff underwater wouldn't mess with him. At least, he thought that's what he remembered.

The call was louder now. Elliot watched his lamp for anything in his path. He decided his time was better spent moving.

He pushed the starter button and experienced a sick moment where he imagined the scooter not responding, forcing him to swim to the surface with no hope of rescue. But the scooter roared to life.

He leaned forward, and sure enough, saw what made the noise. The whale was enormous; definitely a humpback. Another one appeared, then another. Three of them floated maybe ten feet away, their size too big to catch any of them in his beam in their entirety.

Humpbacks were friendly, weren't they? Probably only curious about the light. Elliot pushed away the nervousness and controlled his breathing. He kept his head straight, afraid to look them in the eye. Better whales than sharks. But didn't sharks sometimes hunt whales? Great thought. He squinted into the darkness, searching for dark shapes in a darker ocean.

The whales dropped out of sight, and he wasn't sorry they'd vanished. His anxiety kept poking him, making him breathe faster.

He shouldn't be here. This alien environment didn't want him here. How much longer? It couldn't be long. He couldn't stand it anymore and climbed up. He needed to get to the surface.

When he broke free from the ocean, Elliot watched the water bead down his mask, and stared out at the horizon. The low moon told him sunrise wasn't far off. The silver light shone through nearby clouds and sparkled along the tips of waves.

He floated a moment before unlocking the helmet and pushing up the faceplate. He inhaled the fresh air with a smile, then scanned the horizon. No sign of any ships.

He experienced doubt for the thousandth time since taking to the water. Why hadn't he taken a boat with some of the others? At least, he hadn't walked into an underwater hole and dropped into an abyss, or wherever it dropped them. If he hadn't found a way off the island, he would've stayed behind, and sat on the beach soaking up the sun and waiting for the bomb to fall.

An absurd thought occurred. What if GERI changed its mind and sent out rescue crafts to evacuate the area? Yeah. Right.

Elliot shut his eyes for a minute, listening to the hum of the motor. Then he reached into a plastic pack and pulled out a bottle of water. He chugged it, then threw the container into the waves.

A sudden streak of light flashed across the sky from the direction of Washington. For a moment, Elliot thought it was lightning, but the sky was clear.

A sonic boom blasted, his ears ringing so hard he wondered if his eardrums had blown. The explosion threw the scooter sideways, as if punched by a fist of air, and he struggled to hold on. An eerie ring of blue light bloomed beneath the ocean's surface as a massive column of water simultaneously rolled upward into the sky.

Elliot righted the scooter and kicked it into high gear, hoping he could outrun the advancing water, make it to land, and find cover. But the giant wave gained on him, and he realized it would only be seconds until it swallowed him completely.

This was it. This was how he would die.

He dared a peek over his shoulder and witnessed blue-green light bursting from the water. Snakes of light, thousands of them, spreading out in all directions, enveloped him. Electrified needles penetrated his skin. His entire body burned.

Dark blue, darker, blood red, white with flecks of emerald. The light snakes spat out dots that grew and changed and swallowed one another.

He fell from the scooter, his body rolling over and over from the momentum. Time slowed. Water droplets crawled through space, elongating, snapping into two, then three, or joining with others.

And then he was underwater, surrounded by an impossible cerulean hue. His body seized, and he lost his hold on the world.

Bomb

Maude

MAUDE COULDN'T SEE ANYTHING except white in all directions. It disoriented her, and for a minute she struggled to fight back panic. She reached out an arm, and Bill grabbed it.

"We're alive," she said, and realized she said it with her own voice. It sounded like a stranger's voice, but in a good way.

Bill tightened his grip but stayed silent.

A steady humming attracted her attention, and she listened to a stream of energy all around them, and a lower steady sound she envisioned as a great grid.

Maude concentrated and heard the murmurs of others from the compound, but many were weak, fading away, and past caring. They were being drained, and their identities slipped with each moment.

Breaking away from the netting had exhausted her, and left her frayed, although her emotions seemed amplified. Her memories tumbled through her consciousness out of order, but vivid as real life. Proof that she was still herself, and that she would recover from whatever drain had occurred.

Stay with me, Maude, someone spoke inside her mind.

"I'm afraid," Maude said.

Don't be, you're safe for now.

"No, I'm not."

You will be. If you listen.

And she heard something else far off, but it was more memory than present. "Odd Maude. Odd Maude."

She remembered running into a closet at school, slamming the door shut, and jamming several broom handles against it. Three bitches had chased her; they'd had it in for her since her family came there two years ago.

She'd wanted to be homeschooled. She used to be. But her parents insisted that the school was excellent, and they wanted her to interact more with others.

Things would never change. She'd always be Odd Maude. The darkness was safe. No one could see her cry. The whiteness was safe, too. She was just a speck here, flotsam.

Past and present brushed each other. Odd Maude.

Now it was the first time she went into a thrift shop. It touched her as if it happened yesterday, or as if it was a peek at something in the future.

Stepping into the dusty interior, confronted by clothes arranged in sections by color, she felt she had stepped into Oz, and that slipping over this rainbow she could be anyone. Odd Maude wasn't an insult, it was a blessing.

And in the brown section she found an eight-dollar aviator jacket, and it became a new skin.

She sat in a big easy chair, knees curled up against her chin, as one network featured an old profile on Katharine Hepburn. That's who she'd wanted to be. Katharine "I don't give a damn about what anyone says or thinks" Hepburn.

Odd Maude.

And there was Spencer, calling her after disappearing from her life for two years, and there she was slamming down the phone and crying, and finally picking it back up and giving him hell, but not meaning it. Not really. And he would show up at her door unannounced, with bushy hair and a scraggly beard, and a goofy Spencer smile.

And then emptiness. No Maude. Nothing.

Time twisted around her, and she knew none of it was real, and all of it was. Time. Maude could see it front and back, up and down, inside and outside.

Come back to me, the Molecule Thief coaxed her from the abyss. *Focus on this thread.*

"Odd Maude, Odd Maude, why won't you come out and play?"

Maude, he whispered. The Molecule Thief, Tha. *Maude!* This time, his voice filled with anger.

"I'm here!" Maude shouted back. She couldn't see him, but she could sense him and hear him close by. So close she could punch him.

"I know," Bill said. "Calm down, let's keep moving."

He couldn't hear Tha. Of course, he couldn't.

He's right, Tha said. *Keep moving.*

"There are other things here," she said without speaking.

Many things, Tha acknowledged. *And all of them will kill you, given half the chance.*

"I want to get out of here."

You will, but you can't without Spencer.

Maude tried listening harder to the tone of his thoughts, to his deeper vibrations.

"Is Spencer here, too?"

He is. But you need to have him come here. Reach out for Spencer. Or reach out for The Order. They will find you. And they will find Spencer. Follow them.

The Order. The phrase jarred her.

Tha wasn't being honest. "You don't care about Spencer."

You don't have much time, the Molecule Thief said. *You've got to get up and get out.*

"Bill?" She heard the fear in her own voice and could've been listening to an eight-year-old version of herself seeking solace.

"What is it?"

"There are energy lines all over, and then there are other lines, they're like a giant cage."

"You can see all that?"

"I can hear it. I can get us out of here. It's a matter of gripping one thread and making all possibilities collapse into themselves."

She was terrified he wouldn't believe her, and sighed with relief when he answered, "If you say it, Maude, then I believe it."

"Let's go," she said.

"I'm with you," Bill answered, his voice coming from the whiteness. He stopped, and she sensed his shock. "We're breathing?"

"No," she answered. "We are, and we aren't. I could explain, but..."

"I don't want to know," he answered, and they shuffled off, guided by instinct through the haze, relying on Maude's perception.

The netting and the threat posed by The Contained had given her clarity. She saw her futures and pasts, and now wanted to grab one and surge ahead.

Odd Maude. Time to fight.

Spencer

On the other side of the grid, white landscape stretches out in front of me. The ground is like sand or snow or sea, smooth and wet looking with trails running through it, like someone dragged a large stick along the ground, or like paths left by giant snails.

The air above this flat and sterile plane dances in waves of magnetospheric plasma.

Maybe the desolation and lack of landmarks should upset me, but I feel calm. That's weird, right?

Usually my mind is a thousand places at once, but here the roar has quieted and I'm able to breathe and sort things out. Is this what the universe is like for everyone else?

Unlike the other misty area, everything is in clear focus. In the distance, walls rise out of the ground like partitions, and beyond the walls I see structures rising into a weird skyline.

There's a noise here, a steady thrumming, and my movement is unencumbered.

I think I could fly if I wanted.

The entities, The Order, are with me. They're amused. We're all amused.

—*You cannot fly,* it says.

The comment is met with tremendous humor. It's joyful.

The Order is concerned about me, or about one of my possible futures, or possible pasts. But what they're really concerned about is the Molecule Thief.

They want it dead, destroyed. It's an abomination to them. But I don't know why.

—*It came into being on its own accord. It created itself. It has no past. No future. It is.*

There's a collective memory and history of all that has been and will be. I try to embrace the philosophy, to link with The Other, and I'm washed away by the enormity of the collective consciousness.

Trying to see time as they see it is mind-blowing. I'm not built that way, none of us are.

The Order is self-contained; a merging of form and thought with shared ideas and sensations. One has become another and all have become one.

If a future exists with the present, then things are predetermined, right? Only they aren't. Because I can blink and pick out not just one future, but thousands of them. Millions.

And it's the same with the past. Reality is constantly changing.

The Order explores my memories. They search for something, and although I'm immediately nervous about what it is, I know it's as it should be.

Elliot and I are playing chess. He's never played before, so I'm being patient, helping him think through moves.

His mouth turns down. He likes the idea of a "war game," but there's no physical challenge, and he's frustrated staring at the board, trying to visualize moves ahead of him, and cause and effect.

"This is stupid," Elliot says.

Why is The Order fixed on this memory? I look at the board, see the rows of black and white, the checkered grid.

A pawn drops through a black square. Then, at another spot, another pawn vanishes.

An uneasy ripple surrounds me. The Order shoots through my mind, picking it apart.

—*You're connected with Tha.*

The statement is accusatory, and the words spasm with emotion.

I don't want to respond, but that isn't an option.

My mother calls out and I snap into the present. Behind the glass of her helmet, her face is grim, and she shifts weight ever so slightly. As she reaches out, her arm stretches for yards.

The general is here, too. And there's Castro, gray faced and looking ill inside his suit. This is too much for him. I'm sure he wants to lie down and rest, and wants the pain to stop. The others look around with wide eyes and even wider mouths.

The general steps closer and colors emanate from him, like a psychedelic aura. His concern is a tinge of ochre. It deepens into burnt sienna, then lightens into golden hues. My mother's aura flickers with reds.

Elliot is still here, too, as part of the memory called up by The Order.

—*Tha is something that cannot and should not be. It does not belong. Anywhere, anytime. It is chaos.*

Tha. The Molecule Thief. It doesn't make sense that he picked me. Maybe it does. With all my screwed-up wiring, I'm sort of an anomaly.

I see things, right? And I wanted this, if I'm honest. I've always wanted normal, but I really wanted extraordinary, too. I wanted my differences to have profound meaning.

I invited the Molecule Thief in, maybe without realizing it, but I reached out, gave him something to anchor onto. A core to weave existence around.

I know The Order is eavesdropping on my thoughts. Of course they are.

The Order communicates.

—*Tha slips through realities. It can't stay long in any single one. It is an abomination. It is outside the real.*

But Tha found The Contained, I answer.

—*An unfortunate discovery. That space kept The Contained safe and away from The Order.*

It's a prison.

---*The Contained are in a state of being. They do not belong in The Order.*

I don't understand. Why?

---*The Contained are not part of The Harmony that is The Order.*

And Tha showed them the way out. Tha helped them make use of a naturally occurring rift and then showed them how to make another from the energies of our world.

The new rift would lead here, where they would make a stand against The Order.

What will happen if The Contained escape?

—*We cannot accommodate,* The Order answers.

What does that mean?

If The Contained burst through the rift, disharmony will follow.

The Contained will upset the area it contacts, sending a ripple through the energy schemes, disrupting existence for all. Each disruption, no matter how minute, causes exponentially more disruptions.

As one reality is disturbed, another is necessarily affected. And another. And another.

Tha didn't come into being with the creation of the rift. He's always existed. And he always will. They can't stop that. They can't put him with The Contained, they can't take him into their reality or another. There's nothing they can do to stop him.

"The universe is always dying." That's what a physics teacher once said. "Galaxies spread out until their energy is so diluted they go dark. Eventually they will be nothing."

Does the same hold true for all realities? Is Tha entropy? Does he bring chaos that will end the way everything is?

Communication from The Order jumbles inside my skull as thoughts and images and memory.

"Cute horses, Spencer. Watch this."

Jarod and Lucas Wheeler approach the picnic table where Elliot and I play chess.

—*What is this?*

Jarod's fist crashes down, sending wooden chess pieces flying. Knights, bishops, rooks rain down, but abruptly freeze, stuck in an airborne state of chaos.

"Look, The Atomic Bomb," Jarod shouts. "Welcome to the twenty-first century, motherfuckers!"

—*Stop it.*

"It's happening," I say. "They dropped the bomb!"

Jail Break

Spencer

THE ORDER WITHDRAWS, BUT they are still with me. Several hover near us, blue centers surrounded by a translucent orb of gelatinous matter kept in place somehow.

They can move fast, if they need to, even though they have no legs. They're able to grab one of the thousands of energy streams and get towed along.

They're beautiful, actually. The blue core is serene and the sphere around it, angelic. I can't tell the entities apart.

I'm drifting.

"Spencer," Dawes says. "Are you still communicating?"

"Yes."

"Can you see them here? Outside the enclosure?"

"Yes."

Questions shoot through the speakers inside my helmet. People are curious, excited, scared, elated. I cut through the many voices with my own, and make the pronouncement in a simple statement. "GERI is dropping the bomb now."

All talking stops.

Castro's prayers break the silence. Rod and Jeff share an expletive. The group watched me, but I don't know how much of my conversation with The Order they've picked up. Probably not much.

I know the bomb is in mid-explosion. So do The Order. Time shudders at the disruption, and curls in on itself, like a large lumbering beast that feels pain, but doesn't understand why it's being punished.

Hydrogen isotopes slam together and fuse. It's horrifying and beautiful. Energy rips through the atmosphere, screaming and shredding whatever order it can find to create a new order.

The boundary between our realities shakes and rips, and I can almost feel the fabric rent.

I have an aberrant thought. How many people who stayed behind at the compound have been sucked into the anomaly, surprised at finding themselves in a white mire, an afterthought of a nuclear blast? What would that type of energy change set in motion?

The Order is frozen in this moment, looking ahead, looking behind, calculating realities.

"The Order want us out of here," I say.

The Order is an antibody. We're an infection.

Dr. Alfredson laughs, although it sounds more like nervousness.

The blast gives The Contained what it wants.

The prison tears open. It's a slow process, a fast process. It's happened, it is happening. It will happen forever.

Inside the high-tech suit, my skin itches, and my blood pumps faster. Insane shards of light dash about in unpredictable trajectories. A violet burst rips the area directly in front of us, humming in a way that irritates the tiny hairs inside my ears.

"What is that?" My mother's voice is vibrating.

The beam widens, and then a blue orb forces its way through. Another follows.

The Contained.

They have substance now, too. I can't tell the difference between them and The Order, except they don't move in such an organized way. Their movements are stuttering and chaotic.

My mother stumbles. I catch her before she drops. Everyone in the team struggles; the sensation is like being shaken so hard your head hurts, only there's no reason for it.

"What's happening?" the general shouts.

"The Contained," I respond. I watch them advance. "They're coming our way."

The Contained move with one speed now, and they follow one path. They're headed right for us.

"I can't explain now. We've got to go!"

"I can barely move," my mom says.

I grab her. She blinks, but doesn't say anything.

The soldiers glance at the general for guidance, but he turns to me.

The Contained start spilling through the widening portal.

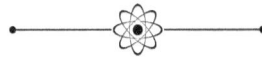

Maude

Maude fell without falling. The surrounding air changed into a gauzy, wet mess, and she gagged. Light flared, such a brilliant white, and everything else burned away.

"What's that smell?" she said. Or thought she did.

The foul odor of rotten eggs assaulted her and between her temples pounded the shriek of cat gut drawn against the strings of an electric guitar.

She landed on soft ground. Beside her, Bill's face screwed up, the skin bunching around his eyes.

He held himself wrapped in his own arms, and his muscles twitched as he rocked. She didn't know what was happening to him, but he suddenly looked young and unable to handle things.

"Come on, Bill!" She grabbed his arm, but he pulled away, eyes wide and glassy.

Although Maude couldn't see them, she heard The Contained on the move. They were a shower of hot sparks that promised the arrival of an inferno. After all that waiting, this was their moment, and The Contained bathed in it.

"Something horrible happened," she said. "Can't you feel it?"

The things were everywhere at once, and their target was a stark violet slash in space that looked like some giant panther had clawed the mist.

"Those are the things that grabbed us," she tried to say, but nothing came out.

She tried taking a breath. It hurt, and nothing entered her lungs.

Ideas came through the cacophony, or maybe impressions; a series of images sliding through her awareness. And she knew he was here. Spencer.

"Come on, Maude!" Bill shook her.

"I'm okay. Are you?"

"I feel like my head is ripping open and my insides are scrambled."

Maude surveyed the surrounding scene, testing the air with each breath.

"Everything's changed," she said.

"There was a burst of energy," Bill said. He took forever to reach his hand to the back of his neck, and then suddenly it was there. "GERI did it. They dropped a bomb on us. Fuckers actually did it. How the hell are we still alive?"

Bill's roar pulsed through her. It hurt. She heard the pain in his voice at the betrayal, and his thoughts came in a single burst;

How-could-they-have-done-this-to-me-I-gave-up-so-much-for   them-and-never-   asked-questions-I-served-I-was-a-good-soldier.

She forced Bill out of her head, his emotions too much to handle. The information rushed over Maude, forcing her to process it at a rate that threatened to fry her brain.

"Head for that." She took charge, hoping to calm Bill's panic.

Her muscles protested as they tried moving faster. The physics were all wrong.

"We're going in the same direction as The Contained," Bill said. "That's where they're going."

Maude kept pulling, his head down, his mouth a tight line. They had only moved two or three steps, and it felt like an hour had passed. Maybe two. But that wasn't possible.

A burst of blue slammed into the surface near their feet. It spread, contaminating the ground, disrupting the lines of energy below.

Heat crawled up her body, and she stumbled back. The heat turned uncomfortable, and then intensified. Unbearable. She broke out in a clammy fever sweat.

The blue light grazed Bill's boot. The leather scattered at the point of contact.

"Holy shit!" He pulled Maude back. "Don't let it touch you."

"That came from the direction we're going," Maude said, panting.

"Are you sure?"

She nodded.

"Then we're not going that direction," Bill said.

"We have to. That's where Spencer is."

"Our chances that way aren't good. And how can you know that?"

"How can you not?" she countered, and realized the absurdity of her statement. "Let's go over our options," she said. "We can hang back and let the action play out while we try to avoid getting dragged in, or we can return to the netting and try to free more survivors."

"If there are any," Bill said.

"There must be. I know it."

Maude's indecision screamed along a hundred thousand paths and branched into a hundred million more.

Another blue light appeared. Bill reacted before Maude did, pulling her back, but instinctively extending his arm as a counter-balance.

Blue touched his fingertips, and they became snowy. The grainy static worked its way up until two of his fingers became nothing but blue dots, and then the dots spread out and joined the paths of energy around them.

"Fuck me!" he shouted.

His eyes squeezed shut, and he clenched his teeth. Then he opened his eyes to slits, peeking at his hand before his eyes flew wide open. He stared at his hand. The two fingers were still there. The fingers weren't there.

"Oh my God, what is this?" he cried.

But he started moving again, dragging her with him. Another burst of indigo and another spot of corruption spread below them.

They twisted away, like dancers who hadn't figured out the rhythm. Maude remembered being a kid, playing Hot Lava with her tutor Amanda, who threw cushions on the floor as they hopped from one to another, laughing. Only here, one wrong step and she would crumble into a million little dots and drift away.

Something stopped her. Maude tilted her head and listened as The Contained rushed to the violet portal, their voices raised in a battle cry. On the other side, the challenge was answered, and two opposing forces met in a violent clash.

Maybe they didn't want to go in that direction. But she saw they already had. And they hadn't.

"What?" Bill asked. "What aren't you telling me?"

He peered over her head at the portal in the distance.

"It's a fight," Maude said. "They're fighting."

Bill held back, but Maude tugged him toward where Spencer was. He had to be there. She felt it. And knowing Spencer, he probably needed rescuing.

Schrodinger's Rift

Spencer

THE PEOPLE AROUND ME can't see what's happening, and describing it in real time is impossible. How do you describe the start of a war?

"My God," Dawes utters. He responds to an eruption of light by stepping in front of my mother, a protective act, and she puts her hand in his.

The change in everyone's postures tells me that people sense a difference. They know without seeing that something horrible is happening.

The creatures spill out of the bright tear and vibrations emanate around us, an alarm announcing the breach. In the distance, from the city beyond this flat area, more of The Order are coming.

I see them as dark blue dots against the energy lines they ride. They're an organized swarm. They move as one.

"The enclosure's gone," I say.

"And The Contained?" Dawes asks.

"They're coming through. The Order is going to try forcing them back, but I don't know if they can without opening a path to their origin."

"Their origin?"

"This space was a buffer against disturbances from the area they held The Contained in."

A ball of silver light appears above us, a projectile lobbed by one of The Contained, and a handful of defenders fall back, crying out, avoiding the targeted area. The other people with me can't see the entities, but they must see this because people struggle out of the way.

The two younger soldiers aren't successful. The light hits, pitting the ground, disrupting the energy lines, and the soldiers vanish.

"Shit," the general says. "Spread out!" He has my mother's hand and pulls her along on a zig-zag path.

Another ball of light lands and takes down two of The Order. Their forms freeze, the blue core within darkens, and then they fade.

They aren't dead, but they aren't alive, either. The weapon isn't meant to kill. Instead, their current state of being is disrupted, which is just as bad.

The Order returns fire, drawing energy from around them and directing it at the entities coming from the collapsing prison.

"What's happening?" Dawes asks. "Where are they?"

"They're all around," I say, and his eyes widen with worry.

"They're fighting. There's The Contained!" I stab a finger to the left, then point to the right as they change direction. "And more are coming. Lots more."

"What are those things? Are they energy weapons?"

"Yes and no," I say. As usual, I'm the only one who appreciates my humor. "The bursts force The Contained or The Order into a lower, defenseless, energy state."

"So it kills them?"

"No, it blasts them into many states, but until they exist in one of those states, they don't exist at all."

"That makes no sense," Dawes says. "Give me something I can use, Spencer. What about if it hits one of us?"

"It'll do the same to us, I think."

It's at once the most humane and cruel weapon imaginable.

Both sides fire dozens of silver bursts. The Contained reinforcements are still pressing forward, slower now. The fighting has disrupted the energy lines they travel.

A bolt from one of the light weapons darts out and slices through Alex's arm, and it's gone. Snap of the fingers. No blood. Below the elbow, his arm doesn't exist.

Alex's screams tear through the com system. All of us move back, wincing at every sign of attack, trying hard to avoid being caught up in the struggle.

"Can we go back the way we came?" Dawes asks.

"I think so." It's a stupid answer, and he crosses his arms, but stays quiet. "I think the bomb closed the rift and made the anomaly unstable."

"So, we're trapped?" Dawes asks.

"No," I start to answer, but stop.

I can't tell him that even though the rift is closed, it's still open. That time is meaningless here.

Once we step through the rift, it will cease to exist. At least for us. In that moment.

"We should have taken our chance outside," Alex moans

"You made your choice," Jeff mutters.

"There was no good choice." Dawes is always the voice of reason.

"How long do we have to wait for the nuclear fallout to subside?" I ask.

"The AMOPP suits will give us enough protection to get out and make a quick crossing through the area," Dawes sats.

The Order is everywhere, as is the escaping Contained. The battle is chaos. No sound, only flashes of silver, bursts of mercury.

I'm the only one witnessing the whole struggle; maybe the rest are seeing the energy bursts, or a flicker as one of the entities is struck and shifts into another state of being.

"We can't stay here," I say. "We have to go."

"Not into the middle of that," the general argues.

I run, but Jeff snatches me back. I can't overpower him, so I try slipping through his grasp, becoming squirmy and hard to control.

The only way is through the battle. There's no choice. I keep struggling, but Jeff is strong and well-trained, and I'm losing.

"Spencer, stop it," my mother says.

I can tell it pisses her off seeing someone wrestling me into submission, and at the same time, she's relieved at not having me march into that fray.

"We have to get back into The Contained's prison before it disappears," I say. "The nuke made it unstable. It's collapsing!"

"And then what?"

"We'll get out. We will. I can get us out."

The only thing worrying me is the Molecule Thief. With me on the inside of the mirror, he can make his way out now.

Wasn't that his intent all along? I've been nothing but a means to an end for him. If he's through the rift, then I'm stuck here, right?

There's so much wrong with my thinking, I can't stand it. Too many holes, too many unanswerable questions.

No time to sit down and think it through, to rationally consider options and consequences. I'm on intuition now.

"We can't stay here," I pronounce.

A calm declaration, and they hear its truth. Everyone talks through the com system, but stops when the general asserts himself.

Dawes watches the scene ahead of us, the silver and blue bursts, the flicker of the approaching horde.

He glances my way, and says, "Let's move."

That's it. Nothing dramatic, two words spoken matter-of-fact. I'm relieved and terrified.

"You know what happens when you die?" Jarod Wheeler once said to me.

He had that grin on his face, the one that warned of his cruelty.

"What?" I took the bait.

"Nothing. You stop being. Snap. That's it. That's what happened to your dad. It's like you never existed. It's like... nothing. Nothing."

"I don't want to die," I said to Elliot during a rare moment when we had a real talk.

"It happens to everyone," he said. "Don't get stuck on it. Don't let it bother you. It doesn't bother me. It's not like I can control what happens."

"But it's going to happen to *me!*"

"It happens to everyone."

Jeff lets me go, and I'm moving, leading the group. We're only nine now, five less than when we started out.

I'm in front. The general can order me back. My mother can call out, but they don't.

I wish I could tell them what I know, but what's true for me wouldn't necessarily be true for any of them. I can't tell them anything else. Maybe I've already told them too much.

No, I've told them exactly what I've told them.

I think about that stupid game of chess, and see partially melted pieces covering the top of the picnic table. I can't see the board anymore; it's shrinking row by row, column by column. Shit.

Like it or not, people are depending on me, and I can't give in to weakness. I'm so scared it hurts all over, but I keep moving.

I stumble and someone catches me. Despite leaning on a crutch, Castro uses his free arm to bolster me.

"You're doing good, Sport," he says.

His words help, but then a silver projectile strikes the ground, blinding me. I stop, and the others pause as well. Everyone talks at once.

Another bomb strikes.

Castro's features are tinged light blue, as is his AMOPP suit. It's like he's been dipped into a vat of indigo. He's beautiful.

His eyes are wide open and trusting as he dissolves into millions of particles, and the particles scatter like seeds into the streams around us.

Death Loop

Jennifer

J ENNIFER STOPPED AND STARED at the milky surface where Castro stood only a few seconds before; now all that remained were flecks of blue. Would it be better if there was blood, or the smell of charred flesh?

No, but this was so impersonal. Just a flash, and then nothing.

Drew squeezed her shoulder. His eyes showed how much that one hurt him.

Spencer was quiet, like he couldn't process what had happened.

Then he shook his head slowly, his upper lip tucked in.

She reached out, touching his back.

"No," he said. "That shouldn't happen."

Then he gave his head a vigorous shake, and trudged ahead.

She kept moving, too. She wasn't about to let Spencer get too far ahead.

He was different, here. Focused. Everyone else was distracted and disoriented.

What if, when the time came, he didn't want to leave? She swallowed hard.

Why would he stay? The idea didn't make sense, but it filled her with panic, and she hated her inability to suppress it.

She never infantilized her boy, though her husband gave into that temptation. He wanted to protect Spencer. Did he feel responsible for his son's oddness? Jennifer too often denied his differences, and she regretted that.

Jennifer peered ahead, frustrated by the lack of visibility. It reminded her of the whiteouts she'd experienced on country roads, when the wind blew the snow from a field, and all she could do was continue through the brightness, trusting that the road continued, and she wouldn't hit an obstruction.

Spencer stopped. He took a step back and tensed up, knees bending as if preparing to leap. Beyond him, riding along the ground, was something bright, surrounded by a violet haze with flecks of yellow. She watched the ground peel away from either side of its glowing form.

"What *is* that?" she shouted.

Jeff shoved Spencer out of harm's way and raised his weapon. He shouted as he fired. The thing swelled and burst. Another bright swell followed, and Jeff kept firing.

Spencer watched, and in his eyes, Jennifer saw acceptance.

"You okay, Spencer?" Drew asked.

"Just scared stupid," he said.

No, he wasn't. She knew her son.

"We can't go in a straight line," Drew said. "Can you lead us around? Try to take us around the edge of the fray?"

"I'll try."

They started moving again, and no one spoke. What was there to say? Drew hurried in front of her, and behind her were Alfredson and Rod. She knew by their faces that the men had assumed some sort of a protective role for her.

Poor Herschel. All this time, she'd never asked him how he was doing. When GERI wrote him off, his world collapsed. Any media coverage of their situation would have him in the role of scapegoat. And maybe her, too.

A series of silver projectiles appeared in the sky, and although most rained upon The Order, two or three landed among their small group.

Alex stumbled, his form looking as though a swarm of blue bees had descended upon him. As he landed on the ground, his leg detached from his body, breaking into dark particles that disappeared into the whiteness beneath him. He thrashed for a moment longer, and then his other leg vanished, and soon the darkness finished his torso, then his head.

Dawes tugged at her. She didn't realize she had started screaming.

Jennifer shut her mouth and gathered what remained of her sanity.

This was the end. She knew it. So did Spencer.

Her son made eye contact with her, and then smiled. While he had meant to reassure, Jennifer only experienced another blast of desperation.

Spencer turned and tapped Rod's shoulder. The man nodded, and Spencer pointed ahead. Rod didn't hesitate. He blasted the area with his plasma rifle. Jeff joined in until Spencer motioned for them to halt.

She heard Spencer through the com: "Stay close, the border's just ahead. That's where The Contained broke through. The Anomaly is still open, but it won't last."

"It's darker there," Alfredson responded.

They took another hit. Philip fell, freezing spread-eagle a foot above the ground, and a large circular hole opened in the center of his chest. A cookie-cutter could have made the wound. No blood. No evidence of trauma. Just a hole.

Jennifer stepped past him as he dissolved. When she checked again, expecting to see little of him remaining, she instead saw Philip whole again and the blast re-opening his chest.

The moment of his death looped.

Spencer touched the tormented man and interfered with the process. Philip collapsed into a thousand blue pieces.

"Keep moving!" he said.

The general accepted his command without question.

"The energy lines here are different," Alfredson said.

"The anomaly?" Dawes asked.

"What's left of it," Spencer confirmed. "It's shrinking."

If the surrounding blasts were any sign, the battle here was fierce, but then it would be. The Order wanted to keep their criminals from breaching the border, to shove them back into containment.

"The physics keeps changing," Alfredson marveled.

"No, it's your perception." Spencer stopped.

He jabbed a finger at the air and ducked away from something. She envied his ability to see their surroundings. The rest of them could see energy trails, shifting colors and sudden lights, but Spencer saw the shapes and the perspectives.

"How close, Spencer?" Dawes asked.

"Close. We have to get through there. There's a path, but it's collapsing. We have to go. Now or never, or we'll be trapped here when the anomaly finishes shutting down."

Spencer ducked down and gripped her hand. "Here! Follow me."

The colors before them blossomed into shades of blue, and sparks of white rained upward. Changes in pressure happened rapidly, and Jennifer's face warmed.

"There. Fire!"

Rod and Jeff blasted away, following Spencer's directions as they moved.

"Down!" Spencer's tone compelled them, and the party dropped, although their bodies didn't follow expected paths.

Spencer jumped back up and waved his arms. The motion left strange trails in the air.

Was Spencer hit? Her heart punched against her ribs.

"Maude!"

Jennifer peered into the light and sure enough, there she was. Along with another figure. They moved in a jittery manner, like bodies illuminated by a strobe light.

Fake Spencer's Vanishing Act

Elliot

ELLIOT WAS NO LONGER in the ocean.

He froze, his body still wrapped around the scooter. The machine sat on the ground, surrounded by a placid gray field.

He slowly rose from the machine, his arms stretching, feeling as if they belonged to someone else. He raised his eyes upward and then peered into a strange and endless horizon.

He should be dead or at least experiencing horrible physical side-effects like they did in Hiroshima. Why wasn't he? What kind of bomb had they dropped?

Elliot kicked away from the machine and experimented with movement. Vertigo gripped him as his body twisted and expanded.

His eyes widened. It was as though someone had injected him with a disorienting drug.

Flashes of blue in the far distance caught his attention. How far had the scooter taken him from the compound? It should've been far enough.

Could the blast have pushed the anomaly, or moved it? That made no sense. Maybe it opened another tear?

Elliot took a long step, then another. He fell, or should have, but his body floated at an unnatural angle to the ground.

He wasn't in the water; but he wasn't on any land that he knew. His heart swelled against his chest, pounded once, and then beat again after an indeterminably long time. He opened his mouth and uttered a guttural comment of fear and confusion.

"Elliot?"

He turned, startled by the voice.

Spencer stood close by without protective gear. That didn't seem possible. His eyes looked serious, and instead of jumping around like usual, they drilled into him.

"Are you okay?" Spencer asked.

Elliot studied his friend for a long time; it literally felt as though hours passed. How was that possible?

"Where is everyone?" Elliot asked.

"They're here. Looks like your chariot didn't get far. You're lucky to be alive."

"The bomb..."

"Yeah, the bomb."

Spencer looked over his shoulder, then back.

"We have to get out," Spencer said.

Elliot didn't like the feel of this conversation. Spencer sounded different; more assured, almost over-confident. His voice was different.

"What's that over there?" Elliot asked, pointing at the activity in the distance. The blue-white flares weren't constant.

Spencer followed his finger and turned back with a shrug.

Elliot stood, knees slightly bent, arms at his sides for counterweights. He watched Spencer for a few moments before saying anything.

"And where did you come from?" Elliot asked. "How'd you get here?"

"Where did you enter from?" Spencer asked. "I need to know. It's important."

"Why?"

Spencer jutted from one spot to another. He didn't move his feet, or his arms, he just went from spot A to B.

Elliot shouted and stumbled back.

"Where did you come in?" Spencer asked again. "Tell me everything you remember."

Spencer's eyes adopted a strange quality. They looked as if someone hid behind them, peeking through a mask.

"We're in the anomaly," Elliot said. But if this was the anomaly, how had he gotten here? If a hole opened, then why wasn't saltwater pouring in?

Spencer tested the air, looking like a mime searching for an invisible door. Finally, he turned around, visibly annoyed. He stared at Elliot and nodded.

"What are you?" Elliot asked. His arms shook as he struggled to process it all.

Spencer shifted. For a second Elliot saw him as a flat surface; it looked like he was a piece of cardboard. Spencer shifted back, and Elliot cried out, falling and landing on his elbows.

"You're not Spencer," Elliot said.

"I'm Spencer," the thing said, "just not your Spencer."

Fake Spencer stretched an arm out and made contact with something Elliot couldn't see, but a slight hum suggested an energy source. Elliot grabbed the counterfeit person, but his palms burned at the point of contact.

They shot through the whiteness at a dizzying speed. Around him, he saw thousands of different colored lines running across the landscape at different heights.

They stopped. There wasn't any physical sensation. One moment they were flying, and the next moment they were stationary.

Fake Spencer slapped Elliot's hand away and looked at him with consternation. "I've wasted enough energy on you," he said.

"Where's Spencer?"

"You better hope he's as far away as possible."

"Why's that?"

"Because you wouldn't want to be near us if we ever got together."

The creature turned away, dismissing him. Elliot's face warmed as his temper rose.

Fake Spencer's fingertips glowed, and Elliot intuitively snatched his arm. He didn't want to be alone, not here.

The counterfeit Spencer snarled and yanked free. His features were Spencer's, but they possessed a darkness Elliot had never seen in his friend.

"Talk to me!" Elliot ordered.

The doppelganger extended a hand and gripped Elliot's forearm. Blue dots spread from the point of contact.

Pain stabbed the spot and Elliot shouted. When the doppelganger pulled away, there was a hand-shaped chunk missing from his arm.

It was as if a shark took a bite out of him, only there was no blood, just a hole where flesh could've been surgically extracted. He looked down at it in horror, a scream running through his mind that he refused to let free.

He swung before thinking about it, his fist striking Spencer's jaw. The fake Spencer reeled back, almost falling over, but righted himself.

Its hand lashed out, the palm a blur of dark blue, but Elliot knocked it away and delivered another punch. He followed that by wrapping his arms around the entity, pinning its arms to its sides.

That move should've been enough to subdue Spencer, but this wasn't Spencer. It strained against his hold, twisted, and broke free.

The thing's form jittered, went flat again, and snapped back. It grabbed at something in the air and then launched a blue globe at him.

He didn't know its purpose, but it couldn't be good. Elliot flung himself down, letting the orb spin harmlessly by.

When he looked up, the fake Spencer was several feet away. It stopped, and surrounding space seemed somehow different. Its expression changed, eyes showing too much white as it glanced about, ducking in one direction, then another.

The entity was running from something, wasn't it? Elliot wished he had Spencer's ability to see things, or even Maude's hearing. He wanted to know what the doppelganger saw.

With the creature distracted, Elliot lunged. He grabbed it about the waist and drove it to the ground. The fake Spencer crawled and stretched until it broke away. It lunged at a particular spot.

Elliot watched its head and shoulders vanish.

"No," Elliot shouted.

He wasn't letting it get away through some hole. He gripped its ankles and pulled, using his body's weight, and digging in his heels. He had to lean back, surprised at how powerful the tug was toward the invisible opening.

The fake Spencer dragged him a few feet. Elliot should let him go. What did he care? But sensing this thing might be the difference between survival and death, he renewed his efforts to keep it from escaping.

One of the entity's leg's kicked free. Elliot's hands slipped and the other leg got away.

And it was over.

The entity vanished.

Elliot cried out, sweeping the air for it, angry at his clumsiness, and angry at Spencer, both the real one and his mirrored self.

Elliot rose, his muscles struggling to adjust to the strangeness around him.

He stopped and looked back. The disturbance was closer now.

He could investigate and find out if the rest of the group from the compound was in that direction. Or he could try to find the hole, and see if it led to the compound, or somewhere else in his world. If the hole still existed.

Fake Spencer had been looking for an exit. Maybe the others would need a way out, too.

Too bad.
He didn't need any of them. He didn't need anyone.

Tha-umaturgy

Spencer

I'M RUNNING, IF YOU can call it that, and the craziness of the battle between The Contained and The Order is all around us. So close. So freaking close.

Maude and the soldier she's with have stopped in front of a stream of silver drawn along the milky surface. Angry blue particles follow in its wake, rising in a fragmented manner.

"Maude! Stay there!" I shout, but I know she can't hear me inside my suit. I gesture, holding up a cautioning hand. A silvery blob shoots out of nowhere and hits the ground at my feet.

I see the end of the silvery chasm between us and make for it, and Maude does the same. We reach one another after what seems like a forever.

"Spencer?" Maude touches my shoulder and I look at her; eyes wide as half dollars.

"You're here," I shout. "I knew it."

I take her hand. My heart is thudding so hard. Her hair is flat against her head, and her eyes are red, puffy; she looks like she hasn't slept in weeks. She's not beaten by the ordeal though; her posture is defiant.

She also isn't wearing a suit. I don't understand how that's possible, but I take the plunge and press the tab that lifts the faceplate on my helmet.

"Spencer!" Mom shouts, but it's too late.

There's no rush of air in or out, but I don't have trouble inhaling. How is that possible? What if time here exists as a *where* instead of a *when*, and we haven't been here long enough to need to take a breath? That makes no sense, because I can breathe if I want. Or not.

"I was afraid," I say.

Maude nods and hugs me, and I'm afraid all over again that this isn't really happening, or that something will come along and mess it up. I'm holding her too tight.

"How did you get free?" I ask.

"Tha."

She ducks away from something to my left, and out of my peripheral vision I see a hundred or more entities charging in our direction. The prison is still emptying as they force their way into this neutral area.

"We have to go that way!" I say, pointing at the approaching onslaught. "It's our way out."

"I just came from there?" she says.

"We need to get away from this fighting and find an escape."

"Not back there," she says, and I hear the panic in her voice. "There's no rift back there."

"There has to be."

The soldier, who she quickly introduces as First Sergeant Bill Martin, asks: "Why? Why does there have to be a rift?"

I can't answer that question, so I answer another. "If there's no rift, we can figure a way to make one."

"The last few rifts took a series of earthquakes and an atomic bomb," Martin says. "Got one of those in your pocket?"

"It doesn't matter. If we stay here, we're dead. The Order doesn't care about us, and neither does The Contained. They're too busy trying to destroy one another, and we're just collateral damage. But once the battle is over? We're as much a contaminant in their reality as Tha. When The Order turns its attention on us, they'll most likely change us so we don't disrupt the system, destroying our current form and dispersing our energy."

No one argues.

I head toward the worst fighting.

"Are you sure? That way?" Dawes asks.

"Not at all," I say, with a ridiculous laugh.

I move, holding Maude's hand.

No, I'm not sure. But now's not the time for indecision, or for weakness. If I pause, I'll freeze.

Maude gives me a look, and I see the same question in her eyes.

"There's a way out," I say. "Tha's looking for it the same as we are."

And we better find it first.

A pack of The Order break away from the main group, and seems to be on a path to intercept us. They don't appear to be moving, but they come closer in spurts, like winking in and out of existence.

I tell Dawes, and he curses his inability to see them. He yells for me to give him a direction, and I point. Gun barrels swing along the path and plasma shots take out several of them.

The surviving pack members lob bursts our way, and thankfully, the silver flashes are visible, and people scatter. We get lucky. We won't be lucky again.

If we keep on the path we're heading down, we're committing suicide. But where the hell else can we go?

I stop. Faces turn to me.

There's no way we'll make it. My legs are heavy, my knees want to buckle. I'm finding it hard to stay focused. I want to shrink away.

Think.

Think.

The prison is collapsing. We can't stand still. We can't move forward.

That's the problem. I'm thinking the wrong way. I'm thinking in three dimensions. I'm thinking as if I'm stuck outside the anomaly.

Think.

"Spencer, what is it?" Dawes asks.

"Spencer!"

I'm turning inward, following my thoughts, giving them freedom from fear and criticism.

All around us are hundreds of thousands of streams of energy, or potential. If we can recognize one flow and commit to it, that potential can collapse into reality. Right?

And there's no time, either. At least, not the linear thing we think of as time. Would time depend on the reality stream?

—*Tha*

An alarm resonates through my body.

—*Tha*

The concept is the single thought of The Order.

—*Tha.*

—*Tha.*

It's a mad hunting cry and a response. It's me they're after, not my double. Something has changed. Some potential in this reality has collapsed. The other is gone and now, in their consciousness, I've replaced him.

"Spencer," Maude calls out. She hears it, too.

I want to scream out, "I'm not Tha!" Only I'm not sure that's true, now.

"We're done," Maude says.

The general's lips tighten. "What's happened?" he asks.

"The Order, they're coming after us. There's too many of them," Maude says.

"I have an idea," I say, and damn if I'm not smiling. Maude nods, and I know she's looking at me with hope.

"What idea?" my mother says.

I don't answer; instead I squeeze Maude's hand and reach into an energy flow. No hesitation. I commit fully.

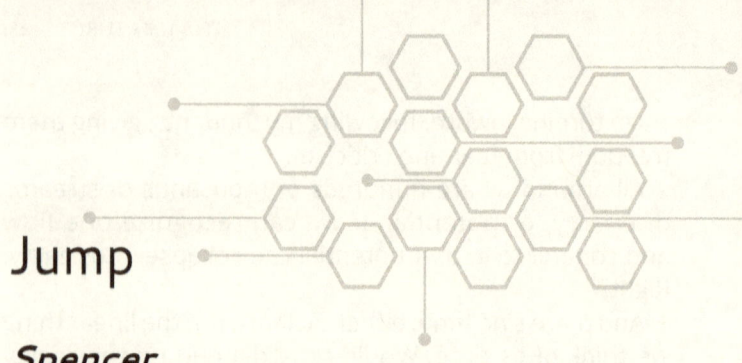

Jump

Spencer

I MERGE WITH THE energy. Exist through millions of points along the way, in millions of time frames.

It's like stepping off a curb, only instead of finding the street beneath your feet, you're endlessly dropping and at the same time securing a step. I break the connection, yanking away as if I'd touched a live wire.

Maude and I are still together, holding hands. But we're alone. She looks like she's about to freak out, but I'm the one who loses it, hyperventilating and shaking.

"It's okay," she says, and her voice calms me. I'm never letting go of her hand again.

"We jumped, didn't we?" I say.

There's nothing ahead of us, just a flat white surface, and it's shrinking.

"That way," she says, and points in a direction behind us. I turn, and over my shoulder I see The Contained. We've skipped past them and abandoned the rest of our party.

"How did you come up with that?" she asks.

"It's how they do it," I respond. "Looking at the potential realities and committing to one is overwhelming, though. I feel like my head is going to explode."

"Can you do it again?" Maude asks.

"I don't know."

I take a deep breath and lean over, hands on knees.

"You have to," Maude says. Her eyes are desperate.

I need to calm down, to focus, but my mind is everywhere at once. I'm still terrified at what I've done, still crazed at the impossibility of it.

In the distance, blasts of plasma respond to bursts of blue. My mother's there. So are other people I care about.

I don't want to let go of Maude's hand, but I reluctantly force my fingers loose.

"I'm going to try to jump again."

Like before, I look around me at the many energy flows and pick one. And like before, I'm seeing all the possibilities they present as I pick through the textures of time and, once again, force myself to totally commit.

I'm digging into one stream, and the potential collapses in a snap. And just like that, I'm back with the others.

General Dawes stares at me in awe.

"What did you do?" my mom asks, her eyes wide.

"No time to explain," I say.

Another series of silver bursts rain down. It's inevitable. We're going to take frequent hits. There's no way out.

"Everyone grab hands."

They do, and I take my mother's hand as I concentrate. Nothing happens. I don't jump.

"It's too many. I need to take you one at a time."

"Jennifer," Dawes says. "You go first."

The soldiers let go, but Alfredson hands on.

"I'll be right back," I say. "I promise."

Alfredson swallows and slowly uncurls his fingers from around my mom's wrist.

My mother hugs me with both arms—the second stretches as I'm back in another stream. The silver is falling where we were, are, will be, and we're there, but we're somewhere else.

Again, the possibilities explode and I'm tumbling, disoriented, until I commit and then we're somewhere on the shrinking white plain. My mother is safe.

I'm not thinking now, I'm acting. Everything slows down, and I'm jumping again, not questioning the wisdom, but trusting instinct.

I don't know how many other people I can do this for, or how many times I have left in me. Maybe I'll jump and that will be the last thing I ever do.

But I don't doubt myself. I don't pause. I do nothing but plunge into the stream.

I bring Dawes. Then Rod. Bill. Jeff. Alfredson.

And then everything around me is silver.

Maude

Maude's head hurt. The jump with Spencer had been a nightmare, a cacophony that threatened to blow out her temples.

When they jumped, it only lasted a second at one level. On another level, it went on for eternity.

In the stream, she heard *everything*. Only it didn't deafen her or dull her awareness. It heightened sensations. Even now.

Not showing her agony to Spencer took almost as much out of her as the jump. She stood, putting on a front, but fighting below the surface to get control of the overload of information flooding her head.

"We need to keep moving," Dawes said. He was bent over, one hand on his knee.

Despite how Bill's forehead wrinkled, he asked, "Where?"

Good question. Spencer would know. He could see things in this landscape, even in this anomaly, that nobody imagined.

Spencer appeared, bringing Rod with him. His face was pale, and he looked dazed. Maude wanted to touch him, to make sure he was okay, but then he disappeared again.

His mother made a strangled sound. Maude heard her pain and worry and turned away to give her privacy.

The pounding in her skull shifted, lessened, faded into something manageable. Thank God.

Maude shut her eyes and took a deep breath, letting the worst of the noise drift away, and realized that like Spencer, she could tell where some lines were. Maybe she couldn't see them, but she could hear the difference in the space around her. Maybe she could jump?

Maude hesitated, listening for one single stream. It meant opening herself up and filtering the noise. She wasn't sure she could stand it.

Spencer flickered into existence, bringing Jeff with him. And then he vanished before anyone could respond.

Spencer's mom let out a shout. General Dawes took her hand and drew her close.

Maude looked across the white plain and saw several figures still behind, one of them surely Spencer. Silver sparks showered down on them, and all the remaining figures collapsed.

"Spencer!"

Dr. Newton saw it, too. She let out a pitiful cry that wrenched at Maude. "Spencer! Oh, God."

"Is anyone moving?" Dawes said.

"I can't tell," Maude said. "It's too far away."

Maude needed to do something. She needed to stomach the pain, the confusion, and listen for the path that would lead her to Spencer.

Only she couldn't do what he'd done. She didn't know how he worked it, what he saw she couldn't hear or visualize.

"Spencer," she whispered.

And he appeared, his body in a crouched position, his arms reaching down to Alfredson by his feet. Maude gave an exhale of thanks.

"Too close," Spencer said.

The air shimmered. Maude's head exploded with sound. They were coming. The Order.

Their fury sang through her temples. She did her best to minimize its roar, but still the intensity of the anger and hatred made her cringe.

The battle against The Contained still raged, but now their attention shifted to a new target.

They were coming for Spencer.

He was the abomination threatening disorder.

Surrounded by a cloud of energies, The Order arrived with a cacophony that almost deafened her. It screamed its demand.

—Tha!

She watched the cloud stutter closer and heard it gathering more energy. It drew strands of power in from the streams, building in intensity, preparing to release the energy as a weapon.

"No," Spencer hissed, and charged at the sound.

"Don't" she cried.

Stupid, impulsive, courageous Spencer.

He thrust his hand into the dense center of the entity, and the volume of emotion increased until the anger gave way to searing pain.

This part of the cloud shrieked and flailed about, seeking escape from the threat of dissolution. Maude shouted for Spencer to stop.

The clouded faded, breaking up.

Worse, his disruption was separating this part of the collective from the whole. Its horror and shock wrung pity from her, even though it felt undeserved.

Bits of identity screamed along the many energy flows as the whole chased after it, desperate to reclaim a portion of its being, if only to save it from complete non-existence.

The universe paused.

Maude listened, anxiety growing as she heard a far-off rumble.

The Order called through the great network it traveled for all units to break off the battle with The Contained.

A more immediate threat presented itself: *Tha*. Spencer.

Death at the hands of this new being shot through this link in which they found nourishment, and kinship, and meaning and existence. They responded as one voice, and the presence within the network built up.

They were coming. Not just for Spencer, but for all the intruders who'd arrived with him.

(Un)happy Reunion

Spencer

MAUDE'S SAFE.

"My God," I say. "Do you realize how close you came to dying? If I hadn't reached in and disrupted them..." They would have killed her.

Maude nods. "But we can't think about that now. The Order is calling for more."

"More what?" my mom asks.

"More of itself. Reinforcements. It wants Spencer. They want Spencer. He's become Tha."

"I hate that word," Mom says

Maude takes my hand and tugs me close. She looks worried and I don't know how to calm her down.

We need to get out of here, find a rift, if there is one, and if there isn't, then maybe there's another option. I don't want to think about that.

"Which way?" General Dawes asks.

The others crowd around, and I fight to keep from feeding off the anxiety in their body language and voices. I need to concentrate. Good luck with that.

"We can't go back the way we came in, and we can't go back across the plain to where The Order is," Mom says.

"And we can't stay here," Alfredson adds.

I look up at the discordance in one of the streams. Something's familiar there.

I reach out and sense him. It? Me? Tha.

"He's been this way," I say.

Maude knows immediately who I'm talking about.

"Where is he now?" she asks.

"When is he now?" I say. "He followed this line."

"To where?" my Mom asks.

"I don't know, but we should consider following it."

"Not a lot of other options," Dawes agreed.

"Do you think it's a way out?" Mom asks.

I shrug. We start moving, and our progress is slow. We could do it the jumping way, but that's exhausting, though I don't know why, and I'm not sure I have it in me right now.

Maude tugs loose and tips her chin up, then tilts her head to one side. She reminds me of an old logo I once saw in a history book, a dog sitting beside a gramophone. I know better than to say that.

"What?" I ask.

"They're close."

General Dawes checks the landscape behind them, then ahead of them.

"I hear them," Maude says. "There's so many of them." She sounds frightened.

Alfredson steps closer to Rod, who's grim as he scours the whiteness. He and Jeff both crouch, adopting a defensive posture, but I sense they're struggling to remain combative. How do you fight something you can't see?

The Order is arriving, moving through the energy fields, so many gelatinous orbs, becoming larger, then larger still. Not all of them are coming, though, not the ones still beating down The Contained.

"Wait," Maude says.

I look at her, and she has a half smile on her face. Her eyes are sad, though, and her posture reflects the enormity of the obstacle before us.

"What is it?"

"It's Elliot," she says. "He's close by, calling out."

"I don't believe it. How did he survive the blast? How did he get in?"

Maude shrugs.

I peer along the plain and see the patterns, watching them flow along, until one attracts my attention. There's a disturbance. It's him, right? It's Elliot.

"That way," I say, and we all move.

It isn't far, but it isn't close either. However, if we're in motion, it makes it more difficult for The Order to get a solid fix on our position.

They have a fair estimate of where we may be based on where we were, but I can't do anything about that. The worst thing that can happen is that they manage to get in front of us.

I want to jump, but I don't have a lot of stamina left, and certainly not enough to do it with members of the party.

I'm leaning forward, pushing against the ground, pumping my arms, sweating, breathing hard. I'm willing myself forward, keeping pace with the others in the group.

I can't tell how far we go, and no one else has any idea, either. We might be fixed in one spot for all we know.

I keep expecting The Order. They're closer. They're much closer.

Sweat runs down the middle of my back. It itches, but I ignore it. My mother is at my side, her face cast in determination; and next to her is Dawes. Maude isn't sweating like the rest of us. The only evidence of exertion is the redness of her cheeks.

And then I see him.

Elliot's wearing a dry suit. He stands, watching us, and I'm ridiculously happy to see him.

Maude breaks from the group, she's flying, launching at him; and he wraps his arms around her in self-defense. The rest of us go over to him.

"How did you get here?" I ask.

There's no time for us to talk, to share greeting, to tell one another how happy we are.

"The explosion, somehow. Good old GERI really screwed us."

"There must be an opening, then."

Elliot is staring at me, disdain thick in his expression.

"So, there's an opening here," Mom says.

"I don't know," Elliot responds.

"I can't hear anything different," Maude says. "Spencer?"

I study the area, looking at the patterns, watching the energy move.

"Your friend was here," Elliot says. "You know who I mean."

Tha? I don't feel him, but then it occurs to me that maybe I do, but thought it was my own feedback singing through the energy lines.

Why isn't the area singing with discordance if we're anywhere near one another?

"He felt you coming and took off. I think you scare him. He doesn't think you can both exist in a reality together," Elliot says.

"If that's true, then how is Tha here, too?" Maude asks.

"Because we're not in a reality," I say. "This is a buffer. It's like a neutral zone. The Order sought it out to build the prison for The Contained."

Elliot shakes his head.

"So are you stuck here?" Maude asks. "Tha is gone, and if you go after him, will you destroy everything around you?"

Elliot glances about at the rest of our party.

"If it makes any difference, I tried stopping him," Elliot says. He doesn't sound too convincing.

Maude looks furious.

Something clicks in my head. Why didn't I see it before?

"Spencer?" Mom says. "Is that what will happen?"

Elliot's looking over my shoulder, and his eyes harden. I turn and see The Order has caught up to us.

We Are Light

Spencer

WE DON'T HAVE A chance. There's no way forward, and no way back. There's no negotiation. No surrender. There's just the sudden combined attack, the conversion of our energy, and our controlled dispersal through the massive network surrounding us.

It's inevitable. We won't feel anything. We'll just freeze and our identity will cease. It sounds cruel, but it's not. It's the way of things.

Except it isn't.

My idea is terrible. But as it hits me, I know there's no other solution.

"Don't," Maude whispers.

I hear her inside my head. I feel her in my heart.

"When I move, you get them ready to move," I say.

My mother watches me, her eyes suspicious. "What's he going to do?"

I can't have a discussion. Not now. I see the distortions in the pattern, the sparks of noise I've left behind. Only it isn't me.

Tha was here with Elliot. Those are his energy signatures, left behind like a trail of bread crumbs dropped on the forest floor.

The only way out of here is to create an opening ourselves. That means upsetting the balance and taking advantage of the instability. If I can make it happen.

I always wanted to be extraordinary. I always was.

I'm scared, and angry, and hurt. And I have no choice. There's no courage where there is no choice, is there?

I lift my hands and reach for the nearest energy line. The hairs rise on the back of my neck and along my arms. My skin burns. Needles plunge into my abdomen.

No time for goodbyes.

I'm traveling a multitude of directions simultaneously. I'm an explosion of Spencers. I'm a giant spider shaking the web, drawing the attention of The Order, luring them away from my mother and the others.

They can't ignore me. My action is terrifying to them. I'm Chaos and they have to stop me.

I'm everywhere and everywhen at once.

I'm a conduit.

All of this is happening faster than the blink of an eyelid, and at the same time, it's unrolling at a ponderous and deliberate pace.

The breadcrumbs left unintentionally by Tha are intense. Can he feel me? I'm tracking him, ripping up the trail in my wake and calling to my own pursuers.

They're trying to anticipate me. I know they'll get me, but not before I reach him.

And just like that, there's Tha.

He's at the spot he's made, digging at the border between the realities.

He's aware of me, and he's surprised. We're both outside time, both converging on the same point, both sharing so much there's a danger of our becoming one and maybe becoming nothing.

"Hello, Spencer," he says.

He doesn't try stopping me. What's the point?

"If you come through, you'll end us both," he says.

He's laughing, it's an unpleasant nasal sound. I don't sound like that, do I?

"You can't get through, can you?" I say.

He doesn't have to answer. I see him stuck there, between the realities, like a fly on sticky paper. He's pathetic.

I'm reaching, and he's pulling back, trying to find a safe spot. He's fighting me off.

"How do you live like this?" he asks.

I pause, afraid of his meaning.

"Like this," he insists, and he struggles in his spot.

He does that laugh again, and it runs through me. "Do you ever wonder what drew us together?" he asks. "Why you? Why me?"

He's wasting time, stalling, trying to figure out how to turn this situation to his advantage. He's a cornered animal, and he's dangerous. And his words are hazardous.

I can't start doubting myself. I can't start guessing, and then second-guessing. That's not how it works. That's not how reality manifests.

"Careful," he says. "If you do what you're thinking of doing, only one of us stands a chance of surviving, if either of us survives. And that's a big *if*."

"I'm not really thinking about it," I say.

"You're nothing," he says. "Look at you. Look at me. I made myself. From nothing. I'm my own god. What are you, Spencer? Who's really the imitation?"

I stretch forward, and he blocks me.

"I won't allow it," he says.

"You and I both know what's going to happen," I say.

"It's happened in the future and the past, and it is happening now," he completes my thought. "It's futile, isn't it?" he adds.

If I don't do this, we're stuck here forever... existing in-between time, a mosquito in amber. I'd rather be nothing than trapped alone in this existence.

"You don't have a choice," I say.

"You do," he snaps back.

"I can't let people down. I have to do this."

The Order is close. We're a blinding light for them; it's impossible for them to not see us.

"If you succeed, do you know what will happen?" Tha asks. He's got that tone again, that edginess that reeks of contempt.

"It doesn't matter."

"You won't be Spencer any longer. Not truly Spencer. Maybe you'll be me. Maybe that's what you've always been."

"You're not me," I say.

Maybe we're both manifestations of the infinite potential forms of the collection of molecules that are the ideal Spencer.

Can Spencer exist independently of that? Spencer the ideal. He's what neither the Molecule Thief nor I can be.

I wish I'd read philosophy. I'm sure Plato might have something to say about this.

I'm hesitating, and that way is death. Worse than death. I can't. I need to find the resolve necessary. If I have to surrender a part of myself, I'll do it. If I have to give up everything, I'll do that, too.

"You think I'm the one to be pitied?" Tha says. "If you go through with this, you'll be the one to be pitied. You'll be a shell. Everything you've always held wonderful will no longer be wonderful. You'll be like one of The Order, seeing things in rigid patterns."

If I listen any longer, I'm lost.

"I can't," I say.

I reach through Tha and I'm flung across the universe and simultaneously snapped back.

I'm screaming. He's screaming. His memories aren't real, but mine are, and then so are his. His needs are my needs, his grief is my grief, his rage is my rage.

And in our collision, is release.

Light surrounds us.

We are light.

I'm overwhelmed by the changes. I see things I never did before.

Diamonds of light flash, overloaded with color. Some are part of a spectrum my eyes couldn't detect before, but I see them now, and that one color, the metallic incandescence I remember in the scale of an oarfish, is everywhere. It flares, and the landscape ignites and reveals billions of particles, each a distinct color.

And I'm spinning back.

My eyes? They feel unformed. Nothing about me is solid, nothing is fixed in place. I still have shape, but it's tenuous; my molecules are a loose assembly of potential.

I'm in a place where I'm born, and I'm in middle-age, and where I'm dead, rotting in the ground. I'm married to Maude, and I'm not. I've never met her, and instead I'm dating someone else, and marrying him. I have children. I've never had children. So many possibilities.

Here, though, where I am, I'm changed. My body and mind no longer trapped by the same needs and limitations.

I'm not even Spencer any longer, not really.

Bits of me keep dispersing, and I struggle to hold it together. How did Tha manage?

I'm in awe of the willpower necessary to maintain identity against such odds. It's so much easier to just let go.

And yet, I keep fighting. Still trying to regain the bits of me that are Spencer. Still fighting to survive.

Focus. Come on, Spencer.

I can't. Imagine wearing a blindfold, and then having it ripped off. Imagine seeing everything for the first time, and trying to place sounds and smells to each image. Imagine trying to reconcile textures with things you've never seen before but only imagined.

And the energy released by our contact shears the fabric. The pain is unimaginable. Every cell is disrupted, singularly and as a whole.

Thought stops.

Everything stops.

Tha and I remain locked in excruciating contact. Time warps.

One of The Order faces me.

Only it isn't The Order. It stopped being that when it became separated. Now an orb hangs in space, the vibrant blue core gone dull. It's disconnected from the collective.

It hovers in meaningless existence; an empty husk unable to connect into a merged consciousness, waiting, without thought to activate it.

Beyond the orb, across the white plain, beyond the partitions, The Order's civilization rises and crumbles, and rises again, cities built with painstaking organization, following patterns so immense it's difficult to discern.

Maybe the buildings are the moments of the collective history of The Order, time its brick and mortar. Maybe it's an illusion.

The Contained are dispersed. They no longer pose a threat and the uncertainties align until they fall into place like a mechanism of a lock.

I am the only remaining threat.

I don't belong here.

I don't belong here.

I don't belong here.

And because of my contact with Tha, the inevitable occurs. A portal opens.

Tha is screaming, and then he's tumbling through the rift, as surprised as I am that he's still here, or that I am, and that we're separate from one another.

I'm screaming now, too. Part of me is still here, and part of me goes with him, and I can't undo the choice I've made.

The others rush out, too: Dawes, Elliot, my mom, Maude.

When they're all gone, I go through, what's left of me, mourning my lost self. But for the first time I can remember, I'm not afraid.

Nexus

Maude

M AUDE WATCHED SPENCER MOVE his arm, reaching out for something, his eyes showing enormous concentration.

She dared a glance at the arriving entities, visible as sparks of silver and indigo, and she heard their uncertainty and alarm.

The Order froze, poised on the lip of eternity.

Spencer's mouth opened, his body spasmed, and he disappeared, screaming.

Maude's knees weakened, and she stumbled a step and might have fallen if Elliot hadn't propped her up by gripping her arm.

"What's happening?" Dr. Newton asked.

Before Maude could respond, the roar of a thousand windstorms deafened her. She covered her ears.

The noise storm continued, running through her spine, spreading out through the bottoms of her feet.

It became part of her, threatening to sweep her away, throwing her into an abyss from which she would never return.

"What did Spencer do?" someone shouted.

The sound was a wall, but there were cracks, and, in one area, the cracks led to an opening.

She crawled for the dead spot; a patch of relief within the madness. Elliot's fingers squeezed her bicep, supporting her, but she jerked free and pointed, trying to make herself understood. A nod and a startled expression showed he got her meaning.

"Spencer!" she shouted his name over and over.

Spencer's mom joined her: "Spencer!"

Elliot shoved Maude aside and barreled into the dead area, his figure elongating until it looked as though he would snap in two. He disappeared, leaving behind only a flash of color.

Everyone in the group stared after him, then started shouting at one another. Maude gripped Dr. Newton's hand and pulled her.

"We can't leave him!" Spencer's mom shouted.

"He's not here," Maude said. "Maybe he went through."

"But what if he didn't?"

"He opened the way for us. We need to honor that. We need to go."

Spencer's mother nodded.

They moved toward the abyss, passing into an area where the pressure increased, and her legs felt leaden. The whiteness of the landscape changed, giving way to muted browns and greens.

Dr. Newton stopped; her eyes glassy, red-rimmed. She had questions, but Maude feared them. Dr. Newton took a last look behind, then hurriedly went on, followed by General Dawes and Bill.

Maude remembered the stupid fish she saw when she first met Spencer, the ones that became dragons, and suddenly didn't want to go. She'd pushed Spencer's mom to leave, and now that it came down to it she couldn't leave. She didn't know where Spencer was, but couldn't leave him behind.

A hand closed on her wrist, and Bill pulled her through.

She couldn't fight it.

Jennifer

It took a moment to orient herself.

They stood in an overgrown lot surrounded by rubble, on a block where heavy equipment and dozens of men and women worked on constructing what looked like a housing project. A few blocks over, she noticed a three-story structure attached to a small strip mall.

They were in Seattle. At the site of their old home. Where it used to stand, anyway. Memories flooded back, and she swallowed her anguish.

She never thought she'd come back here. Too much pain linked to this spot. She'd never really dealt with it, not completely. She'd avoided facing the loss of her husband, yet here she was.

"Jenn, are you okay?" Drew spoke in a soft tone.

"We're in Seattle," she said.

His eyebrows rose, and he studied their surroundings. "We can't be."

She shrugged, and he stepped back. Bill and Alfredson wandered over to them, looking dazed. Rod and Jeff kept still, trying to look soldierly. After what they'd been through, it was amazing they could still function.

Drew called the soldiers over and gave instructions; suits were to be stripped off and stashed in the lot, where they'd remain hidden unless someone knew where to look for them. Jeff and Rod jumped to follow his command, probably relieved at the restoration of some sense of normalcy.

Drew spoke to them all. "We need to stick close to one another, within earshot. If anyone sees, or feels, anything out of the ordinary, and I don't even know what that means anymore, I want you to speak up. Immediately."

Alfredson shrugged. "No one's looking for us."

"We don't know that," the general insisted. "Until I can contact people outside GERI and find out who authorized that bomb, and what's going on with the power structure within the organization, we need to assume the worst."

Jennifer kept scouring the area, waiting for Spencer. She sat down on a large block of concrete and let the tears flow. Maude came to stand over her.

"I don't hear him," Maude said.

Jennifer took Maude's hand and pressed it to her forehead. They stayed that way as the morning sun warmed them, and the sounds of the city pressed in. How unnatural this felt; how empty.

"Why did we end up here?" someone asked.

"Because this was Spencer's home," Jennifer answered, and then broke down.

Spencer

I'm descending, as if through water, and as the world comes up at me, I can see it, like surfacing from the ocean. I come out, rising into dirt and grass and trees and clouds and sound, to everything that is around me. *Everything* is here. Everything but *me*.

I feel the ground beneath me, see the blue of the afternoon sky, hear the rustle of the trees. But I see multiple versions. Not just here. I see every potential landscape. Every universe where this place exists the way it is, the way it was, the way it will be. It exists a different way. It doesn't exist at all.

And I am afraid that I'm not Spencer anymore. I'm afraid I'm every Spencer. I don't know who I am. I don't know *when* I am.

But I know where I am. I'm in Seattle. I don't know why. Maybe because Seattle is some sort of touch point for me, a nexus where distinct possibilities intersected. It doesn't matter.

I end up crouching, then squatting where our old house once stood, in the living room where the mirror would have hung upon the wall. I find a fragment of silver and tilt it, looking for reflections.

I hadn't expected to live. I'd guessed that combining energies and drawing in forces along the power streams would de-stabilize the environment long enough to get out, but I also expected it to kill me.

Tha's not gone. Not that he ever properly existed. But he deserves as much a chance at survival as any living thing. He'd been manipulative and self-serving, but only because he wanted to survive. That didn't make him bad.

I look up. The others haven't noticed me yet, so I stay in place and explore whatever it is inside myself that has changed.

I see multiple wind currents moving through the upper atmosphere. I see a single bit of paper as a path, occupying every position where it could exist. It has different speeds and different positions at the same time as it rolls along and wedges against a rusty signpost. Where I used to see a thousand things happening at one time, connecting through my brain, making me scattered, now I see the infinite. And somehow, seeing all the possibilities at once, I feel calm and focused.

So much has changed, and so much is the same. The Order is still the Order, and The Contained, as decimated as they are, will grow again as the dominant society continues toward finding impossible perfection.

And Tha? He and I aren't done yet.

"Spencer!"

Maude charges across the lot, and I rise to meet her. The others join us, my mother covering her mouth as her tears flow. Elliot keeps his distance, watching with an aloofness that strikes me as alien.

"I thought you were gone," Maude says, leaning in to kiss me.

Part of me still is, I almost say.

Maude

Maude caught her breath as Spencer's lips met hers. His fingers slid through her hair before pulling her closer. Maude shut her eyes and ended the kiss long before she wanted to. This intensity of feeling was so new, so overwhelming. She rested her forehead against him and was surprised by her own tears, hot against her cheek.

Still, a smile formed on her lips. Maude listened to his breathing, then turned her head and pressed her cheek against his chest to feel his heartbeat.

She seared this moment of peace into her memory, then stepped back to really look at Spencer. His kiss had felt different than the first one they shared. Confident. Assured. Present.

They'd both been through so much these last few days. She wanted to kiss him again, but held back. Not yet. She still had so much to process. She'd lost so much and didn't want this new intimacy tied to the pain she experienced. She wanted to hold this away, to cherish it as a beginning, and not as part of an ending.

"Your eyes," she murmured. "They're different."

"Different?"

"They look older."

His gaze held a sadness that she hadn't seen before. And with the sadness, determination. And strength.

She didn't know what to say, and suddenly felt stupid. But he was different. And she was, too.

Spencer scooped a remnant of mirror from the ground, peering at the surface, holding it in different ways.

"What are you looking for?"

"Checking if The Anomaly's closed," he said.

"Is it?"

He nodded.

"Well, that's good news, right?"

He didn't answer, and in his silence, he seemed a thousand miles away.

Spencer looked at her again with his full attention. He didn't drift off, didn't rush his words, or slow them down. He didn't stretch his neck awkwardly, or shuffle in place as if uncomfortable in his body. He was Spencer, but it seemed that, in passing through the anomaly, something had clicked into place.

Maude threw down her reservations and wrapped her arms around him. They held one another, no talking, no need for it. Her gaze went to the silver glass, where an irregularity caught the sun's reflection. She shut it from her mind and concentrated on him.

Spencer tossed the shard to the ground and held her.

Tha

I *am* Tha, and I *am* here. All the seeds of the dandelion cling, quivering, to the seed head.

Dead fish bob in the ocean. Stiff birds, squirrels, insects, and bats lay among toppled trees. The air smells like steamed meat and salt. The buildings of the Vancouver Island compound are demolished, ripped open, their innards spilled across broken pavement and grass ripped up by the roots and washed away from the soil. A nuclear wasteland. There are no people. Not one. Only me. Tha. The Molecule Thief.

The dandelion seeds turn vibrant yellow as they solidify into a hearty flower. Difficult to get rid of. For the moment.

TIME RUNNER

THE MOLECULE THIEF BOOK 2

The adventure continues. Order now!

lpstylesbooks.com/timerunner

SCAN ME

EARTHQUAKE

THE MOLECULE THIEF PREQUEL STORY

Find out what happened to Spencer before Vancouver Island in this short story about the megaquake that destroyed Seattle and his home.

lpstylesbooks.com/freestory

Acknowledgements

Writing may be a solitary activity, but the writing community has given more support that we can ever show enough gratitude for. Our deepest thanks to our early readers: Jennifer Lycette—the world's most dedicated reader, James Parenti, Caitlin Sweet, Mario Aliberto, Christy Moceri, Jeremy Dunckel, Brian Drozdowski, and Josie Patalon. Also, to those who have been on our cheering squad for this book: J. Thorn, Zach Bohannon, Claire Winn, and JP Rindfleisch.

And finally, special thanks to our partners, Jamie and Sean, our first readers for life.

Thank you all for your support.

About LP Styles

LP Styles writes science fiction, fantasy, and horror. With a limitless and sometimes twisted imagination, LP Styles gives readers quirky and inventive worlds to escape into.

For more info check out:
   lpstylesbooks.com

L.P. STYLES

)

www.ingramcontent.com/pod-product-compliance
Lightning Source LLC
Chambersburg PA
CBHW051126190726
48290CB00006B/1707

* 9 7 8 1 7 3 8 7 7 3 5 0 3 *